HEIRESS IN RED SILK

HEIRESS IN RED SILK

MADELINE HUNTER

THORNDIKE PRESS
A part of Gale, a Cengage Company

Copyright © 2021 by Madeline Hunter.
A Duke's Heiress Romance #2.
Thorndike Press, a part of Gale, a Cengage Company.

Thorndike Press® Large Print Romance.
The text of this Large Print edition is unabridged.
Other aspects of the book may vary from the original edition.
Set in 16 pt. Plantin.

LIBRARY OF CONGRESS CIP DATA ON FILE.
CATALOGUING IN PUBLICATION FOR THIS BOOK
IS AVAILABLE FROM THE LIBRARY OF CONGRESS.

ISBN-13: 978-1-4328-9410-8 (hardcover alk. paper)

Published in 2022 by arrangement with Zebra Books, an imprint of Kensington Publishing Corp.

Printed in Mexico
Print Number: 01   Print Year: 2022

For my sons Thomas and Joseph

CHAPTER ONE

Eccentricity ran through the Radnor family much like an orange thread weaving in and out of a tapestry. Some members showed none of the color, while others were ablaze with it. Kevin Radnor was still a young man, so it remained to be seen how much the orange would dominate his section of the tapestry.

He already displayed some evidence of the trait that so marked his father and his uncle. When a subject captured his attention, he investigated it thoroughly with a notable singlemindedness. Thus, at not yet thirty years of age, he had acquired an extraordinary expertise in fencing, mechanics, engineering, moths, ancient Greek, chemistry, and carnal sensuality.

It was the last of those investigations that brought him in late March to a brothel in the neighborhood of Portman Square. His attention had been distracted of late by a

7

business problem he faced, and only pleasure might relieve his brooding. The house he visited was known for women who had joined their profession out of enthusiasm, not desperation. That absolved his conscience of furthering the ruin of some poor female, and also appealed to him because with enthusiasm came both invention and joy.

He sat stripped to the waist in the chamber of a prostitute who used the name Beatrice while the pretty, redhaired woman slowly removed her own garments. Already his concerns had receded, especially because Beatrice turned disrobing into an art. At the moment, down to her chemise and hose, she was bending over to roll down one stocking. Her pose revealed her round, plump bottom which, Kevin noticed, had been rouged along the cleft.

A scratch at the door caught Beatrice just after she pulled off the stocking.

"I've a gentleman here," Beatrice called out.

"I only wanted you to know that it has come. The new bonnet," a muffled woman's voice said. "It is so lovely."

Beatrice began on the other stocking, but Kevin could see that the news of the bonnet had most of her attention now.

"Go and see it," he said. "I don't mind."

She skipped over to him and gave him a kiss. Then she hurried to the door and opened it halfway.

"See?" the other woman said.

"Oh my, she outdid herself this time," Beatrice said. "Look at that ribbon and how intricate she wove it."

"Rosamund is the best," her friend said.

Rosamund. The name might have been shouted, it garnered Kevin's attention so thoroughly. He stood and joined the women at the door. "I have a fancy for pretty bonnets," he said. "Let me see it."

The bonnet was indeed handsome, with blues and pinks appropriate for the coming spring. Some cream cloth had been neatly sewn to cover the high crown, and the ribbons around its base showed painstaking effort to create little rosettes.

He admired the bonnet, but it was the hat box on the floor of the corridor that interested him much more. He lifted it, so the bonnet might return to its home. A label pasted to its side carried the words Jameson's Millinery, Richmond.

He kept his expression impassive, but as soon as the door closed, he strode to the chair and picked up his shirt.

9

"What?" Beatrice exclaimed. "I thought —"

"I suddenly remember I must attend to something this evening. Do not worry, I will pay Mrs. Darling all the same."

Beatrice pouted. "I was expecting some fun. You are one of my favorites."

"As you are one of mine. Another night, however."

Fifteen minutes later, Kevin pulled up his cantering horse in front of a house on Brook Street in Mayfair. He tied his mount to a post, then bounded to the door. When it opened, he pushed past the servant and ran up the stairs, ignoring the bleating objections sounding behind him.

He barged through an apartment, throwing open doors until he entered the dimly lit bedchamber.

A woman cried out in shock.

"*Hell,* Kevin," a man yelled.

That brought him up short. Two pairs of eyes glared at him from the bed. The woman's peered over the edge of a sheet pulled up to her nose. "Honestly, Chase, sometimes your family is not to be borne," she said furiously.

"My sincere apologies, Minerva. Chase. Truly. Only I have found her. I have finally found Rosamund Jameson."

Rosamund hoped the lady hovering outside the window of her shop would enter. She looked to be of quality, judging by the blue, woolen pelisse that fit her as only the best-made clothes did. Her bonnet had cost a good penny too, although Rosamund could not help reworking it in her mind. She would have found a stronger shade of blue, with more brilliance that would contrast better with the woman's very dark hair. The brim could use a touch of trimming too. The lady had a lovely face and impressive dark eyes, and it was a shame to use a brim that made so much shade.

But unfortunately the lady walked away, and Rosamund returned her attention to Mrs. Grimley, who had decided to purchase one of Jameson's Millinery's last remaining winter hats. Mrs. Grimley had demanded a lower price because the season was over, and Rosamund had agreed. The hat sported some fur, an indulgence she regretted. That fur had been admired by her patrons, but it made the cost too high for her clientele. That meant her own money had sat in that hat all winter.

"Can I interest you in commissioning a

bonnet for the spring garden parties?" she asked while she placed the hat into one of her special boxes. They cost more than she liked, but all the good milliners used them, and her ambitions required she swallow the expense. She had enjoyed choosing the pasteboard with its purple hue that contrasted nicely with her cream, printed label.

"I will think on it," Mrs. Grimley said. "I am traveling up to London and will be visiting shops there with my sister, but I may still have need of something when I return."

Rosamund smiled, but her heart sank. She would have never been able to open this shop in London and was grateful that Richmond afforded her the opportunity to start her business. Richmond was very close to London, however, and her best patrons gave her one commission to every five they left in London. One day she would have a fine shop in Mayfair that could charge double what she did in Richmond, but she needed to take matters one step at a time.

"I will look forward to creating a masterpiece for you, should you have that need." She tied the cord over the top of the box and handed it to Mrs. Grimley. "I'll have them caps you wanted in a day or so and will send them to your home. They be almost finished."

She did not find much artistic fun in caps, but she sewed a great many of them. Even her wealthiest patrons felt there was no need to pay London prices for such utilitarian items. Caps kept her shop alive, in fact. That and the commissions that came from London, from old friends like Beatrice.

She thought about the bonnet she had sent there two weeks ago, and pictured Beatrice wearing it in the park. She had invented a new way to make grosgrain rosettes for it, a method she would not share with anyone else. Perhaps one day fine ladies would seek her out in London because of those rosettes.

Mrs. Grimley took her leave. Rosamund tidied up the counter, then turned to rearrange some trim on a shelf. She always let the ends fall out of their boxes and baskets, reflecting the light to show off their color. She used them as lures, hanging down to catch the eye of wealthy fish swimming by.

She was dusting the looking glass set near the window, the one on the table where she fitted hats and bonnets to patrons, when she noticed the lady in the blue pelisse was peering once more through the shop's window. Rosamund smiled while she dusted, to encourage her to enter.

Enter she did. She paused inside the door,

her gaze taking in the shop, moving from the bonnets to the shelves and counter, and finally resting on Rosamund. She looked Rosamund up and down, then stepped closer. "Are you Rosamund Jameson? Did you of late live on Warwick Street in London?"

"Yes. That be me."

The lady fished a card out of her reticule. "My name is Minerva Radnor. I have been looking for you."

Rosamund read the card. *Hepplewhite's Office of Discreet Inquiries.* "It says here your name is Minerva Hepplewhite."

"I married, but the office remains in my given name."

"I think you did not come here because you want a new hat."

Mrs. Radnor smiled. Her dark eyes brightened. "No, although yours look to be very nice. I have been trying for many months to find you and tell you about a legacy you have received. A substantial legacy."

"You do not need to close your shop," Mrs. Radnor said. "I will wait if someone enters and needs attention."

"As if I could talk to a patron now." Rosamund drew the curtains over the window and locked the door. "I can barely

14

breathe."

"Perhaps some medicinal spirits . . . ?"

Rosamund looked over her shoulder at her guest. "I don't be needing spirits. Just an explanation . . ."

"Of course." Mrs. Radnor moved a second chair to the table with the looking glass, so that they could both sit.

"Who would leave me this . . . legacy?"

"The Duke of Hollinburgh." Mrs. Radnor looked intently at Rosamund. "Did you know him?"

Rosamund took a moment to absorb this astonishing news while she collected her wits. "I was acquainted with him. We had but one conversation." She realized why Mrs. Radnor was looking at her so closely. "We were not lovers. It was nothing like that, if you be thinking that way."

"I am not thinking any way. You see, he also left me a legacy. We were not lovers either. In fact, we had never met. I am fascinated that you and he spoke at least once."

"It wasn't a long talk, but he learned something about me." She had confided too much, perhaps, but that conversation had occurred when she was weary and only because he had shown kindness to a friend of hers that he hardly knew. Rosamund had

15

known who he was, and was surprised how easy it was to chat with him. "He was so very kind. He gave me a purse that held ten guineas. That was how I was able to open this shop."

Mrs. Radnor looked around the shop again. "When did this happen? The only address given in the will was the street in London, but no one there knew of you."

"I lived there for a mite bit over a year. I took it over from a woman I knew, and I confess we did not inform the owner because he might have increased the rent if we did. I kept to myself as a result. I lived there while I worked at a millinery shop in the City, learning what I could about accounts and finding sources for fabrics, notions, and such. It takes more than a dream to make a go of something like this."

"And you figured out what it took and set about obtaining it."

"Something like that. Then I moved here, because letting a place in Richmond would be much less, and there weren't so much competition."

"Where were you when you met the duke?"

Rosamund's back stiffened. "Is it a requirement of receiving the legacy for me to give my whole history?" She regretted how snappish she sounded.

Mrs. Radnor seemed not to notice. "Goodness no. I, for one, was most grateful for that. I did not mean to pry." She removed two more cards from her reticule. "Here is the solicitor you must see to obtain the inheritance. This is my personal card. We are sisters of a sort, aren't we, as two women to whom the late duke gave unexpected gifts? When you come up to Town, please call on me if I can aid you in any way. In fact, if you write to me when you are coming, I will invite you to stay with me."

Rosamund took the cards with unsteady fingers.

"Are you in such shock that you are not even curious about the amount of the legacy?" her guest asked gently.

"Whatever it be will be more than I've got now." Maybe it would be enough to open that London shop she dreamed of, though. Or even to help with her sister's future. Those ideas gave her thinking firmer legs. "It would be nice to know if it comes close to a hundred. That would go far with some plans I have."

"It is a good deal more than that, Miss Jameson. You have inherited many thousands of pounds."

Thousands of pounds. Rosamund had to concentrate on breathing in order to get any air inside her body.

"Furthermore, there is a business in which the duke was a half owner. He left his half to you."

"The duke . . . had a millinery shop?"

Mrs. Radnor reached over with a smile and laid her hand on Rosamund's. "Not a millinery business. Quite different. Please arrange to come up to London as soon as possible. I will help you settle all of this in a timely way."

Rosamund let out a laugh, and then had the horrible suspicion that she was about to burst into tears. Instead she grasped Rosamund's hand with both of hers and said, "I will leave for London as soon as I can stand without fainting."

CHAPTER TWO

Two weeks later, Kevin Radnor again rode his horse through Mayfair to his cousin Chase's house. Despite his agitation, which more than equaled that on his last visit, his progress was slow. Society had begun arriving in Town for the Season and roads that had been blissfully peaceful for months were now clogged with wagons and carriages.

He jumped off his horse upon arrival, threw the reins to a groom, and showed no more ceremony than the last time in entering. The butler merely pointed him toward the morning room.

Chase and Minerva had only moved here recently, so he strode through chambers sparsely furnished until he arrived at the light and airy morning room that overlooked the garden.

"Where is she?" he asked by way of announcing his abrupt arrival.

His cousin Chase glanced at him, then

finished drinking the coffee in the cup at his mouth.

"How good to see you, Kevin. And so early too." Minerva made a display of turning to look at a clock on a small corner table. "Why, it isn't even ten o'clock."

He was in no mood for Minerva's sarcasm. "Chase wrote that Miss Jameson was coming up to Town yesterday, and that you had offered her hospitality, so I know the woman is in this house."

"She is at that," Minerva said. "Only she came two days ago and yesterday visited the solicitor. Right now she is in her chamber, probably sleeping."

He pivoted toward the door.

"Stop." Chase's command caught him in mid stride.

Chase's blue eyes glared when Kevin looked back at him.

"Sit. You cannot go up there, throw open a door, and have the conversation you want," Chase said. "I understand your impatience, but you will have to wait a little longer."

"I have waited a year, damn it. And *I found her." He* had. Not Chase, the investigator charged with finding these mystery women their uncle had bequeathed fortunes to. Not Chase, whose profession was to conduct

20

inquiries. Not Minerva either, who also had that profession, peculiar as that was.

Minerva gave him a sympathetic look that reminded him of the kind a nurse gives a tired child throwing a tantrum. "Why don't you have some breakfast?"

He grudgingly went to the sideboard and made a plate of eggs and cakes for himself. The footman brought coffee when he sat across from Chase. His mind, however, was preoccupied with the upper floors of the house, where the woman who held his future in her hands slept peacefully, unlike his own sleepless nights of late.

The food helped him find some equanimity.

"When was the last time you had a decent meal?" Chase asked.

Kevin looked down at his plate, now empty of a mound of eggs and two of the three cakes. "Last night. No, wait. The night before. I have been busy."

"Still working out the problem with gambling odds?"

"Not problems. Probabilities. And yes, I have been doing a bit of thinking about those."

"It doesn't seem right, somehow. To gamble with a mathematical advantage."

"I'm certainly not going to gamble *without*

an advantage. The point is to make a lot of money fast, not lose it."

Chase, who knew why he needed that money, gave a little shrug. "You will find a way."

"It may not matter. You are harboring a woman in your home who may make it all pointless." He forced calm, even nonchalance, into his tone as he turned to Minerva. "How did the visit to the solicitor go?"

"Very well. Miss Jameson is overwhelmed, of course. Mr. Sanders was his usual, calm, fatherly self and explained everything clearly. He answered her questions completely."

"What questions?"

Minerva's mouth opened a bit, then shut. She glanced askance at Chase, who returned a look that said, "That was a mistake, darling."

Minerva drank a bit of tea. "She had typical questions about accessing the funds. Unlike mine, hers are not in trust. The duke knew her, and probably saw what anyone can see, that she is a very levelheaded woman and quite practical. He would perhaps not worry so much whether she could manage the money on her own."

Kevin felt a very thin smile form. His uncle, the late duke, had left a woman who was almost a stranger more money than he had left one of his favored nephews, Kevin. Free and clear, no less. "And the rest? The business enterprise?" *His* business enterprise.

Minerva cleared her throat. "Yes, that. Well, she did ask Mr. Sanders what she should do with it. He was duty bound to tell her the options." She grimaced. "The notion of selling her half did seem to appeal to her."

Hell and damnation. He would kill Sanders.

"I must see her," he said. "Go and get her. Either that or Chase will be fighting me with swords on the staircase to try to keep me from going myself."

Minerva's eyes narrowed. She turned to Chase, looking for equal annoyance, only to see Chase decide to drink more coffee right then.

Minerva stood. "I suppose I can see if she has risen yet. However, I will not wake her for your convenience, and if she is not yet dressed, you will have a long wait. You should call again this afternoon, as a civilized person would."

"I don't care if it is a long wait. I'll stay in the library until she comes down."

Minerva left. Chase pulled over a stack of

mail and began flipping through it. Kevin availed himself of the sideboard again.

He settled back into his chair. All the Radnor cousins had their own strengths, and one of Chase's was the ability to find information and assess its worth. He also could size up a person quickly. He had made a profession of those talents.

"What did you think of her?" Kevin asked.

Chase set down a letter and considered the question. "She is sensible and independent. She has established herself in a shop and appears to be making a success of it. At least enough of one that she has an assistant and an apprentice, which allowed her to leave it in their hands while she journeyed here. She is common born, but she has little of the rustic left in her. She seemed intelligent, but I did not speak with her very long."

"What does she look like?"

"She has blond hair. Other than that, my opinion would be subjective at best. Does it matter?"

Blond hair. He had assumed it would be gray. He didn't know why he thought that. Perhaps because most modistes were advanced in years before they could afford to open their own shops, and he assumed it would be the same for milliners. Of course, most women did not have a duke giving them a small purse that could be used to establish a business.

"Minerva thinks her hats are very fine. Dramatic without being vulgar, in her opinion," Chase said. "You look annoyed that I have nothing more."

"You know how important this is, so I assumed you would examine her closely and ask a few discreet questions."

Chase smiled broadly while he picked up his interrupted letter. "I knew you would be able to conduct your own investigation soon."

Kevin returned to his breakfast, wondering what his cousin found so amusing.

This was without a doubt the finest house Rosamund had ever entered. She marveled again at the drapery on her bed and the windows and the elegant paintings on the walls. The size of the chamber had impressed her, as had those of the public spaces below. Although still sparsely furnished, the furniture that did exist was of high quality.

Even the Copleys did not live like this, and they were gentlefolk. Not of the degree of Mr. and Mrs. Radnor, of course. Chase Radnor was grandson of one duke and cousin to the current one, after all.

She rose from the bed with regret. She had laid there awake for at least an hour, thinking about her change in fortune and what she would do with that money. She would put some aside to make sure her sister never had to do as she had done and go into service in a strange house. Lily would receive a proper education, too. That she could now provide for Lily was her greatest joy about this legacy.

Some of the rest she would use to open her London shop. Mrs. Ingram could continue with the one in Richmond until it was decided whether to keep both. She would need some help here in Town, though. That was one thing she needed to start looking into.

She could not stay forever in this house, so she needed a place of her own, and soon. But this was the point where her thinking changed from practical, sensible, and clear to something more muddled.

Now she looked out the window at the overcast day. Below the garden showed green starting to form near the ground. Bulbs sending up shoots, most likely. She continued considering her new home while she pictured tulips and narcissus fully up and blooming. A small apartment would be enough, even when Lily visited her. She had no need for more. And yet — it all depended on the purpose of the home, didn't it?

If she intended to be a milliner, a modest abode would do. However, if she intended to —

She hesitated giving the dream words. She always feared that hoping too much would destroy the hope itself. Yet if she were going to consider this other step, she needed to face why. Her heart stretched with ache and yearning while she forced herself to do just that.

The question was, if she were wealthy, if she lived in a fine house and wore fine garments, if she were more than a servant or a milliner, would she then be good enough for Charles to marry her?

She closed her eyes while she thought of his name and saw him clearly in her mind, so handsome and fine, with a smile that made her heart beat faster from the first day she saw it. The memory of his face had been preserved carefully over the last five years. True love preserved it, and faith and loyalty. Such a love deserved to have a life if it could, didn't it? A future? Even his parents might accept her if she was rich, and Charles — he had never forsaken her of his own choice. He'd been forced, and sent away, just as she had been forced from the Copleys' house.

She relived the last kiss he had given her before the carriage took him to the coast. She had crept back to the house and waited in the street's shadows to watch him go. He'd seen her, and walked straight to her, ignoring the glares of his parents and the command of his new tutor. He'd taken her in his arms and kissed her fully, and promised they would be together some day.

She was not a dreamer by nature. She knew better than to depend on that day arriving. After all, he was the son of a gentleman and she was the daughter of a tenant farmer in Oxfordshire. Such matches were not made. With her situation she had little time to think of it even if she wanted to. Yet she continued loving him and secretly hoping against all reason. And dreaming.

Now, with this legacy, there was a chance to make the dream real.

Her thoughts ran. The first items on a list came fast, then she cast a more serious mind on some others. Would this work? Should she risk it? Like those bulbs out the window, her dream sent up shoots that wanted to grow tall and flower.

A scratch on the door interrupted her. She bid the person enter, and Minerva opened the door with the maid next to her.

"I see you are awake. Mary here has brought up water and will help you to dress."

"It be late, I suppose. Past time to start me day. I have some places I want to go this afternoon."

Minerva entered and closed the door behind her, shutting out the maid. "I need to tell you something. Your business partner is below, waiting to meet you."

Business partner? Oh, yes. "The other Mr. Radnor, you mean. Kenneth."

"Kevin. As I told you, he is my husband's cousin."

"Then I must see him, so your husband is not insulted."

"You should see him because you are tied together in that enterprise, not because of my husband."

She hadn't understood anything about that business when nice Mr. Sanders explained it. Not that she'd listened much. She was still so stunned regarding the money she'd inherited. Nor did she want to meet this other Mr. Radnor yet. Not today. She wanted to go walk the streets around this house, looking for shops and homes to let. She wanted to imagine herself riding along in a carriage with Charles . . .

"I will dress and be down soon."

Kevin paced the library for half an hour, then chose a book from a shelf and threw himself onto the divan. He read a while, then realized he did not remember one word his eyes had scanned. He threw the book aside, rested his head against the cushion, and closed his eyes.

This was hell. He had learned how to talk business with men. He had even adopted the bonhomie that industrialists used with one another, even though it did not come naturally to him. But a woman? Not for the first time since his uncle the duke had died, he wondered if the man had gone a little mad at the end.

The old sense of betrayal began to well up inside him, but he swallowed it. It was Uncle Frederick's personal fortune to do with as he chose. If, in a gesture of bizarre largess and insurmountable eccentricity, he decided to give half a promising enterprise to a little milliner of dubious background and no knowledge of machinery and engineering, that was his right.

He had also considered this often enough, and long enough, to accept that the decision perhaps spoke of a lack of faith in

Kevin himself. Much as he preferred to disregard that notion, it was difficult to reject completely. It entered his mind now. Only this time he *could* reject it. If Uncle Frederick had not trusted Kevin with the enterprise on his own, he could have left the other half to a successful man of industry. Not Rosamund Jameson. Just finding her had cost him a year of progress at a time when matters of industry moved faster each day.

The library door opened. He immediately rose, as Minerva advanced on him with a determined look in her eyes. She got that look a lot. It was a wonder that Chase didn't find her a bit shrewish. Kevin certainly did.

"She will be down soon. Mere minutes. Before she comes, I want to make something *very* clear to you." She strode until she was so close she had to tilt back her head to look him in the eye. "She is my guest, and I expect she will become my friend. I like her. You are to treat her with the same respect you would give a lady. You are not to browbeat her, or lose your patience, or let her know you find her a trial even if you do. If you in any way insult her, either by word or action or brooding sigh or dismissive tone, I will make your life miserable."

"I never insult women."

"Oh, for the love of grace, your mere presence insults women at times. But I've had my say. Behave."

With that she turned and marched out of the library.

Kevin shook his head in exasperation. Insult women? What a ridiculous thing to say. He never insulted women. He barely spoke to them.

A faint rustle penetrated his awareness. He turned to the sound. A woman stood just inside the library door. He stared at her, and she stared back.

Rosamund Jameson was no little milliner. She wasn't a little anything. She stood taller than most women, and the simple, gray pelisse dress she wore revealed a body that held the promise of being extremely well formed and voluptuous. Lithe was not a word anyone would use to describe her.

The rest of her appearance struck him like so many smacks to his shocked consciousness. Blue eyes. Blond curls. Porcelain skin. Full lips.

The woman was beautiful. Deliciously so.

He was looking at her as if he examined her for flaws. No doubt he would find plenty if he wanted to see them.

She conducted her own examination while

he delayed greeting her. Like his cousin, Kevin Radnor was tall. His full, dark hair hung to his jaw and cravat. She didn't know if this was a new fashion or if he had neglected to have it dressed recently.

Unlike his cousin, he had dark eyes. Very dark and deep set. They and the hair made him appear somewhat dramatic. She could not deny that he was handsome and had a fine nose and mouth. A somewhat hard jaw kept him from looking too fine. His features had none of his cousin's ruggedness, so that jaw saved him from being . . . beautiful. Minerva had warned her that he was given to brooding, and Rosamund could imagine him doing that, and then appearing very poetic indeed.

He did not begin to measure up to Charles, of course. There was none of Charles's bright smiles and sparkling eyes. Kevin Radnor had more in common with the strict, distracted tutors that passed through the Copley house, men who were still young but had forgotten how to have fun. Rosamund had not been able to imagine a woman of spirit wanting any of them, and she now had the same opinion of the man facing her.

Finally, growing uncomfortable at how he just looked at her, she walked farther into the chamber. "I am Rosamund Jameson. You be wanting to speak with me."

He came to life. "Yes. I thought we should meet, considering you now own half of my enterprise."

"If I own half, isn't it *our* enterprise?"

Whatever had occupied him, it now disappeared. He smiled the smile of a proud, confident man showing forbearance. "Why don't we sit and talk about that?"

She perched on the edge of the divan. He took an upholstered chair nearby and angled it so they could speak directly.

"I expect that inheriting half a business surprised you," he said.

"Inheriting anything at all surprised me. But, yes, that part was especially astonishing."

"Did the solicitor explain the enterprise?"

She kept her face impassive, resisting intimidation. "It has to do with an invention to improve machines," she said confidently.

"Steam engines."

"His explanation was brief. I confess I did not understand the details."

"That is not surprising. Even men have difficulty understanding it."

He sounded very superior saying that. "Perhaps if it is hard for *even men* to understand, you should show them how it works. I would think that would clarify everything."

He smiled indulgently. She did not care for that smile either. "I can't. If I do, anyone might steal the design and duplicate it."

"Mr. Radnor, forgive me if my next question is too womanish, but if you can't show it to anyone, how does this enterprise make money from this invention?"

"I intend to manufacture it myself."

Me. My. I. "You mean *we* intend to manufacture it. Do *we* have a factory?"

"Not yet. I am waiting on an enhancement. Once that is procured, it can be manufactured."

So this enterprise was based on an invention that had never been built and had no factory and still lacked its final enhancement. "I should tell you that I be thinking of selling my share."

His eyes turned stormy. He leaned toward her. "You can't do that."

"The solicitor said I could."

"It would destroy everything. If you sell, whoever buys it can then sell part shares to others. Each one would demand to see the invention, which means any of them could steal it. This is an enterprise that must be closely held for it to amount to anything."

35

"You are concerned someone will steal this idea?"

"Of course I am. It is so valuable that I dare not even patent it, lest others see the drawings."

"Are you concerned I will somehow steal it?"

He subtly resettled in his chair. "Not steal, as such. You can't steal what you already own."

"I'm glad you admit that I in fact be half owner of it."

"But . . ." He seemed to think twice about what he was going to say. She saw the exact moment when impulse conquered whatever better sense had made him hesitate. "You are an heiress. There will be many men pursuing you. You might be unduly influenced by one of them."

"Lose my head, you mean."

"Yes."

"Become so drunk with love that I do something not in me own interests."

No response, but a vague nod.

"You are a man who thinks women are half-witted and ruled by emotion, me thinks."

He frowned peevishly. "Men lose their heads too. It has nothing to do with your being a beautiful woman."

She startled at the word "beautiful." He did too, once it was out of his mouth. "And you might marry," he quickly added. "Your husband might demand to know all that you know. He might even browbeat you in order to learn the enterprise's secrets."

Charles would not do that. She immediately scolded herself at that thought. It was one thing to allow a dream a bit of room to grow and another to become as befuddled as this Mr. Radnor assumed love would make her.

"Mr. Radnor, I could worry about you in the same way. You might become enthralled with some woman and be influenced by her to share the secrets. Or maybe you would use company money to keep her happy, or to pay off her gambling debts."

He found that amusing. "I never become enthralled, so you have nothing to worry about."

"Never? Not once?"

He shook his head. "Not even once. This invention has the potential to make you a very rich woman, Miss Jameson. Rich beyond your imagination. Every steam engine built will need this invention. Already they are putting them into vehicles that ride on rails. In twenty years those will be everywhere. Then there are machines in factories and other applications. Steam engines will be used by the thousands soon. You would be foolish to sell out now."

It sounded like she would be better off putting her money in one of those rail vehicles than this invention. For one thing, she would not have to see this man on a regular basis. He unnerved her when his gaze became intense like it be now. She had to struggle to hold her own ground, let alone give as good as she got.

He smiled. A nice smile. A bit seductive, if truth be told. "I will take care of everything. You can tend to your other affairs until the money starts pouring in. Then you can worry about how to spend it all." He reached into his frock coat and extracted a folded paper. "Because we are equal partners, we both need to agree to decisions regarding funds and developments. However, I can relieve you of that obligation after you sign this."

She took the paper and read it. While she did, he rose, went to the writing desk, and returned with a pen and the inkwell. He set them on the table next to the divan.

"Do you understand it?" he asked.

Partly. Mostly. There were some big words that interfered, but she thought she had the main points. "This document would give you full control of the enterprise, and the right to make contracts, spend money, and decide on this invention's future use and cost without my signature." She looked up at him. "Do I look like a stupid woman to you, Mr. Radnor? If I do not sell my share — and nothing that has happened here today has convinced me to keep it — I will be involved in the decisions going forward. I have no intention of signing this."

She let the paper slip from her fingers and onto the floor.

He stood abruptly, turned, and muttered. She thought she heard the words "impossible female" between a few colorful curses. She let him regain control, which took several long moments. Finally, he turned back to her, his face still reflecting his anger.

"It will take anything three times as long to accomplish if you insist on being involved. I'll spend hours explaining the details of every decision and tutoring you in mechanics and mathematics," he bit out. "Even finding you took too long and left this in limbo to the whole plan's detriment."

She stood. "And yet I be here now. Let me ask you something, Mr. Radnor. Have you ever run a profitable business?"

He did not respond fast enough, so she knew the answer.

"Well, I have. Now, I have things to do

this afternoon. Good day to you." She sailed out of the library, head high, and waited until she was back in her bedchamber before she vented her frustration by screaming into her pillow.

CHAPTER THREE

"Well, I have." Kevin mimicked Rosamund Jameson's last words while he finished describing the irritating meeting with that most annoying woman. Only he knew he had pitched her voice wrong. Hers was softer, almost velvet in its timbre. Still, the words were what mattered. "As if managing a hat shop for women compares to running an industrial company."

He felt better having gotten the entirety of it out of his head by telling Chase and Nicholas. They sat in Nicholas's dressing room, on those ugly, blue upholstered chairs that had been inherited along with the rest of Whiteford House when Nicholas became the new duke. Nicholas had just come up to Town after a month at his estates. His baggage still littered the chamber because he had sent the valet away when Chase and Kevin walked in.

Now they shared a bottle of claret, and

after much talk of politics and of Chase's marital bliss, Chase had asked about the enterprise.

"In other words, the conversation was a failure," Nicholas said.

Kevin watched how the fire created orange ghost flames in the wine in his glass. "She would not listen to reason."

His cousins remained silent for a stretch. He knew what that meant. They didn't approve. Now he would have to listen to them explain how and why they didn't approve, like two fussy aunts.

"I in no way insulted her," he felt some obligation to say, because Chase might report to Minerva the substance of the meeting. He didn't really think Minerva would make his life miserable, but if she truly put her mind to it, he suspected the potential was there.

"You also in no way flattered her," Chase said.

"Not true." He had called her beautiful, hadn't he? Not that he would tell these two that. It had slipped out, surprising them both, the result of how very aware he was of her beauty even while he negotiated with her. That had put him at an unfair disadvantage. He would have come away with that document signed if not for the way her appearance and presence interfered with his clear thinking.

"In fact, I implied she was a very level-headed, smart woman." He was stretching with that, but since he had not said that she was half-witted, ruled by emotions, or stupid, he had in fact implied the opposite.

"That is good to know," Chase said with some relief.

Hell, Chase *had* been charged by Minerva with finding out what had transpired.

Nicholas stretched out his legs. " 'Implied' may not have been enough. It doesn't sound as if it ended well, and she apparently left abruptly, much irritated. You should make amends. Stop scowling at the idea. You are attached at the hip to this woman unless you can buy out her share, which you cannot afford to do. You need to find a road forward. A friendship will smooth the path, while mutual vexation will make it very rocky and perhaps impassable."

"He is right," Chase said. "If it were anyone but yourself, and if it did not involve that enterprise and your bitterness over Uncle's bequest to this woman, you would see the truth of it at once."

Kevin grudgingly acknowledged that Nicholas made some sense. "I suppose I can call on her in Richmond and suggest we try to accommodate each other's interests."

"No need to journey there," Chase said. "She is remaining as our guest for a spell and will be looking for a home in London."

That was not welcome news. He had assumed she would at least be out of the way. "Then I will call on her at your house."

Nicholas turned to Chase. "What is he facing? What do you think of her?"

"I think she is no one's fool. Also, it bears mentioning that she is attractive. Wouldn't you agree, Kevin?"

Kevin nodded indifferently, like a man who had not really noticed but now, upon it being mentioned, had to agree.

"Is she now," Nicholas said with interest. "How attractive? Middling attractive or very attractive?"

"As a married man I should not notice . . ." Chase said. "However, the word that entered my mind on first seeing her, was . . . luscious."

Kevin kept his expression impassive.

Nicholas grinned. "Well, that should make being friendly all the easier, Cousin."

"Enough about me," Kevin said, eager to change the subject now. "I've been wondering something, Nicholas. As an unmarried duke not anywhere near your dotage, you should be a much-pursued fox among the husband hunters this Season. Being in mourning spared you the worst of it last year, but this is a new day. How do you plan to get through the next few months without some girl's mama nailing your tail to her wall?"

Rosamund checked the long list of errands she had made for herself. She had chosen the most pressing for today's outing. She needed to find her own place to live and had a meeting with a man in the afternoon for that purpose. She could not impose indefinitely on her hosts' generosity.

First, however, she would browse the best shopping streets. She checked her bonnet in the looking glass, smoothed the bodice of her crimson pelisse, and picked up her gloves and reticule. Accepting that her appearance was the best she could muster, she descended to the reception hall.

The servant on duty bowed. "Would you like me to call for a carriage? I was instructed to have a groom drive you in the cabriolet if you should desire to go out."

"I think I will walk, thank you."

"But I was instructed . . ."

The poor young man worried about disobeying a command, one that she had not requested be given. She did not want a groom beside her in a cabriolet, waiting impatiently when she left the carriage to do what she needed to do. Her errand was better accomplished on foot anyway.

"If you have the cabriolet brought around, I will drive the lady."

She turned toward the voice. "Oh. It is you."

Kevin Radnor made a faint bow.

"What are you doing here?"

"Waiting for you to come down."

"I be thinking we have spent enough time in each other's company this week, do you not agree?"

"I agree that I was not gracious or friendly, if that is what you mean."

His admission made her pause. Men usually did not admit to being wrong. That he did so disarmed her.

"You will not find me errands of any interest to you. Most will be better done on foot."

"Then I will drive you to where you must walk."

The butler had already sent for the carriage. She could think of no way to get rid of Mr. Radnor without being ungracious and unfriendly herself. She did not object when he accompanied her outside.

"That is a very attractive bonnet," he said.

He was only flattering her, but she touched its brim and could not stop a small smile.

"Is it one of yours?"

"I always wear me own creations."

"The colors suit your ensemble, and you. Do you design like that with your patrons as well?"

"I do." She launched into an explanation of how different faces required different shaped brims, and some women looked lovely with thin ties under the chin while others were flattered by broad ones. He seemed to be paying attention, but as the carriage pulled up in front of them she wondered if he was truly listening.

"I have it in me mind to go to Oxford Street," she said. "To see if there be shops to let."

He got the horse moving. "You intend to open a shop in London?"

"Possibly."

"What about your shop in Richmond?"

"I may keep that one too. It all depends on what I learn in the next few days."

"Chase said you think to live here in Town."

"That also depends on what I learn." She would have to remember that those two were cousins, and Chase would probably tell Kevin most anything he wanted to know.

"Shouldn't you be looking at homes to let instead of shops?"

She wondered if he was going to offer unwelcome advice all day. "First I am going to look at some shops, if that be acceptable to you."

He turned onto Oxford Street and stopped the carriage. He tied up the reins, passed a boy a coin to watch the conveyance, then helped her down.

"Thank you, I can manage now," she said hopefully. "I will hire a hackney to get me-self back."

"I will accompany you so you are not walking the streets alone. Town is unsettled these days, and not safe. Besides, I have never shopped for a shop before."

There were not any street-level shops available in the area she wanted, but she found a few on cross streets. She bent close to the windows of one a few feet down Gilbert Street to peer in. Then she walked around the corner back onto Oxford and strolled down, angling her head to look up.

Beside her, Kevin Radnor did the same thing. "What are we looking for?"

"Space above that be available, like this one here." She stopped below a window that had a "To Let" sign in it. The shop was on the second story.

"Most women's shops in London be up like that," she said, more to herself than to him. "It be cheaper, of course. However . . ." She stepped back and examined the shop below, at street level. It sold jewelry. "It also be more private. A woman enters a door and becomes invisible until she emerges. No one peers at her while walking past the window. The question —" She walked back around the corner, then crossed the side street to see what would be noticeable when one walked by on Oxford.

Kevin Radnor followed her like a shadow. "The question is what?"

"Is one at an advantage having a shop on the street or a disadvantage? In Richmond I have me own at street level, and having wares visible to passersby brings new patrons me way. The milliner's shop where I worked in the City did as well. However, in Mayfair the modistes and milliners might be up there for reasons besides the cost of letting. A more public establishment might be looked down upon. I don't suppose you know if street level be considered too common here?"

"I don't buy women's things, so how would I know?"

"Lots of men buy women's things, Mr.

Radnor. I daresay you be an unusual gentleman if you never have."

"Oh. You mean for mistresses and such. I don't buy gifts like that."

She had to smile. "You said you have never been enthralled and now you claim to have never had a mistress or lover for whom you bought gifts. Are you a monk?"

He looked her right in the eye. "Hardly."

For a moment, while their gazes connected, she saw a different Kevin Radnor. Smoldering more than brooding. Frankly sensual. It surprised her that he revealed himself in such a way, until she recognized that what she really witnessed was masculine interest. In her.

She was not prepared for that from this man. Nor did she expect her own reaction. His hooded, piercing gaze compelled her attention in spite of herself and evoked warm little trembles in her body.

He gestured to the shop. "Whatever is normally done, I would think a lady would prefer not to walk up two sets of stairs. Just because something is not commonplace does not mean it can never happen."

"I will ask Minerva about this, but you may have the right of it. Why should women have to climb stairs to buy a bonnet or dress?" She began walking back to the carriage, all too aware of Kevin Radnor in stride beside her.

The man who represented building owners was waiting outside when Kevin brought the carriage to a stop in front of the house on Chapel Street. Kevin took in the façade while he tied the reins. It was not a modest abode. It rose three levels above the elevated entrance doorway. In this neighborhood it would cost a good deal to let.

Apparently, Miss Jameson was eager to spend her inheritance.

He helped her down and introduced her to the agent after receiving his card. Mr. Maitland smiled and opened the door. "We will tour the cellar kitchen and chambers last, if that will suit you, sir. Most couples are more interested in the public rooms. The library is right here."

"You have misunderstood, Mr. Maitland," Miss Jameson said. "Mr. Radnor escorts me today, but I alone will be living in the house that is let."

Mr. Maitland expressed no surprise, but he sent a gleaming glance in Kevin's direction before extolling the proportions and airy space of the library.

Miss Jameson paced around, unaware that the agent had formed his own conclusions about her. Nor did Kevin see any reason to alert her or to correct the man. When it came time to sign the lease, Mr. Maitland would learn the truth of it.

She positioned herself in front of the empty bookcases that spanned one long wall, flanking the fireplace. "They look rather bleak."

"They won't after you have filled them," Mr. Maitland said.

Miss Jameson barely nodded. She followed Mr. Maitland out to see the dining room and morning room. They went above to view the drawing room and gallery, and a large apartment. The next level held more bedchambers, and the top one the servants' quarters.

"It is a handsome house," Kevin said while they came down the stairs. "Large." What could one woman need with all this space?

Miss Jameson slowed her steps so he came up behind her on the staircase. "This be a very good street, yes?" she asked quietly.

"An excellent street. This house will require at least three servants, however. More likely five or six. That does not include any grooms for horses or staff for a carriage if you have one."

She stopped outside the library and allowed Mr. Maitland to pace farther away. "It be the sort of house a lady would live in, you mean."

"Anyone could live in it who wanted to and could afford it. But, yes, a lady would be comfortable here."

"I think so too." She cocked her head. "Where do you live?"

"In my family home when I am in Town."

"You be with your family still?"

"It is only my father, and it is a very large house. If I did not agree to dine with him on occasion, we would never see each other."

"How interesting." She walked toward Mr. Maitland, who waited patiently by the door leading down below.

When all was done, Mr. Maitland left them alone to walk through again if they chose, or, Kevin assumed, to discuss the suitability of the house for a man looking to keep a mistress contented. Miss Jameson returned to the library and again pondered those bookcases.

"I never thought about a library." She glanced at him as if suddenly remembering he stood there. "I don't own any books. These will look odd if they be empty."

"You will simply purchase some books. Just buy what you like. Or, if you prefer, a

bookseller will choose a selection for you."
He noticed she now frowned. "Do you
know how to read?"

"I know well enough. Probably not so
good as to read what a bookseller would
choose." She strolled past him, toward the
entrance. "I think I'll try to get better at it,
so I'm sure to understand the details of any
fancy documents that are put before me."

He cursed himself for his question. He
had actually watched her read the fancy
document *he* had set before her. "Like
many things, it comes easier with the doing
of it. What do you enjoy reading?"

"Years ago I began reading a book that
had pictures in it of knights and ladies. I
did not get far before I couldn't borrow it
no more, but I did enjoy it. Perhaps I will
see if a bookseller has a copy of that book."

Mr. Maitland locked the door and took
his leave. Miss Jameson bent back her head
and looked up the height of the house, giving Kevin a view of her very fine profile.
The word "lovely" came to his mind. Her
face was more elegant than pretty, more
classic than sweet. As for Chase's description of her being luscious, that mostly
pertained to her form beneath the neck.
Even in her pelisse he could see evidence of
full breasts and a narrow waist. His imagina-

tion had spent too much time during the last day disrobing her to discover just how luscious she might be.

That would have to end immediately, unless he wanted to be an idiot while trying to lead her in the direction the enterprise needed to go. It had entered his mind that saddling him with Miss Jameson had been the duke's idea of a fine joke. Uncle Frederick's sense of humor had taken peculiar turns sometimes.

She turned to the carriage. "I think this will do."

"It is very large." The last thing he wanted was for her to let a house that cost so much she went looking for more money. That would only encourage her to sell her half of the enterprise.

"So you said. Three servants at least, you said. I like that it be the kind of house that a lady might live in, though."

"Is it your intention to live like one?"

She allowed him to hand her into the carriage. "I think me intention might be to live like the heiress I be now. I will decide after I do me sums."

That evening after dinner, Rosamund settled into the library with Minerva.

"The house sounds like just the thing,"

Minerva said, continuing a conversation started at the table. "That street is quite fashionable."

More fashionable than this one, her tone implied. Being gentry born, and married to the grandson of a duke, Minerva did not have much to prove. Her blood, and that of her husband, made her acceptable.

Rosamund had loved the house and was well on her way to reconciling the cost. She had pictured Charles coming to call, and being impressed by it. Instead of Kevin Radnor, she had imagined the man walking along with her was Charles, taking it all in and being glad that she was no longer the farmer's daughter in service to his family, and whom his family denied him.

"Mr. Radnor thought it too big for me. I believe he was surprised I even considered that neighborhood. I suppose folk such as me don't normally live there."

Minerva leveled a gaze at her. "If such things matter to you, there are other places to live where you will be comfortable."

Rosamund liked how frank Minerva always was. She heard her new friend's warning. *It is not for such as you, and some neighbors will pretend you are not there. If that will hurt you, then live elsewhere.*

She wished she could be as frank in turn,

and confide why she wanted that house, and why she would be asking Minerva for help in other things that were not for such as her. But she didn't dare give voice to her secret dream, a dream she feared has no real possibility of coming true.

"If I be ignored, I won't mind. Hopefully, when my sister comes of age to join me, she will be better accepted if I have been there a while."

"When are you going to see her? I look forward to meeting her."

"I intend to go north in a few days and bring her to the school you recommended. Perhaps during the next school holiday we can call on you here."

Minerva had been so helpful already. She had learned about that school and even written Rosamund's letter to the mistress who owned it so the spelling and manner of writing would be correct. Rosamund hesitated to request more aid, but she had nowhere else to turn.

"I would like to have some dresses sewn for Lily. I have her measurements and the garments do not need to be fancy. Might you recommend a dressmaker who can do good, practical clothing quickly?"

Minerva smiled mischievously. "I have been waiting impatiently for this question.

Only I expected the wardrobe to be made for you, not your sister."

Rosamund laughed. "I suppose I might order a few things for meself too."

"Then we must visit a good modiste so whatever you order is not only practical, but also fashionable. For your sister as well as you. The other girls at that school may wear simple gray while in the schoolroom but will arrive and leave in far better." She tapped her jaw while thinking. "I believe I know just the place. We will go tomorrow."

"Mr. Radnor spoke of calling again tomorrow, to escort me to the warehouses. Perhaps if we leave before he arrives —"

"No, no. Let him come along. I will send a note to him to be here early, so we have enough time. We will take our coach, so we all can ride together." She leaned in and grinned. "We will bore him senseless. He will not be so quick to try to keep a close watch on your movements after sitting for hours in a modiste's reception chamber."

Was that what he was doing? Keeping her in his sights? How silly of her not to have realized it. Of course Minerva was right. Kevin Radnor was not simply being friendly. He wanted to make sure she was not meeting with investors who wanted to purchase her share of his company. Of *their* company.

Perhaps she had been wrong about that male interest she thought she saw in him too. No doubt he had only been calculating how to manage her. To him, she was merely a problem complicating his plans. In that case, what a relief — she had enough trouble just being in business with him, let alone having to fend off unwelcome advances.

She looked over at Minerva, who sat so comfortably with her now. Minerva had never, not once, done or said anything that implied they were not equals, even if they weren't.

"We met because you and your husband do inquiries," Rosamund ventured. "Do you find that interesting?"

"Each one is a puzzle to be solved. It can be very engaging, and sometimes exciting."

"Do people tell you secrets in order to receive your services?"

"At times it is necessary. Hence our profession being one of *discreet* inquiries. Other times the search is very simple, and all I ask is that I be warned if it might be dangerous." Minerva eyed Rosamund with curiosity. "Do you have an inquiry that you want me to conduct for you? It sounds as if you do."

"Perhaps . . . Could be I do."

"Rest assured that any confidences regarding it, and even the request itself, will never be spoken of to anyone else."

Rosamund decided to trust Minerva. "I do want your help. You will know how to go about it, while I will spin meself in circles." She took her biggest step yet toward the dream. "I want you to find someone, or at least learn what became of him."

CHAPTER FOUR

Kevin found it entirely exasperating that Minerva had inserted herself into his scheme to befriend Miss Jameson. Yet here he was, handing them both down from the coach on New Bond Street after enduring all that chatter about fashion and fabric.

He gazed up at the first story, where this modiste plied her trade.

"Come along, Kevin," Minerva said. "We may want a man's opinion. If so, you will have to do."

His face impassive, he followed them up the stairs and entered the modiste's salon. Madame Tissot knew Minerva and, upon learning two wardrobes were required, swept the ladies away, leaving him to pass the time in a room with uncomfortable furniture.

It occurred to him while he surveyed the feminine chamber, with its frail tables and chairs, that this was what Minerva meant by making his life unpleasant. Well, she would have to do better than this. She did not know with whom she dealt.

He tried the one upholstered chair. It had not been built for a man with his height, but after sprawling this way and that he managed to find some accommodation. He then closed his eyes and retreated into his mind. His last thought before giving all of it over to his probability calculations was curiosity on whom the second wardrobe was for.

Some time later, he emerged from his reverie and checked his pocket watch. They had already been here over an hour. He could hear feminine laughter and conversation behind one of the doors. He considered leaving a note and taking himself off, but he was on a campaign to win over Miss Jameson's trust and friendship. That required he spend time with her. Which, if Minerva had not waylaid his plans, he would be doing now.

The voices rose, and he heard a few snippets of conversation. "Oh, you must, Rosamund."

"Isn't it too daring?"

Lots of laughter then.

"Not at all," Madame Tissot said. "The dress will be very modest, and the color will be fashionable this year."

"I'm not sure . . ."

It sounded like a decision was required in that room. He might not know about fashion, but he knew when a woman dressed to enhance her beauty, and also the difference between acceptably daring and scandalously daring.

It was better than sitting out here for Zeus knew how long. Besides, she was, in a manner of speaking, spending *his* money. With that thought, he walked to the door and opened it.

Three women turned shocked expressions on him. Madame Tissot patted her chest above her heart. Minerva's astonishment turned to amusement. Miss Jameson — Miss Jameson made his breath catch.

She had been swathed in fabric from breast to toes. A deep red fabric, with a light sheen to it. Her creamy shoulders showed, and from the way she held the cloth he guessed her back did as well. She just stared at him, clutching the red closer.

He wondered if she was naked beneath that red silk. She looked it. Possibly not, though. Maybe the straps of her chemise had merely been lowered —

The modiste clucked her tongue. "Sir, it

63

is not customary to have men here while I drape."

"Really, Kevin." Minerva sighed dramatically. "I said we might need you, but I would have told you if we did."

What nonsense. One would think he had never seen a half-naked woman before. "It was clear that Miss Jameson was undecided, so I concluded you did need a man's opinion, in order to speed up the decision." He gestured to the red fabric. "It is lovely and you should use it." He turned to Madame Tissot. "You must be careful with the dress. Nothing vulgar. Red can be risky."

Madame Tissot looked at Minerva. Minerva at Miss Jameson. Miss Jameson shrugged and nodded.

"The red silk it will be," Madame Tissot said.

Kevin paced to the table where Minerva sat with fashion plates lined up in front of her. He examined each one, then paused. "What are these plain ones for? Even in a shop, women wear better than this."

"Those are for my sister, to wear at her school," Miss Jameson said.

He looked over at her. Madame Tissot had draped her further, in a bulky muslin mantle that covered her so thoroughly that only her pretty head showed now.

"Your sister?"

He had no idea she had a sister. Actually, for all he knew she had four of them, and three brothers, and two aunts. She might even have parents in the country somewhere. She might have a very good reason to let a large house.

He knew nothing of her family because he had never asked her about that. Or anything about herself. He could picture Nicholas and Chase shaking their heads at him. Clucking their tongues. *Badly done, Kevin. Badly done.*

"Perhaps if you leave us, Rosamund can get dressed and we can depart soon," Minerva said.

"Certainly." He opened the door. "Carry on."

"After two hours in those warehouses, no doubt you could use some air." Kevin broached the idea while the coach rolled back into Mayfair. "Why don't we ride in the park a while?"

Minerva plucked a tiny watch from her reticule. "I cannot. I must meet with one of our agents regarding an inquiry. Just have the coachman leave me off."

"Perhaps a short ride," Rosamund said. The warehouses had been very dusty, but then, they usually were. She had examined the new products for milliners and bought a straw form for a hat, as well as some notions, all of which would be delivered in the morning. More importantly, she had ingratiated herself with the owners and some of the men who served customers.

The day had cooled, but she opened the coach window anyway. The crisp breeze felt good against her skin. She looked out but could see Kevin Radnor out of the corner of her eye.

For a man born to the ton, he was not especially observant about etiquette. His sudden appearance in the fitting room had stunned them all. He must have noticed, yet he'd treated his intrusion as perfectly normal, even when Madame Tissot specifically said it wasn't.

She'd had nothing more than loose silk covering her undergarments. He had definitely looked, but he had not ogled. He'd reacted as if he walked in on women in dishabille all the time. Perhaps he did. Not lovers, though. Not mistresses. He had been most clear about that.

Which meant something else if he was "hardly" a monk. She added another item to her list of things to do in the next few days.

After dropping off Minerva, the carriage entered Hyde Park and took a spot in a long line of carriages inching along while their gentlemen and ladies enjoyed the fashionable hour.

"If it is too crowded we can go elsewhere," Kevin said.

"I don't mind. I like watching the ladies. I steal ideas from their bonnets and hats and envy their ensembles."

"You have been here before?"

"We shop girls come all the time. You never notice us because you ride in coaches or on horses, and we are down below, on foot along the edges."

"I'm sure I would have noticed you if I rode past you on my horse."

"When you are lost in your thoughts, me thinks you don't notice anything at all."

He did not argue the point. He opened the other window so the breeze could waft through. "How many sisters do you have?"

"Just one. Lily is fourteen, much younger than me. She was a child when our father passed away. I had to leave her in the country while I found employment."

"Now she will attend a school, however. That is why those plain dresses were ordered, you said."

"Minerva helped me find a school. Lily

67

will have a fine bit of catching up to do. But she will come out of it with an education. I am hopeful that when she be grown, she will make a good marriage. I have settled some of the inheritance on her, to help with that." She realized she was talking too much again, about things of no interest to this man. "Anyway, that be me plan."

"That is generous of you, to have thought of her first, even before indulging yourself."

He seemed sincere in saying that. "Do you think it will work? If she be educated and finished, and has a settlement, that she might marry well? I'd like it to be a gentleman, so she would not have to worry about money. It could be a middling sort of gentleman."

"It could happen that way. You have made a friend in Minerva. When the day comes, she can help ease her into the company of such gentlemen."

"She'll still be the daughter of a tenant farmer. I can't change that."

"A fortune has a way of obscuring the details of one's birth."

She hoped so. Not only for Lily, but for herself. She was counting on a big fortune obscuring quite a lot. Yet there were things she could not hide. She knew that. She had not been educated, for one thing. She didn't

68

speak like the ladies she heard. Her reading was only passable and her hand when writing not elegant.

You make hats, her inner voice said. *The nicest wardrobe, the biggest house, will not change who you be. Charles will never marry you.*

"You are brooding," he said.

She looked over to see him smiling, as if he knew how peculiar it was for him to make that accusation instead of receive it. She had to laugh.

"Let me see if I can guess what occupies you." He leaned forward and looked into her eyes in that disconcerting, piercing way of his. "You are thinking that you will hold her back, no matter what you do for her."

It touched her that he guessed. That he knew. She could not agree and keep her composure, so she only looked back at him. That connected gaze and their close proximity sent a little buzz to humming through her.

"It is not so hard to imitate a lady. It merely takes a bit of practice. Such a change does not make you one, but it prevents people from marking you otherwise too, until they know your history." A slow smile broke. "Even that has been known to be altered."

What an astonishing suggestion. It was too late to create a new history for herself with regard to Charles and his family, but for her sister's sake —

"Chase? Is that you in there?" The woman's voice all but shouted in Rosamund's ear. She looked over to see another coach so close that she could serve coffee to its inhabitants.

"No, that's Kevin," a younger voice said. "Kevin, how odd to see you here. You never come to the park at this hour."

Two women's faces filled the other carriage's window. An older woman with dark hair squinted to see Kevin. A younger woman with blond hair looked directly at Rosamund herself. They both wore bonnets that did not flatter them, in Rosamund's opinion. Expensive, though. She took note of the intricate pleating on the underside of the dark-haired woman's brim.

Across from her, Kevin stifled a groan. He slid to the window. "Aunt Agnes. You are looking well."

"You are probably shocked to see I am alive. It isn't as if you ever call when you are in Town."

"I have been very busy."

Her gaze shifted from him to where Rosamund sat. "I can see. Isn't that Chase's coach?"

"It is. I am escorting one of his house-guests this afternoon."

"Are you going to introduce her? Bad enough you have reduced yourself to trade, but must you also adopt the rude behavior of your fellow tradesmen?"

Rosamund saw how Kevin's smile formed a thin line. He looked back at her with something akin to an apology. "Aunt Agnes, Felicity, may I introduce you to Miss Jameson? Miss Jameson, this is my aunt, Lady Agnes Radnor, and my cousin's wife, Mrs. Walter Radnor."

Two frowns. Two pensive faces. Then two startled expressions turned to each other. "Did you hear, Felicity? That is *Rosamund Jameson,*" Lady Agnes said.

"I heard. Oh my." The younger woman stared hard at Rosamund. "Oh *my.*"

"How dare Chase not inform us all that she has been found?" Lady Agnes said loudly.

"You will have to ask him," Kevin said. "Now, we are due back at his house —"

"Nonsense. Stop that carriage so I can make Miss Jameson's acquaintance." Lady Agnes loudly ordered her own carriage to pull out of the stream. "A whole year we have been waiting. I had come to believe she would never be found. Dolores will be — well, shocked to say the least."

Kevin cursed under his breath. "There is nothing else for it now. Allow me to apologize in advance, Miss Jameson." He shot open the carriage trap door to give the coachman directions to turn out of the line at once.

"Must we do this?" Rosamund asked while the carriage maneuvered to a place to stop.

"Why would they want to talk with me? Lady Agnes did not look happy even to *see* me."

"My aunt never loses an opportunity to feed her own bitterness." He opened the door and stepped out, then offered her his hand.

She climbed down, then set her skirt to rights. "I don't understand."

He scratched the side of his head. "The thing is this. If you had never been found, eventually your inheritance would have been split up among all of us."

In other words, the whole family had been hoping she was dead.

After examining her from head to toe, Lady Agnes deigned to speak. "Well, Miss Jameson, it took long enough to find you."

"Had I known a fortune waited, I would have been found sooner."

"Indeed." Again that long inspection. Her expression said she was not impressed. Rosamund noticed those eyes narrow and pause on her bonnet. *Too good for such as her,* those eyes said.

"She lives in Richmond," Kevin said. "Hence the delay. She never saw the notices in the London papers."

"The major papers can be had all over England," Lady Agnes said.

"I suppose if someone hopes to inherit an unexpected fortune from a stranger, that person would arrange to procure and read every edition," Kevin said. "Miss Jameson is not that person, it appears."

His aunt was no fool and knew he was mocking her. A nasty glare flamed above her pursed smile. "Apparently not. You are rather old to be unmarried, Miss Jameson. Considering that there is little to complain of in your appearance, I find that most odd."

"Aunt Agnes," Kevin admonished.

"I have been devoting meself to other things, Lady Agnes," Rosamund said. "I've a millinery shop that requires attention. Looking for a husband has fallen aside as a result."

"A shop girl. Well. Did it not astonish you to discover the duke's bequest? It was certainly most peculiar to us."

"To me as well. I scarcely knew him."

Deep, penetrating inspection now. "And how, may I ask, did you scarcely know him?"

"No, you may not ask," Kevin said. "Let us all take a turn before Miss Jameson decides the entire Radnor family is odder than the bequest." He turned with deliberation and stared at his aunt until she fell into step with him.

That left Rosamund walking beside the younger woman named Felicity, who was the wife of one of Kevin's cousins. She was a pretty woman, with fragile features. She reminded Rosamund of those little china sculptures, the ones that always had tiny, pointed noses and blank, blue eyes.

"That is a very handsome bonnet you are wearing," Felicity said.

Rosamund immediately felt guilty for her unkind thoughts. "Thank you. I made it meself."

"What a talented person you are! Of course . . . you won't have to make your own anymore, will you?"

"Oh, but I want to. It is me trade."

Felicity laughed. "Come now. With your fortune you can purchase any hats or wardrobe you want for yourself and can give up being in trade altogether."

"I don't think so. I enjoy it too much."

Felicity blinked hard.

"How sad that you are unmarried as yet. I expect that will be quickly remedied."

"The solicitor warned me about fortune hunters. I think it be best to avoid them, don't you?"

"It depends on their own fortunes." She slowed her pace, dragging Rosamund back with her. "Kevin has probably been rude about part of that inheritance. I would apologize for him, but I have given up doing so. Although this one time it is perhaps understandable. He didn't care about the money, you see. Only that invention, and that the duke left half of it to a stranger."

"We have come to a right understanding about that, so he has not been too rude."

"Are you going to give him your half? I can't think of any other understanding that he would find acceptable."

"I am not planning to do that, and he knows it." Rosamund noticed how they kept falling back from Kevin and Lady Agnes.

"I suppose you could turn it back to the estate. One is not forced to accept bequests."

"Why would I do that?"

"To rid yourself of it, of course. My husband explained to me that although it isn't worth anything, it could cost a person dearly. A partner is accountable for debts and additional investments. It would be such a shame if that happened to you."

Felicity was showing herself to be a sly woman. Rosamund wondered why she offered all this advice. "If I do turn it back, who would receive it instead?"

"I suppose it would be split among the cousins, although most likely the others would sell and take the pennies offered. Kevin, of course, would keep his portion."

Having her half broken up like that was the one thing Kevin did not want. And if it was so worthless, she could not imagine why Felicity cared what happened to it.

"Well, I think I'll keep it for a while, to see what's what with it first. That will spare all those cousins from having to bother with it."

Felicity appeared dismayed. "Miss Jameson, when I said you might want to rid yourself of it, I did so only for your benefit." She looked around, as if to make sure no one walked close by. "You really do not want to be Kevin's partner. He will probably ruin you. And . . ." She lowered her voice. "You may not have been told this, but his last partner died under suspicious circumstances."

Rosamund was so startled by the revelation that she almost tripped over a fallen branch on the path. Felicity took satisfaction in that reaction. Up ahead it appeared Kevin and his aunt's conversation had turned contentious.

"What do you mean?"

"It was called an accident, but no one in the family thinks the duke had a mishap and fell off that parapet. Nor do we think he jumped. That only leaves one way he ended up on the ground below."

Rosamund decided she did not care much for this woman. "You have implied that Kevin Radnor is the reason the duke fell. Please speak plainly now. Do you have any reason to believe that, or do you merely dislike him?"

Felicity's lids lowered. Her head rose so she could look down her nose. Rosamund knew that expression very well. A lady was about to put an inferior in her place.

"He is most dislikable, but I do not suspect without cause. It happened at the duke's estate, Melton Park. None of the others were there. Kevin claimed he was in France, but he was really in England. I saw him myself in Town the next day. If he learned about the will, and the disposition of the duke's half of his company, he had a reason to be angry enough to act rashly. Is that plain enough for you?" She began walking with sulking determination. "It was my hope to spare you. I can see that was a mistake."

Rosamund matched Felicity's strides until they drew up behind Kevin and Lady Agnes again. They got there just in time to hear Lady Agnes say, "I'm only advising that the sensible solution is for both of you to sell whatever exists for whatever someone will pay. It is unlikely to be worth more in the future, and this would spare you this unseemly partnership."

Her arrival caught Lady Agnes up short. Unaware she had been overheard, she retreated into pleasantries. "Look at how nicely the ivy has revived here in the park, Felicity. I was just telling Kevin that my new gardener has started some vines on my back wall."

CHAPTER FIVE

Rosamund never thought she would find herself asking Kevin Radnor to call on her, but the next morning she sat at the writing table in the library to pen a letter doing just that. A long night of grappling with her thoughts had led her to conclude that she would turn to Kevin this time for advice rather than Minerva, since Minerva had already helped her so much.

This meeting might also give her a chance to find out if there could be any truth to Felicity's suspicions. The woman was the sort who took pleasure in making trouble.

She labored over the letter, leaving too many cross outs and splotches of ink on the paper. The whole thing was a disaster before she finished. Minerva entered the library just as Rosamund was pulling out a new sheet of paper.

Seeing her writing a letter, Minerva sat with a book and did not interfere. Rosamund tried again, muttering with annoyance when things began to go badly again. She set down the pen and covered her eyes with her hands.

"Are you weeping?"

She uncovered her eyes to see Minerva standing right next to her.

"No. I be trying not to scream." She gestured to the paper. "My hand be bad, my spelling be bad, and I can't seem to use a pen without dribbling ink all over everything."

Minerva examined the letter. "If you want, I will write what you tell me to write. Or we can just send one of the servants with a message."

Rosamund picked up the pen again. "You wrote the one to the school. I can't have you doing them all. I need to learn."

Minerva's hand covered the one that held the pen. "I will help you to practice. You cannot learn it in one hour, however. Let us send that messenger for now."

So it was that at eleven o'clock, Kevin Radnor arrived in a fine coach, complete with a footman standing in back, to escort her to the solicitor's office. "It is my father's," he explained. "He never uses it."

She settled on her cushion, while he sat facing her. Dark clouds darkened the sky.

She hoped it didn't rain.

"I am flattered you sent for me," he said. "It has been my hope that we may be friends, and that you will ask for my help in any way that I can be of service."

"I thought it be best to have someone with me, what with it being legal doings." She also wanted to broach something with her business partner. She would wait for the right moment, and hope that she had the courage.

She took the opportunity while they rode through Mayfair to examine the women strolling in the streets. Through one open window she spied an attractive hat with a broader brim than was customary. She removed a little piece of paper and a pencil from her reticule and quickly jotted down a rough drawing of it.

Kevin leaned forward and peered at her paper. "Were you taught how to draw?"

"Taught? No, I just try and get it close enough to remind meself of what I seen."

"It appears you have a natural talent for it, then."

She looked at her little drawing. It did capture the hat's shape and angled brim fairly well.

They arrived at Mr. Sanders's chambers in the City before the rain fell. She liked the solicitor. He reminded her of a kind uncle in his manner and appearance. When she first met him and he explained her inheritance, he had taken pains to do so slowly, perhaps knowing that in her shock it would be difficult for her to take it all in.

Now he greeted Mr. Radnor, then turned all his attention to her. "I have the lease for the house right here. The owner was amenable to most of the changes I requested." He gave her a wink. "What he first gave me was less than favorable, on the assumption presumably that a woman would not have the experience to recognize its deficiencies."

"That was why I asked you to advise me." She had been an inexperienced woman when she signed the lease in Richmond and regretted not being more forceful in her discussions with the landlord.

"I congratulate you on your good sense. It is so much easier to establish these things at the outset, rather than try to fix it later." He handed the large vellum document to her. "You will see that the rent has been lowered to match that of others on the street. Also that the terms are changed somewhat. A few draconian provisions have been removed. For example, there is nothing extra for the furnishings. They are now included, in keeping with how the house was described."

She began to read, guessing that the word "draconian" was a fancy way of saying "bad." The penmanship used in the document distracted her. Perfectly formed with dramatic flourishes, the letters all but sung through the words. A clerk had penned this, of course, but she still envied how beautiful it looked.

"Do you understand it?" The low voice came from her side, where Kevin sat. She glanced at him. Mr. Sanders smiled slightly in amusement.

"I do. Thank you for doing this for me, Mr. Sanders. I see the owner has already signed it."

"He has signed all three copies. If you put your name to them, it is done."

She removed her gloves. One by one she signed her name as neatly as she could on each copy, trying not to dribble any ink. Mr. Sanders blotted then folded one and handed it to her. "You are now a resident of London, Miss Jameson."

This was a bold step. A daring one. There was no turning back now.

Her imagination soared, rearranging the furniture and purchasing more. Picturing Lily in that nice bedchamber on the second story. Seeing Charles walk up the front steps to the door.

Mr. Sanders brought forth more documents. "This is the lease on the shop. That was far more straightforward. It includes the first story, along with the shop at street level." He set down the vellum.

She read through the terms. Kevin tried to read over her shoulder.

"You are taking that shop on the cross street?" he asked.

She nodded. "Someone told me that just because something isn't done, that don't mean it can't be done." She picked up the pen and signed her name.

Mr. Sanders finished with those documents too. "I would say you are going to be a busy woman, settling into both places."

She took her leave of Mr. Sanders. Once in the anteroom, she whispered to Mr. Radnor, "Should I ask the clerk about the fee now?"

"A letter will be sent to you."

The rain started as soon as they sat in the coach again. She looked in dismay at the rivulets it made on the windows. Her plan for the rest of this outing would not work now.

"I have something for you." Kevin held a box covered in cloth. He gave it to her.

It was not a box. She unveiled a book. She

opened it to see it was a novel by Walter Scott.

"I don't know if that is the one you were reading. However, it is very popular and perhaps you will enjoy it. There are knights in it."

She slowly rubbed her palm down the brown leather cover. It had been carved to show a pattern all along its edges. "I will read it at once so I can return it soon."

"It is not from my library. It is a gift. It is yours."

She looked down at that lovely cover. It was the first book she had ever owned. "I will give it a special place on me bookcase. Thank you so much." She looked up to see him smiling at her. Such a handsome smile he had. It softened the highborn angles of his face and affected his eyes so they did not appear so serious and thoughtful.

His generosity gave her courage. "I wish the rain had not started. I intended to ask that we go to the park so that I could talk to you about something."

He glanced at the rain falling hard outside. "We can go to my family's house. My father has already demanded to meet you. We can complete that chore, have a luncheon, then escape him to talk privately. Is that agreeable to you?"

She nodded, although the part about his father gave her pause. After his aunt Agnes and Felicity, she did not expect good things from these relatives.

Kevin weighed the good and the bad of the day. He had not been needed at Sanders's chambers, that was clear. Perhaps she had wanted an escort because legal matters intimidated her. He decided to accept that, although he didn't really believe it.

Her request to have a conversation revealed that perhaps she had wanted his escort for reasons besides letting that house and shop. His solution to the problem caused by the weather came without hesitation, however, even if it meant suffering his father's interference. He embraced the notion quickly because it had seemed an easy way to continue spending time in Miss Jameson's company.

Acknowledging that, admitting it, pushed him into silent thought for the rest of the ride. *The goal, you ass, is to make her more manageable, not to make you an idiot.*

She spent the time poking around in her reticule, then opened the book and turned the front pages. It was not an expensive tome, but she handled it as if it were precious. Her surprise in receiving it

86

touched him. He guessed that she had not often received presents.

He tried not to look at her, but there she was, lovely, self-possessed, *luscious*. Chase had chosen the right word with that one. She could wear a dress as shapeless as those schoolgirl sacks she'd ordered for her sister and still make a man half mad. As it was, her yellow dress and pale green pelisse revealed her form despite the ensemble's modesty. Her proximity alone had him close to a full arousal that would be difficult to hide. He began forming his thoughts in ancient Greek in order to avoid such an embarrassing development.

He really needed to conquer his inconvenient attraction to her, which promised to interfere in numerous ways. It shouldn't be too difficult to do that, though. There were hundreds of beautiful women in London, and he rarely noticed any of them. He prided himself on not being the kind of man who wasted time or money on pointless infatuations.

They couldn't arrive at his house fast enough for his comfort. He bounded out of the coach as soon as the footman opened the door, then handed Miss Jameson down rather than allowing the footman to do it. She had not yet put her gloves back on, and the warmth of her hand permeated his own glove, sending his thoughts where they should not go again. How annoying.

She pulled on the gloves while they walked to the door, all the while looking up at the house's height and down its breadth. "I don't know how you could have thought me new house big when you live in such as this."

"This one is far too large, especially for what is often one person." It had been purchased with many more occupants in mind. His father had anticipated a large family, only to have his wife die while giving birth to their first child.

The butler opened the door to admit them.

"I should warn you that my father is an original. Eccentric, actually."

She opened her eyes wide. "Is he? I don't see how that is possible when you be so conventional." She crossed the threshold wearing a self-satisfied smile.

Kevin followed. He had warned her. If Miss Jameson thought *he* was eccentric, she was in for a shock.

He brought her to the library. Its size amazed her. She gazed at the massive bookcases that filled three walls. The fourth one was hung with paintings. . . . And something else.

She went to stand in front of ten frames enclosing rows of gray and beige moths. Each one had been labeled. It must have taken hours to collect and sort all of these. Yet, with them lined up like this, she could see the differences between them.

She felt Kevin's presence next to her.

"Moths, not butterflies," she said.

"Everyone has butterflies."

She looked at the frames, then at him. She chuckled.

"You find this amusing, do you?"

"*Moths?* It must be quite a struggle for your guests to say something polite when they see these." She imagined a young Kevin Radnor, serious and studious, reading off the names and explaining how this moth was different from that one. No doubt he had enjoyed the social discomfort he created. "It is all a joke, isn't it?"

A slow smile formed. "Don't give it away. No one else has guessed."

"That is because your humor is too sly."

"Not for everyone, it appears."

She laughed and walked away. Moths.

The bookcases drew her attention. Her gaze moved over them, and the many books they held. "Are these all your father's?"

"Some are mine. Some he acquired. Others he inherited. My grandfather was a bibliophile and had his library broken up among his sons when he passed."

"Your family history be on those shelves."

"I never thought of it that way, although I have discovered a few rarities that have probably been in the family for generations."

Side by side they perused the leatherbound volumes. If she purchased one a week she would never own this many books.

Suddenly, something poked at her bum, startling her.

"Mr. Radnor, you surprise me. Please remove your hand."

"My hand?"

"The one on me bum."

"Appealing though the notion is, I assure you that I am never that crude." He held up both his hands to prove his innocence.

She frowned. "What —" She turned around abruptly. "I have never —" She backed up.

He also turned, and sighed. "Father, you really shouldn't," he called out, reaching down to stop the apparatus from advancing further.

She leaned down to peer at a metal contraption with a painted metal face, wearing old-fashioned clothes, boots, and a tricorner hat. "It looks like a big doll."

"It is an automaton. An unusual one, because it rolls." He lifted it to show the wheels at its base. "A flawed idea, because once it is set off, it keeps moving unless it unwinds or hits something. Like your, um . . . like you." He pointed to the salver held in one of the mechanical man's hands, projecting out.

As he held up the mechanical man, its eyelids opened and shut, and a smile formed and unformed while a low, metallic hum sounded. The wheels continued to turn.

"Father, show yourself! Come meet my guest."

"Did you build this?" she asked, examining those wheels and trying to peer inside the figure.

"It was built for my uncle, the late duke. However, I fixed it once my father got hold of it. Part of the mechanism had broken. Ah, there is the mischief-maker."

She looked up to see a tall, lean, white-haired man standing right inside the doorway. He was smiling broadly, clearly pleased with his joke. She looked from him to his son, and then back again. It was like seeing the same man at different ages, they were so similar.

He proceeded into the room, and Kevin made the introductions.

His father took the little man from Kevin. "It wasn't supposed to hit you. The intention was for it to roll past."

"Hardly," Kevin muttered under his breath. "Perhaps you need to work on your aim, then. It always moves in a straight line."

"Yes, well, perhaps I should. Welcome, Miss Jameson. My son has told me that you have finally been found. He is much relieved, as you can imagine. As am I. You seem fascinated with my mechanical butler. Come and I'll show you the others."

Down a stately corridor they strolled. Up a grand staircase with pale blue walls and finely carved white moldings. The senior Mr. Radnor opened two doors with a flourish to reveal a huge chamber full of tables and pedestals, all of them holding automatons.

"This is his drawing room," Kevin murmured while his father strode forth and began turning keys and levers, making the contraptions come alive.

"He must be very fond of these," she whispered back.

"Oh, yes."

"Come in, come in, Miss Jameson. No need to be timid," his father called out.

"Unlike the little butler automaton, these don't move around the chamber."

She entered and admired the variety of the collection. There had to be close to a hundred of them. Large or small, each one had specific movements. A little squirrel fluffed its tail and bit a nut. A clock rang the hour and a group of figures emerged from within and began sawing and chopping wood. Two men sitting on either side of a table appeared to be playing a game of cards.

A large swan in particular fascinated her. At least four feet high and made out of hundreds of pieces of shiny, painted metal, it crooked its neck, turned it, and preened at feathers that rose up and down. Then it turned back, dipped its head, and lifted it with a tiny metal fish in its bill.

"I have the finest collection in England. The biggest too. Quite likely the largest in the world, but I dare not make that claim lest there is some secret hoard of which I am unaware. This one here is from Bavaria. That one came from Naples."

"What are they for?"

"For? Why, they give delight. They amuse. They show the ingenuity and art of their creators." He glanced askance at her. "Ah. You mean how are they useful. I see you have found a kindred mind in your partner, Kevin. Someone else who believes something has no value if it is not producing something or making someone money."

"She did not say they did not have value, nor that they did not make anyone money. After all, you paid handsomely for them. And should you ever sell them, their value, which is considerable, will be apparent."

That received a deep frown. "Parsing through my words, as is typical of you."

"Have you seen your full, Miss Jameson? I believe the cook will be sending up a luncheon soon."

"I be both done and dazzled. Thank you for sharing your rare collection, sir."

Kevin escorted her out. His father, to her dismay, came right along with them.

The luncheon was delicious but a trial. She tried mightily to use the right implements for each dish, and to speak properly. It progressed fairly well, with the senior Mr. Radnor filling the time with one-sided speeches about how the rabble were making Town unlivable, what with their demonstrations and complaints. The meal was punctuated by sharp, brief arguments when father and son disagreed.

The inevitable question came, just as the footman brought in a cake.

"I am curious, Miss Jameson. How were you acquainted with my brother, Hollinburgh?"

She chose her words carefully. "We had a mutual friend. When she became ill, I cared for her."

"And for that he left you a fortune?"

She shrugged. "I cannot know what his thoughts were. Because he was your brother, perhaps you can."

He speared her with a long gaze, then smiled and chortled. "Explain his mind or intentions? As if anyone could. Besides, I barely saw him the last ten years and not at all the last five."

"Yet you lived so close by. Surely you would have seen each other in the park, if nowhere else?"

"My father has not left this house in five years," Kevin said in a matter-of-fact manner.

His father noticed her surprise. "Too crowded in Town now. Too dirty. My friends visit me here. My family has chosen not to."

"Your sisters think *you* should call on *them,*" Kevin said.

"Spoiled girls, the lot of them. Now, Miss Jameson, you have a fortune and half of my son's enterprise. Pity you aren't married. Dare I trust you will be soon?"

95

"Your isolation has made you forget the most common courtesies, Father. One does not ask women that."

"I'm sure Miss Jameson doesn't mind."

"Actually, sir, I do."

He startled at that response. "Well, then, I must apologize. However, let me tell you why I asked. You see, if you were married, you might have a husband with a good knowledge of trade or mechanics, who could take this invention my son has and actually do something with it, thus relieving him of the obligation to spend all his time on such ignoble matters."

Kevin's jaw hardened.

His father looked back, stone-faced and equally belligerent.

Rosamund looked from one to the other. The air fairly crackling with the impending storm.

It was Kevin who chose to stand down. "The meal is done," he said to her. "Let us take our leave and find a place where we can speak of déclassé things out of my father's hearing. It has stopped raining, so the garden is available."

She rose quickly and made a clumsy curtsy in her host's direction. Kevin escorted her out of the chamber.

"I apologize for my father's atrocious

behavior," he said as soon as they were alone.

"It went better than I expected. I thought he would insult me directly. I never expected him to save that for *you.*"

"He loves nothing better than to instigate a row. I'm sure he's keenly disappointed that I refused to rise to the bait."

"That must be tiresome on a daily basis."

"I assure you that I manage not to see him very often."

"Why still live here if he enjoys baiting you?"

He brought her to the morning room and opened the door to the garden. "The family never visits him and friends ceased doing so years ago. If I did not live here, he would be completely alone."

It had been a short rainfall and already the breeze dried the grass and paths as he strolled beside Miss Jameson.

He stole a glance in her direction. Although she looked at the new growth showing on the plants, her expression showed her preoccupation about something. Also perhaps a little fear, as if she hesitated now.

"You said you wanted to talk about something."

"Two somethings. The first one be awkward. . . . When we were in the park, Mrs. Radnor said something to me about the late duke's death being a bit mysterious. She said . . . it was perhaps not an accident."

Felicity was an interfering little fool. "No one really knows what happened."

"She said — she said the family thinks he may have been done in."

"The Home Office looked into it and determined it was an accident."

"Do you think it was?"

Damnation. "I leave it to others who are wiser about such things. Chase made inquiries, I know, and he has not declared it other than an accident, so it appears it was just that. And the other matter you wanted to talk about?" he asked lightly, hoping she would now move on. After a precarious pause, she did.

"I am in need of some help. I do not want to impose on Minerva." She stopped walking and faced him. "I want someone to show me how to be a lady. Like you said it could be done. Minerva is going to help me with me penmanship, and you said the doing of it will improve my reading, but all the rest — I can't do the doing of it until I learn what the doing is. The speech, the walk, the quality way to do things." She flushed. Her earnest expression touched him. "I thought maybe you know of someone who does that. Who fixes people like me."

"You don't need any fixing."

"I do. Even for my shop, I do. I've tried. I had some friends, and I copied them and got better, but I know I still make mistakes, especially when I be flustered or excited. Do you know anyone like that? Who would give me lessons?"

"I can find out. And if there isn't one person, several might do. One for speech, for example. Others for other things." He pictured her attending to the tasks as they were given, mastering them, becoming lady-like in the ways she wanted. The image made him a little sad. "I hope that you will not let such a program of improvement ruin you."

"Ruin me?"

He groped for a way to put it. "When you put on a very expensive hat, does it change who you are? I don't think so. Let any of these improvements you seek be like a new hat."

"You mean don't put on airs."

"I mean don't forget the value of who you are no matter what kind of hat you are wearing."

Her expression cleared. He tried not to be affected by the gratitude he saw in her eyes

99

as she gazed at him. "I think I understand," she said. "I should remember that I be just as worthy now as I will be when this is done."

She smiled at him then, and there was so much sweetness in that smile that something ached in his chest.

"Exactly," he said, perhaps a bit harshly. "Now, are you sure you want to do this? Because it will be criticism after criticism once you start."

"I am sure."

They might as well find out now if she had the stomach for it. "Well, for example, while your speech is probably much different now from when you were a girl, and you have shed much of your accent, you still hold on to some notable errors. 'I be,' for example. 'I be just as worthy.' It is 'I am.' Never 'I be.' "

He watched the impact of his words on her face.

As she absorbed what he was saying, to his surprise, she did not display any embarrassment or shame.

" 'I am,' " she repeated. "I am just as worthy. Not 'I be.' "

He nodded.

She beamed at him.

"Yes. Like that. Just like that. You must do

100

it again whenever I slip. Right away."

To his astonishment, she stood on tiptoe then and kissed him on the cheek.

Her face was so close to his. Dangerously close.

His own kiss came in that instant, without thought. He merely brushed his lips on hers, but in that moment he felt their warmth and velvet softness and inhaled her scent.

Her hands went to her lips as she took a step back. He too stepped back.

She tore her gaze from his own after what seemed a long count, but that probably only lasted one more second after the last.

She began walking back to the house, and he fell into step next to her.

After a few moments, she said, "Do you think it will take long, the lessons?" As if nothing had happened.

He followed suit. "It will take some time to find tutors."

"I be — *am* leaving Town for a spell, to take my sister to her school. I hope to start when I return."

He held open the morning room door. As she passed him, she gave him a long look that all but said, *It would be best to forget whatever just passed between us.*

She was absolutely right. As far as he was

concerned, nothing had happened. He had never believed in infatuation, and he wasn't going to start now.

Chapter Six

Rosamund could not help overhearing the discussion taking place on the terrace. The window to the morning room had been left open, and Minerva, Chase, and four of their agents sat less than twenty feet away.

A young man in a nice frock coat with blond hair appeared to be the object of their current instructions.

"Don't accept any situation except one that has you in his offices, Jeremy. You do not want to be flogging his wares out on the road or anything like that. We need you close to him," Chase said.

"I'll refuse anything else."

"Good," Minerva said. "You, Elise, will apply to work in his house. Chambermaid would be best. You can move around then."

The young woman named Elise nodded.

A thin, sparsely haired man with a pursed mouth raised his hand. "And I?"

"Ah, Brigsby," Chase said. "You are not

here for this inquiry, but for another purpose."

"I don't understand. You said I performed
without exception on the last one."

"True, but this one does not require your
talents."

Brigsby looked dejected. "I think I know
what you want to discuss. I have been waiting for it. You think to let the apartment go,
now that you are here, what with that valet
and all these servants." He straightened his
posture and put on a brave face. "I trust
you will give me a good reference."

"He is not going to let you go," Minerva
said. "Could you just be patient, until we
are done here, and all will be explained?"

Brigsby retreated, leaning out so the others could lean in.

"And me?" a stout woman asked. Gray-
haired and buxom, she wore a lace-trimmed
cap under a large bonnet. The result framed
her soft, creased face twice over. Rosamund
would very much like to sit that old woman
down and show her how more restrained
headwear could flatter at any age.

"You are needed for another inquiry,
Beth," Minerva said. "Mr. Falkner lives
more modestly than Mr. Chillings-worth.
He is not far from Rupert Street, and ac-
cording to Mrs. Drable, he is in need of a

cook. She will put your name forth for that."

"Hard to poke around from the kitchen."

"You are ever resourceful, and it is the only way in at the moment." She looked at Chase, then at all the others. "Questions? Do we all have a right understanding of what is needed?"

Heads nodded. Chairs scraped. Chase and Brigsby walked into the garden. The blond young man went around the house. The old woman and the girl came through the morning room, followed by Minerva. They left, but Minerva sat down at the table where Rosamund still ate her breakfast.

"Is your baggage ready?" she asked after calling for some coffee.

"It is already down. The coach comes in an hour."

"Eat a good breakfast. It will have to last you some hours, and you may find the food at the coaching inns distasteful."

Rosamund looked down at the meal she had barely touched. She had spent the last hour planning what she would say to her sister, and also wondering about Kevin.

She relived that kiss, although she tried not to. The memory had intruded without warning a number of times since she left that big house. She could still feel that soft, warm skim over her lips, slow and sensual.

Her own lips had throbbed in response, and her cheeks had tingled. For an instant, she had not been able to move.

Two seconds, maybe three. At most five or six. None of it took longer than that. And yet, it was difficult to put it out of her mind.

"I want to speak to you before you go," Minerva said. She gestured for the servant to leave.

Rosamund turned all her attention to her friend.

"I have conducted the inquiry you requested. I have some information."

Charles. She immediately felt guilty about that moment in the garden with Kevin and how she kept reliving it.

"He is not in London," Minerva said. "Nor do I think he will be here this Season. He is in Paris. He has been living there for some years now."

Her heart sank. She had let a big house to impress a man who would not see it. She was going to have tutors in speech and comportment to improve for a man who did not even live in the same country. *Clever, clever girl.* "Is his family still here?"

"Oh, yes. The Copleys remain in the same house you gave to me. They are in residence now."

She wondered if she would pass them in

the park one day, while she rode in a fine carriage and was dressed in one of Madame Tissot's dresses. She would greet them and pretend they had not been cruel to her. What would their reaction be? She pictured astonishment, even confusion. That would be worth something, although not nearly enough to justify the funds she was laying out.

"He is not married."

Minerva mentioned that ever so calmly, as just another bit of information gleaned from an inquiry. Nothing in her tone indicated she thought it signified much.

Only Rosamund knew Minerva guessed that it was a very important detail to the client in question. She knew from the studied nonchalance in Minerva's expression, and from the way she chose right then to sip some coffee.

How much did her new friend know? The woman had a profession in conducting inquiries. Had she made some about Rosamund herself recently?

A servant entered, carrying the morning mail. He set a tall stack in front of Minerva, and another one at the place used by Chase. Then, to Rosamund's surprise, he set a large letter in front of her place, along with a much smaller one.

The small one was from Beatrice, she knew. She had written to her friend with a question, and here was the answer. She set it aside to read in the carriage. She stared at the big letter. The hand that wrote her name had formed elegant letters.

"Oh, dear," Minerva murmured.

Rosamund looked over to see Minerva extracting an identical letter from her stack.

"Oh, dear," she said again. This time firmly. Almost like a curse. She slit open the letter and read it, then looked hard at the one in front of Rosamund.

Rosamund picked up hers and opened it. Such a lovely hand. Feminine. Just as impressive as the clerk's penmanship, but clearly not a scrivener's style. "It is an invitation to a dinner party, a week hence."

"Indeed it is," Minerva said. "You can decline."

"Lady Agnes Radnor. Oh, I met her. In the park."

"You did? How unfortunate. Really, you should decline. You will have just returned from a trying journey and cannot be expected to meet all those people so soon."

"All those people?"

"The family. I'm sure the whole lot of them will be there to examine you. I would not wish them on an enemy and do not want to think of you enduring them, let alone all at once."

"I suppose they are only curious."

"You are too kind. *Truly.*"

It touched her that Minerva wanted to spare her, but from what? She would end up meeting these relatives of Kevin's eventually. After Agnes, Felicity, and Kevin's father, how much worse could it be? Declining this invitation would only delay the ordeal.

"I believe I will attend this party. Once it is over, they may lose interest."

"Unlikely."

She laughed. "I must go above and prepare to leave. Thank you for the report. Your inquiry was quick and thorough. You must let me know what fee I owe you." She stood. "I also thank you for your hospitality with my whole heart."

"I wonder why we say, 'I am' instead of 'I be.' After all, the verb is 'to be.' Yet, when we conjugate it in the present tense, there is no 'be' to be found." Kevin shrugged. "Although something similar occurs in most languages. Still, it begs for an explanation."

"That is what has preoccupied you on this ride?" Nicholas asked. "I thought you were brooding over something of consequence. I will have to remember that sometimes when you look deep in thought your mind is wandering through the same kind of mental debris that mine does."

They continued trotting through the Middlesex countryside outside of Town, passing fields showing early growth and trees festooned with blooms. The air smelled of spring as only April air did.

"Did you badger me for this ride in order to discuss linguistics?" Nicholas asked.

"Not at all."

"Then why?"

"Perhaps I just wanted company and thought you could use some too."

"Kevin, you never want company. I have never met another man so comfortable without society."

"You, on the other hand, crave it. I am only thinking of you and being generous."

"You are not being generous. You want something. But I am a patient man and can wait for it."

He had to wait ten minutes. By then they reached a crossroad with a good tavern, and dismounted to refresh themselves.

"I could use some advice," Kevin said once their ale sat on the boards between them.

"First company, now advice. You are full

of surprises today. I can't think of any advice you would need from me, unless you suddenly find yourself with an estate you can't maintain due to lack of income. I've become the expert on that."

Nicholas did not sound bitter, exactly. However, just as Uncle Frederick had disappointed Kevin in that will, so too had he left his heir in financial discomfort. Nicholas had inherited the title, and the properties, but insufficient money. The last months had required he apply himself to solving the dilemma.

"I have agreed to help Miss Jameson, but I have no idea how to do so. Worse, I have at most a week to find a solution."

"What does she want you to do?"

"Find instructors and tutors who will engage her in a program of self-improvement. She thinks to complete a transformation very fast too."

"Is there a lot of improving to do?"

Kevin almost insisted there wasn't, but he considered it. His own interest in Miss Jameson might be coloring his view of things. He liked her the way she was, except when she became stubborn about the enterprise.

"She has been at it for some time on her own, I believe. Imitating the way others speak and dress and such. As Chase mentioned, she does not come off as a rustic. However, there can be moments when she reverts." Charming moments. Moments of vulnerability in a woman who had made her own way for some time and who normally wore the armor of self-possession. *You keep forgetting she is the enemy, you fool.*

"I expect that will give the aunts something to cluck about next week."

"Aunts?"

Nicholas called for more ale. "The dinner party. Aunt Agnes's. We were all invited, and Miss Jameson was too. It will be a chance for us all to give her a good look." He waited while the publican set down the ale. "You appear astonished. Weren't you invited?"

"No."

"An oversight, perhaps."

"I doubt that."

"Well, perhaps Aunt Agnes feared you would start a row with her, what with her getting half the enterprise. Picture the aunts discussing it, and envisioning your brooding and scowling the whole evening, glowering at your enemy from the corners of the drawing room. I wouldn't have invited you either, come to think of it."

"That isn't why she did not invite me. She wants poor Miss Jameson there alone and helpless when their rudeness is visited on her."

"Poor Miss Jameson? *Poor?* She probably has more money than I do."

"That's not what I meant."

"What then? Is she delicate? Easily cowed? I haven't heard such a description of her. She will manage as well as anyone, and perhaps better than most. After all, she probably doesn't give a damn what our family thinks of her."

Kevin frowned over the truth of that, and its implications. She most likely did not give a damn, although she wanted acceptance in a larger way. "It would have helped if this invitation came after the program of self-improvement, is all. With whom do you suggest I make arrangements?"

"How should I know?"

"You are a man about town. Surely you have heard of people who do this kind of thing. Perhaps you have met someone who has already completed such a program and can direct me there."

"I don't know why she charged you with this. If I needed to find such instructors, I would ask Minerva. It is her business to find people, isn't it? With several letters, she probably can have all the names you need."

Which begged the question of why Miss

Jameson had *not* asked Minerva. She might feel she had imposed too much already. Minerva was going to help her with her penmanship, if he remembered correctly. Miss Jameson might think it unseemly to ask for more generosity from that quarter.

That would be understandable. Miss Jameson would not want to take advantage of that friendship.

He, on the other hand, had no compunctions at all about doing so.

The Parker School for Girls inhabited an old manor house in Essex, off the main road that led into London. It really might have been a manor house a hundred years ago, but only its size suggested that now. In appearance it more resembled a very large cottage, and to Rosamund's eye it required some maintenance this season.

Lily fell silent as soon as she saw it, and remained that way all through the introductions with the mistress, Mrs. Parker, and the tour of the school rooms and refractory. The girls were sitting to a meal when they visited there, and Rosamund had her first good look at the other students. Finally, a chambermaid brought them to the chamber that Lily would use.

Rosamund set about unpacking Lily's

clothes while her sister sat on the bed and watched. Rosamund kept glancing over, marveling at how much Lily had changed in the last year.

Taller now. What had been awkward, over large features had suddenly found harmony on Lily's face. Rosamund examined that face, young still, but now lovely and fresh. She pictured her sister a few years older, blond hair up and curled and her lithe body encased in a column of white.

"I'll put your nightdresses in this drawer here," Rosamund said. She closed the drawer and went to the window to peer out. "You've a nice prospect." She glanced back at her sister. "The other girls looked nice too."

"They looked proud. They'll be saying things about me soon if they aren't already." She glared at Rosamund. "I said I be wanting to stay put. I don't need no schooling. Not here, at least. This place is not for such as me."

"It is for anyone who can pay, Lily. Mrs. Parker knows you have not been schooled much yet. She is willing to help you catch up."

"I'll be with the children, you mean. In that room with tiny desks. I won't fit in one."

"They will bring in one that you do fit."
She knelt in front of Lily and grasped her
hands. "If you try, in a year you will be in
the other room with girls your own age. You
are smart and will learn fast. I know it."

Lily shook off her hold and looked down
belligerently. "Seems I should have some
say in all this. It be me life, after all."

"Well, you don't. I want you to learn to
speak well, and write well, and know how to
read better than I do now."

"So I can be putting on airs like you do?"
She gave a derisive snort.

"Those airs mean I can sell a bonnet for
fifteen shillings when without them I
couldn't sell one for more than three."

"I'll be the best-spoken farmgirl in England, then."

"You will be far more than a farmgirl if I
have my way."

"Being a farmgirl not good enough for
you?"

Rosamund rocked back on her heels and
stood. "Not good enough for *you,* Lily." She
moved aside the valise she had unpacked
and pulled up another one. She set it on the
bed. "Look here, what I have for you. When
you come to visit me, you can wear this in
the carriage."

She opened the valise. Lily peered in. Her

frown softened to an expression of wonder. She reached in and lifted the garment resting at the top of the valise's contents. "What's this here?"

Rosamund took it and let it drop so she could hold it up. "Stand up so I can see if I got the length right."

Lily stood. Rosamund held up the dress against her. Lily looked down at the beautiful, soft muslin. Cream with blue sprigs of flowers, it boasted a thin line of lace at the bodice and the sleeves.

"There be — *is* a blue pelisse to go with it," Rosamund said, pleased at her sister's reaction. "When you visit me in London, we will have more made."

Lily ran her palm down the fabric. "It be beautiful. Nicer than what you be wearing."

"I had some made for me too but asked this be finished first so I could bring it. Along with these." She lifted out the school dresses and set them down. "There's another nice dress that I will send to you once it is finished."

Lily examined the school dresses, then returned to the cream muslin. "Where'd you get the blunt for this, Rose? Mrs. Farley said —" She stopped abruptly.

"What did she say?"

Lily shrugged. "When she saw you come

117

up in that carriage, she got a funny look on her face. *Last time a root cart, and this time a closed carriage,* she said. *Your sister's done made the devil's bargain.* Now this fancy school, and this dress."

Rosamund had not missed that look on Mrs. Farley's face. It had remained there the whole time she visited and gotten worse when she explained she was taking Lily out of the Farleys' care and putting her in a school.

She took the dress from Lily and set it aside. Then she made Lily sit beside her on the bed. "I have made no devil's bargain." She wondered if Lily even knew what that meant. "I inherited a lot of money, Lily. It came as a surprise. An unexpected gift. And it changes everything for me and you. Everything."

She described it all, then. About the legacy, and the new house, and her plans for her shops. "I would have written and told you but decided to wait so I could explain it all at once."

Lily appeared skeptical. "That devil's bargain is more likely than this tall tale."

"I suppose so, but this is the truth. When you visit me, I will show you the documents."

"Why would that duke leave you all that

118

blunt after one talk?" She gave Rosamund a very mature look. "You can tell me if you were his woman. I won't go scolding or acting like you be doomed."

"If I had been, I hope I would have rolled up on the Farleys' farm in more than a dirty cart last autumn when I came to see you. If I ever did make such a bargain, I'm not so stupid as to wait on getting my due till after the man died."

Lily seemed to accept the logic of that. "So I be the sister of an heiress. That might make it easier, being here with those girls we saw." She stood and lifted the muslin dress. "I want to try it on."

CHAPTER SEVEN

Rosamund stepped out of the cabinet maker's shop. Beatrice followed.

"That is a fine table you just bought." Beatrice fell into step beside her, the ribbons of her bonnet flying in the breeze. "Big enough for a banquet."

"I don't think I be needing — *I'll be* needing it for that, but the chamber it goes in b— *is* large, and anything smaller would have looked stupid." She had been trying hard to catch herself on this small part of talking properly. Even after a whole week of it, sometimes mistakes slipped by her.

"You'll be needing a side cabinet too."

"Mrs. Radnor owns an old one with beautiful inlay, and I hope to find one like that."

Beatrice slid her arm through Rosamund's own. "Shall we go to one of the warehouses? I've a list from the girls."

They spent the next hour shopping. Rosamund bought some materials for hat-making while Beatrice filled her basket with scents and laces and a few undergarments. Rosamund saw her admiring a chemise and joined her.

"Lawn," Beatrice said, palming the smooth, finely woven cotton. "It is so nice in summer. So much cooler than linen."

Rosamund took the chemise and folded it. "I will buy it for you. As a gift."

"That is too generous."

"It is not without cost to you. I want to ask you something." She leaned in close. "Is Kevin Radnor a patron of the house?"

Beatrice pursed her lips. "You know we don't —"

"I know. However, I really want to know and am willing to bribe you with this chemise."

Beatrice strolled away. Rosamund moved in closely again.

"I suppose it really can't hurt. He is. Actually, he is one of my gentlemen." Beatrice turned her attention to some silk flowers.

"How long?"

"He began visiting after the duke died. Hollinburgh favored the house, but then you know that. Anyway, Kevin Radnor told Mrs. Darling he wanted the same woman his uncle had, but she refused. Marie had left by then, so any further such pursuits would come to naught anyway. He did ask about him, though. After. When I might be likely to be indiscreet. Wanted to know which of the women he preferred. I had to keep my wits about me." She lifted one of the flowers, a yellow rose. "He asked about you, actually. Wanted to know if a woman named Jameson worked there."

"What did you tell him?"

"I said no. Because you didn't, then. Nor had you ever, the way he meant. I'm not sure he believed me. I sort of let him think there might be more to it, but being discreet is a house rule."

"Why would you do that?"

Beatrice smiled slyly. "I thought if he was convinced you had never been there, he would stop coming by. Oh, he took his pleasure, but that was not the real reason he was there if you ask me. He was looking for you. Now we know why! Had I guessed there was all that money waiting for you to be found, I'd have told him right off, even if it meant —" She strolled away.

Rosamund hurried to catch up. "Even if it meant what?"

Beatrice looked right and left, to make sure no one could hear. "Even if it meant he didn't return. Which I would have regretted. He is my favorite, Rose."

"Oh my. Have you fallen in love with him, Bee? I never thought you —"

"Not in love. You can be a child at times. So much that I'm not sure you will understand."

"I will. I'm not ignorant. How could I be?"

"Fine, here it is. He knows what he is about. Do you understand that?"

"Of course."

"Nor does he treat me like a whore. Oh, he is masterful and even demanding, but I get my due, if you understand. I get my turn. And he knows things I never learned." She giggled. "I'm going on, aren't I? Only I never speak of it to the others, so it is a relief to do so now. I don't want any of the others trying to steal him, see. They would too, if they knew."

Rosamund wondered what things Kevin knew that Beatrice hadn't previously learned. From what she knew of Beatrice, it would take some doing to best her expertise. "And you are not in love with him? You are sure?"

"Rose, in some houses there are little sparrows who make that mistake, but we don't. Did you ever see one of us pining over some patron? Anyone starts down that path and we remind her what is what. You know that."

She had worked as a chambermaid in Mrs. Darling's brothel for almost two years after the Copleys threw her out. She had never seen one of the women there act like she was in love. She had heard them comparing carnal information, however. How to derive pleasure from what was a financial arrangement. "If you did not tell Kevin Radnor about me, I wonder how he found me."

"I expect it was the bonnet. I hadn't much thought of it, but he was there when it came, and left fast after I looked at it. Maybe he saw the label on the box."

"I don't think that would do it. There are a lot of Jamesons."

Beatrice pondered that. "Your first name might have been mentioned. I'm not sure. It was just a quick look, interrupting what had promised to be a very enjoyable night. But he left so fast — yes, I think your name was spoken, so he would have known all of it."

They brought their purchases to the counter. Rosamund paid for the chemise but had it wrapped with Beatrice's items. Arm in arm, they returned to the street.

"Has he visited since and asked about any of that?" Rosamund said. "The bonnet?

How you know me?"

Beatrice shook her head. "I regret to say I haven't seen him since."

"If he asks —"

"I will say that you make hats that we favor. He'll get nothing more out of me."

Rosamund didn't bother asking the other question she had for Beatrice. If Kevin Radnor had not started visiting Mrs. Darling's house until after the last duke died, there was no way he was there on that fateful night last year. Pity that. She had hoped Beatrice could put her mind at ease regarding just where he had been when his uncle died.

Kevin disliked being in anyone's debt, least of all Minerva's. Yet in her debt he now was. That did not sit well with him. It was one more way that Rosamund Jameson's arrival in his life had created complications. And they had not even started discussing the enterprise yet.

After spending three days trying to locate the necessary instructors for Miss Jameson to no avail, he had swallowed his pride and laid his problem at Minerva's feet. Two days later — only *two days* — she handed him a list of appropriate hires. Now he waited in the library of that new house on Chapel

Street with the tutors in question, in order to make introductions.

He noticed that the bookcases remained empty, except for one shelf. A Bible rested there, flanked by the Walter Scott novel he had given her and a thin manual on penmanship. From the evidence of the well-used blotters on the writing table, she had been practicing a lot.

Mr. Davis, the dancing master, kept taking out his pocket watch while he paced impatiently. Dark-haired and dressed in the latest fashion, he walked as if each step belonged in one of his dances.

Mrs. Markland, the finishing governess, bided her time reading a newspaper she had found on a table. With gray hair beneath her very large bonnet and a very thin form, she appeared both friendly and stern at the same time.

Mr. Fitzgibbons, the bespectacled, portly, balding elocution tutor, smiled amiably at Kevin, then rose and advanced on him.

"I was told the young woman requires grammar and diction as well as form," he said, enunciating with clipped precision. "Do you know from which county she hails?"

"Oxford, I believe."

"Well, thank heaven for that. If it had been

Cornwall it would be nigh impossible to improve her accent sufficiently."

"You will find that she has already gone far on her own, through imitation."

"To your ear, perhaps." He tapped his own earlobe. "My ability to identify a person's origins from their speech is never tricked by that."

"Fortunately, only imperfect ears such as mine must be convinced."

Fitzgibbons's expression fell, then his smile resumed. "I assure you that in a few weeks she will be presentable, and in ten she can pass any test you require."

Like the house agent, this man had made assumptions. "I require nothing at all. This entire course of action is Miss Jameson's own idea. Ah. Here she is."

Miss Jameson had just entered the library. Kevin's spirits lifted at the sight of her. She had not been gone long, but he had noticed her absence even if it did allow him to spend his days in more usual ways. He had grudgingly admitted to himself yesterday that he looked forward to her return. He resented that, because it made no sense and didn't fit his plans.

She wore a subdued gray pelisse over a muslin cream dress. Both were modest in the extreme, but she appeared ravishing

127

anyway. The quiet colors allowed her beauty to shine. Out of the corner of his eye he saw Fitzgibbons's reaction. For a moment, the man appeared as if someone had slapped the senses out of him.

Kevin introduced her to the tutors.

"Thank you all for coming." She went to the writing table, sat, and extracted a clean sheet of paper from the lap drawer. "I would like to make arrangements for when we will meet. Shall we say mornings at nine o'clock? One morning per week for each of you."

Mr. Fitzgibbons had cocked his head as soon as she spoke. Now he shook it. "I will need at least two mornings, I think." He did not hide that he made that judgment upon hearing her speak. "Mondays and Wednesdays will suit my schedule. Two hours each day. One for elocution and one for grammar and syntax."

"I couldn't possibly be here by nine o'clock," Mrs. Markland said. "Eleven would be the earliest, and a sacrifice at that. I will claim Tuesday, because there are rarely parties on Monday that would require I sleep in the next day."

"She can have Tuesdays if I have Thursdays. Afternoons would be far better," Mr. Davis said. "There will be a better opportunity to find partners to bring at that time. Musicians will be difficult enough, but dancing partners —" He shook his head.

Mr. Fitzgibbons peered at Mr. Davis. "Newcastle?"

"Excuse me?"

"It is most subtle, but I heard the voice of Newcastle when you spoke."

Mr. Davis just glared at him.

Miss Jameson looked at each of them in turn. "Forgive me. I made the mistake of thinking that with me being the patron, I would be the one to pick the color of me bonnet." Mr. Fitzgibbons cleared his throat. "*My* bonnet."

She just looked at him. Kevin suppressed the urge to punch the man.

Mr. Fitzgibbons smiled indulgently. "There is no time like the present to begin."

"Monday and Wednesdays at nine o'clock it will be." Miss Jameson dipped her pen and slowly wrote on the paper. "Mrs. Markland, Tuesdays at eleven for you?" She looked at the woman. "Yes? Good." She wrote again, then set down her pen and turned to face Mr. Davis. "I regret that afternoons will not suit me at all. I have many things I must do in the afternoons. Surely you can find partners who will come in the morning."

"It is very difficult to find anyone to do

so, especially during the Season, especially at nine o'clock." He chortled when he mentioned the early hour, as if surely that had been a joke.

"Perhaps you can try. I am willing to delay until ten o'clock."

He sniffed. "The hour is hardly civilized."

"How unfortunate," Miss Jameson said. "I had hoped we could reach an agreement, because you came highly recommended. However, if me expectations are too inconvenient, I will have to find another."

"*My* expectations," Mr. Fitzgibbons murmured.

"I suppose, this once, I could make an exception and give lessons in the morning," Mr. Davis said with an expression of forbearance.

"How good of you." Miss Jameson smiled brightly and stood. "We are all decided. How fortunate that I begin tomorrow with you, Mrs. Markland." She opened the door. The tutors filed out.

She closed the door and faced Kevin. "Do you think Mrs. Markland can pile in enough in one day to get me ready for that party your aunt is hosting?"

"Unlikely, since no amount of tutoring will appease my aunt, or the others."

"Minerva suggested I decline the invitation."

"Minerva can be wise at times."

She strolled over to the window, which permitted the light to bathe her face. Her lips appeared very dark in that wash of illumination. Darker than the ones he had kissed in his imagination the last few days.

"I do not look forward to it, but putting it off will not make it any better. Eventually, they will each demand to see me and meet me, seeing as how me inheritance — *my* inheritance, made them poorer. Better all at once so I am well armored than introductions when I don't expect it."

"That is one way to see it."

"Minerva and Chase will bring me, so I won't be alone when I walk in." She cocked her head. "Will you be there?"

"Of course. You will have three guards."

"Minerva said that the duke will attend. She said he will not allow them to browbeat me. Will that help?"

"He may be younger than my aunts and one cousin, but he is Hollinburgh. That carries a lot of influence even in the family. Now, tell me about your journey."

She sat on the divan, so he did too. "Lily was skeptical of my plan. She did not want to leave what she knew as her home. She did not like the school, and worried about the other girls laughing at her. I think before I left that she felt better, though." She gave a little shrug, as if she really wasn't sure. "She has grown up. Even since I saw her six months ago, she changed. She is very beautiful, too. I was a little envious of that." She laughed lightly. "The dress helped her come around. She tried it on and she was the equal of any girl coming out this year, I'm sure."

Not more beautiful than you. He had to swallow the words hard and resist the impulse to reach over and caress her face. Hell but he was being an ass today.

"And you?" she asked. "Were you busy with our enterprise these last days?"

"Of course." A lie, that. He wasn't really sure what he had done these last days besides think about her too much. "I'll tell you about it after that party."

"I will be glad to hear of any progress. Shall we say Friday? I'd like you to show me the invention then too."

That smacked him out of his stupid, poetic pining. He looked at her. Still beautiful. Still desirable. But now, also still trouble. He had been a fool to allow all this friendliness to distract him from *why* he was being friendly.

"Oh, dear. You look stormy. You had to know I would want to see it eventually."

"Of course. Friday."

"Friday morning. Unless you need to sleep in because of a party, like the rest of Mayfair except me."

"I doubt Aunt Agnes's party will last that long."

"Won't you attend another after? I thought such as you went to three or four of a night."

"Many do, but I don't. Shall we say at ten o'clock? You seem to prefer uncivilized hours, and I don't care."

"That would suit me. Now, I must visit a cabinet maker to see about more furniture for the house, and a few pieces for my shop."

She walked with him to the front entrance. "I will see you at the party. Be sure to bring your sword," she said.

Kevin braced himself, then followed the butler into the drawing room. Two women waited in it, sitting on either end of a long divan. The garments and jewels they wore to receive visitors probably cost enough to make strong headwind in what he needed for that enhancement.

"Well, this is a shock," Aunt Agnes said. She leaned her substantial form and ample bosom toward the other woman, who resembled her enough to prove they were sisters, but whose own bosom barely showed due to her extreme thinness. "Isn't it a shock, Dolores?"

"Quite a shock." Dolores's throaty voice contrasted with Agnes's shrill one. Despite their obvious differences, to Kevin's mind they were two sides of a double-edged sword. Both tall, both dark of hair and eye, both spinsters, both annoying as hell. "It must be — how long has it been, Agnes? I never dared presume he would ever visit me at my little cottage, but *you* . . ."

Little cottage, hell. These two had bled Uncle Frederick for decades, feathering their nests with allowances and demands. Deciding it was their due, they sent bills aplenty to their brother for the duke's accounts.

"Years. My goodness, I can't remember how many." Agnes speared Kevin with a sharp gaze. "Won't you sit, Kevin? I'll send for refreshments so we can celebrate this rare honor."

He suffered her call for the servant and their chatter about some ball they anticipated attending. Finally, the coffee and cakes arrived.

"Have you come up to Town for the Season?" he asked Dolores.

"She brought enough trunks to say she did, even if she claims it is only a brief visit," Agnes said. "I told her she would be more comfortable if she let her own house for the Season. Don't you agree with me, Kevin?"

"It is wasteful to let a house for a fortnight, Sister. It isn't as if Frederick left me the funds to squander that way."

"I'll be stunned if you leave after a fortnight. You are here for the duration. You can't fool me, Sister. It was all I could do to get you to go home the last time, and I know your sly plan. I say she should stay with Hollinburgh at Whiteford House, Kevin. Don't you agree? That is where she used to stay when Frederick was alive."

"I'm not sure —"

"I would be imposing, Agnes. Nicholas needs to be attending to his own matters this Season. It is time for him to woo and win a wife."

"You can advise him if you are there," Agnes said seriously. "He will need your help. How much better if you were in the house so he could consult with you about these girls whenever he wanted? Truly, Sister, it is *your duty* to move there."

Kevin roused himself at the direction this was taking. Nicholas would have a fit. "I think that he would rather discuss such things with both of you," Kevin said. "You each bring special insights into society and the families in question. Better if he called on you both here."

"I agree," Dolores said. "It is unfair to expect him to seek us out separately, as if he had nothing else to do."

Aunt Agnes's mouth pursed. She did not look on Kevin kindly. "Is there any special reason for your visit, dear boy? You too have much to keep you busy, what with your trade and such."

Your trade. Agnes and Dolores, indeed most of the family, made it a point to refer to the enterprise that way. It was their idea of a subtle insult.

"Although I thought it past time to make a social call, as long as I am here there is something I want to talk about. I am curious why I am the only member of the family who has not received an invitation to your dinner party. I would think it was my trade, as you put it, but since the guest of honor is my partner in trade, it can't be that."

Agnes resettled her thick body on the divan. Her expression shifted as well, from chagrin to petulance. "I did not think you would want to come, Kevin. I assumed that while she might be your partner, she was also your enemy. After all, this woman has half that invention now, doesn't she? You must resent her. Hate her. I didn't want to have a scene at my dinner."

"I would never make a scene."

Agnes laughed. Dolores joined in.

"Oh, that is too amusing," Dolores said. "At best, you would sit there brooding silently, ruining everyone's enjoyment. At worst, you would use that cutting wit of yours to create unbearable awkwardness. We would all be rushing to cover it up with chatter, lest it get worse."

They all but said he was too rude for decent company. How insulting. "I would never do that. If you doubt it, let me inform you that Miss Jameson and I are good friends, not enemies. I have spent quite a lot of time with her since she came up to Town."

"Good friends?" Agnes trilled the words incredulously. "Dear boy, you do not have good friends, at least ones that any of us know about. You are too . . . *you* for good friends."

"That is not true."

"Indeed? Who is your good friend among the gentlemen I know?"

Just like her to demand he name one. "Stratton."

They both veered back in shock. "*Stratton?* The *Duke* of Stratton?" Dolores sent a sidelong glance at her sister. "I find that hard to believe."

"He and I are *very* good friends." He spoke with Stratton on occasion, but he was seriously stretching the truth. However, the man was so formidable, and so quelling a presence, that he did not worry about being found out. Bold though his aunts might be, neither one of them would dare to quiz Stratton on his friendships.

"Well." Dolores looked a bit cowed.

"Indeed," Agnes murmured.

"He has a garden party every Season," Dolores said. "Do you have any influence there? I should like to be invited if you can manage that. He so rarely entertains."

He was getting in deep now. "I will see what can be done, but I can promise nothing, of course."

"Of course."

"Me *too,*" Agnes said petulantly.

Kevin just looked at her. Barring two possible exceptions, none of the family was stupid, least of all this relative. Agnes immediately saw the problem.

"And of course I will send around an invitation to the dinner," she said. "I only sought to spare you. I had no idea you might be disappointed."

"Thank you." He stood to take his leave.

"You will remember about the garden party?" Agnes said.

"Of course."

CHAPTER EIGHT

Rosamund stood. Her new maid, Jennifer, held the dinner dress so she could step in. The raw silk slid up her body, and Jenny settled it on her shoulders. Rosamund remained motionless while the maid fastened the dress in back.

She had never been dressed before. She wondered if she was even doing it right. Who would have thought that in addition to those tutors she had met the other day, she would need one in order to learn the proper way to have servants.

Jenny was new, as were the housekeeper, cook, footman, and chambermaid. All had started since she returned from seeing Lily, but she had interviewed them before she departed. Minerva had a friend who placed servants in homes, and nice Mrs. Drable had sent her excellent candidates. In one afternoon she had acquired the people needed in this big house.

That made her feel both important and wasteful. She could do all of it herself, especially getting dressed. She had to admit that Jenny had an artful hand with dressing hair, though, and knew how to fold or hang the garments coming from the modiste just so.

She ran her hand down the dinner dress. Madame Tissot had made sure it was finished, after Minerva informed her an event was imminent. "I want you to look your best as you enter the lion's den," she had explained. "It may delay the attack for ten minutes or so." Minerva did not like most of Chase's relatives, that was obvious.

How bad could it be? She had survived Kevin's father, hadn't she? And that horrible wife of Walter Radnor. She doubted anyone tonight would be ruder than they had been. She had a plan too. She intended to stay close to Minerva, using her as a shield, and say nothing at all unless spoken to directly. If she did have to speak, she would do so very carefully, and hope to avoid those slips in grammar that plagued her.

"There now." Jenny stepped around and gave Rosamund an inspection with her pale blue eyes. "Have you any jewels you want me to clasp on for you?"

141

Rosamund shook her head.

"No mind. You are lovely without them. They would be a distraction." Jenny lifted a wrap and a tiny reticule. "Would you like to go down now?"

"Yes. You don't need to accompany me. I'll make me own way." She took the wrap and reticule while she mentally kicked herself. *My own way.* She chanted the correction in her mind all the way down the stairs.

Minerva had insisted she and Chase bring her in the carriage with them, and soon it arrived. Chase came to the door, escorted her out, and handed her over to a footman who helped her into the coach.

Another man sat within. A very handsome man who looked much like Chase, but whose features possessed fewer of Chase's strong bones. Another relative, apparently.

Minerva introduced him. Not just any relative. This was Nicholas, Duke of Hollinburgh.

He smiled amiably while Chase joined them.

"Hollinburgh may save you for another five minutes of battle if you walk in with him," Minerva said. "So we have fifteen minutes covered now."

"I should be insulted, only she is correct.

My influence in the family is only good for that long, at best," the duke said.

"I will be grateful for even that much," Rosamund said carefully. "Although I am hoping that it will not be as bad as I have been warned it will be."

"I said she should decline to attend," Minerva said. "I am still of that opinion. We can bring her home right now and announce when we arrive that she is ill."

"She will have allies there, darling," Chase said. "The three of us and, hopefully, Kevin."

"He will be there?" Minerva appeared perplexed. "I thought —"

"He received an invitation yesterday," Chase said. "He mentioned it in a message I received before you came down. But, being Kevin, he neglected to mention if he had accepted it."

"Things have been going well between the two of you, Miss Jameson?" the duke asked. "I only ask because the others we can quell easily enough, but Kevin has a way of speaking his mind too frankly at times."

"He is saying he can be rude," Minerva said. "But you know that already."

"I believe we have a friendship of sorts. He has helped me as I settle in here in Town."

That reassured the duke. "I say, Chase, if Kevin will be there as a friend of Miss Jameson, we might find ourselves protecting the relatives from *him,* instead of protecting her from the family."

"It would be like him to draw their fire," Chase said.

"What an interesting development," Minerva said. "This may be an almost enjoyable evening instead of the utter disaster I had anticipated."

Kevin entered the drawing room. For a moment, the chamber silenced as curious eyes looked to see who had arrived. Then conversation started up again. Two of his cousins' wives showed disappointment. *Oh, it's just you,* their expressions said.

Everyone had come, at least the ones who ever attended any family event. His own father had not bothered, nor his father's brothers, most of whom lived in the country and rarely came up to Town. But his cousins had graced Aunt Agnes with their attendance, all of them wearing their privilege and position as obviously as ever.

The family members who thought they should have received the money that Miss Jameson inherited were here to take a good look at the thief who had deprived them of their long-awaited expectations.

Aunt Agnes and Aunt Dolores were in an animated tête-à-tête on the divan. Agnes saw him and gestured for him to join them.

"We've a disagreement." She sighed, as if arguing with her sister were something unusual. "When we line up to go below to dinner, we are in conflict over where Miss Jameson should be put."

"I say she is the guest of honor and receives some precedence for that," Dolores said. "Agnes insists she be at the end of the line of females."

"She has no social standing, nor the birth to place her anywhere at all," Agnes said.

"Did you in any way indicate to her that she was the guest of honor?" Kevin asked. "We all know why you are hosting this dinner, and we all know that she is the victim du jour, but that is not the same thing."

"I did not write to *her* that she was the guest of honor."

"You did to the others," Dolores said. "You may not have used that phrase, but you made it clear that this dinner was an opportunity to meet this Miss Jameson."

"Sister, truly, you can be such a trial. I think you disagree because it gives you perverse pleasure. As Kevin says, that is not the same thing. She will be last, as is appropriate."

Dolores shrugged. "I am sure she won't know the difference, so I'll not belabor my view of it. What would such a woman know about order of precedence anyway?"

Nothing, Kevin thought. Not yet. Some day, however, Mrs. Markland would explain all that. Tonight, however, Rosamund would be ignorant of any slights. And he, Kevin, would walk beside her, with Chase and Minerva right ahead. Protection on all sides, then, except behind her, where Cousin Philip would be making a nuisance of himself.

As if called forth by his thoughts, Philip approached. The youngest of the cousins and, everyone agreed, the least promising among them, Philip sported a new waistcoat with gold buttons and bold green and yellow stripes. His frock coat looked new too, and the latest fashion, one which Kevin disliked because the snug sleeves constricted movement too much.

"So where is this Miss Jameson?" Philip asked loudly enough for Walter, the eldest of the cousins, to hear from his nearby perch on a chair. Philip's soft face arranged itself into a comical pretense of curiosity. "A milliner, I hear. Uncle must have been going mad, after all, to leave all that to a woman who makes hats."

"How much better to leave it to you, of course. Only it would be gone already if he had, so at least this way it might be useful for a while longer." Kevin gestured to Philip's chest. "Interesting waistcoat."

Philip preened. "Harrington's."

Kevin detested people who told you where they purchased their luxuries. Philip did so all the time, as if expensive garments made him a worthwhile man.

"I suppose that means you have had luck at the tables recently."

Philip blinked hard. "Of course."

Hardly *of course.* If ever a young man had bad luck when gambling, it was Philip. He took after his father that way, as he did in his spendthrift habits and lack of fiscal common sense. He'd gotten in deep with money lenders last autumn, and only God's grace had spared him a hard lesson. That and the suspicious disappearance of a rare Renaissance sculpture from Whiteford House. Chase had tracked down that small bronze, and the description of the person who had sold it bore a strong resemblance to their youngest cousin.

Nicholas had chosen to ignore the theft and not confront Philip, but this particular cousin no longer had free access to the duke's house. Or any family member's residence, for that matter.

"It may have been sewn by Harrington's, but you chose the fabric," Kevin said. He gave the waistcoat a long examination. "Nicely made. Too bad it is in bad taste."

Philip's face flushed. "As if you would know fashion. I doubt you have been able to afford a new waistcoat in years. That one you are wearing has made so many appearances as to be threadbare."

"At least it isn't vulgar."

Walter had risen and sidled over to watch the show.

"Vulgar?" Philip sneered. "You have no sense of style, clearly."

"It looks like something a rustic would buy on coming up to Town in the hopes of appearing fashionable."

Philip was very red now. "You are unbearable. Everyone thinks so. Doesn't everyone, Walter?"

"Oh, yes," Walter drawled. "But the waistcoat really is vulgar. That can't be denied."

Philip gaped, speechless now. He strode away.

"That was unkind of you," Walter said. "And of me."

"I should apologize, but I don't think I will."

Walter took a look at his pocket watch. "I assume this Miss Jameson is coming with Chase and Minerva, because they aren't here either. Deliberately late, I would say, so she is not forced to endure us too long."

Walter, unlike Philip, was not stupid. He could be just as insufferable in his own way, however. It forever chafed that while he was the eldest cousin, his father had not been the eldest brother of Uncle Frederick. That meant Nicholas, not Walter, had inherited the title. None of that kept Walter from trying to position himself as the head of the family anyway, to little avail.

"My wife says she is not what we expect," he said. "Miss Jameson, that is. She saw her with you in the park and they had some conversation. She said the woman is quite young and pretty."

"Pretty" was not a word Kevin would use. Pretty implied something fleeting, dependent upon youth and innocence. Miss Jameson was so much more than pretty.

"Pretty enough, I suppose."

Walter gave him a long look. "You suppose? I guess when you look at her all you can see is a problem, eh? Her having half of that enterprise must gall you."

"We have a right understanding about the enterprise. Because the alternative was to

149

have every person in this drawing room as a partner, I count myself fortunate in only having someone as sensible and pliable as Miss Jameson to deal with." Brave talk. He had no idea if she would prove pliable when the time for such accommodations arrived. Nothing thus far had said so. He enjoyed sowing the seed among the relatives that everything was settled, however. That would gall *them*.

Indeed, Walter did look disappointed. His attention was averted to the entrance of the drawing room, however. "Ah, Chase is here."

Chase and Minerva strolled into the chamber, chatting with each other. A few nods aimed their way, but conversations continued. Then, like a slow-moving wave rolling through the space, silence fell.

Nicholas had entered, escorting Miss Jameson. He walked her through the drawing room toward the hostess. Aunt Agnes waited, sitting like the queen at a presentation at court.

Every eye followed their progress. The women appeared interested. The men looked stunned. Miss Jameson wore a beautiful dinner dress, one that Kevin recognized as being commissioned at the modiste's that day. Its pale lilac hue, subdued but shimmering, had been enhanced by cream embroidery and two tiers of lace near the hem. Someone had dressed her hair differently, so curls dangled somewhat recklessly alongside her face. She wore no jewels.

He tore his gaze away. He looked at Walter, who seemed incapable of blinking, while Nicholas introduced Miss Jameson to Aunt Agnes. He noticed Walter's wife, Felicity, watching her husband's reaction, and her smile growing tighter.

Walter must have sensed the attention. He looked over and smiled broadly at his wife. Then he glanced askance at Kevin. "Pretty enough? Damnation, man."

It was, Rosamund decided, a very pleasant party. The Radnor family was full of opinionated people, some of whom assumed the entire world ached to hear their views on social and political events. The result was a noisy gathering, with a few arguments making for good theater until the eldest male cousin, Walter, decreed they end.

"Enough of that now," he would intone, like a schoolmaster calling for order. In most cases he succeeded in ruining a very lively discussion.

Rosamund held to her plan of speaking

briefly and carefully. It worked because little conversation was expected of her. The rest of them probably concluded that she was dull. As for her manners at the meal that would follow soon, Mrs. Markland had drilled her in the deployment of all that cutlery upon hearing she would attend a dinner party.

"Let us go down," Lady Agnes finally announced.

"Time to go down," Walter repeated, as if doing so required his agreement.

Because all Kevin's cousins were male, and two others besides him were unmarried, the men outnumbered the women even with the two aunts helping to balance things. When they all lined up to go to dinner, she found herself last in the female line next to Kevin. Behind her straggled the youngest cousin, Philip.

Philip appeared to fancy himself as a fashionable man about town, from the way he dressed and also how he managed to pose rather than just stand normally. He kept sending her amiable smiles, and twice in the drawing room tried to start conversations. In both cases Minerva quickly crowded him out. "Trouble, every mincing inch of him," Minerva had whispered the second time. "Profligate, indebted, and a wastrel. If he gets the chance he will ask you for money."

At dinner she found herself sitting between the duke and yet another cousin, Douglas. She wasn't sure she had met Douglas in the drawing room. Indeed, she could not remember seeing him before. All the Radnor men looked a bit alike, however. Clearly all peas from the same pod, each with his own distinction. Chase had that large-boned, rugged handsomeness and the duke a smoother, more typical kind. Kevin's deep-set eyes and regular features set him apart, and Walter's version of the Radnor appearance had a very predictable look, as if one had seen him a hundred times before. This one, Douglas, managed to be unremarkable, despite owning the same eyes and dark hair, the same height and good looks.

Kevin, she noticed, was placed across the way and farther down, out of earshot. Far away from her and from their hostess, who sat very close to her indeed. After a bit of eating, Lady Agnes's dark eyes settled on her. "Tell me, my dear Miss Jameson. From where do you hail? I hear some accent. Subtle, but there nonetheless."

Agnes's voice shrilled through the noise at the table. Right across from her own place, Rosamund saw the other aunt, Dolores, abruptly stop talking to Walter and focus anew.

Not everyone gave Agnes center stage. Minerva kept chatting with Walter's blond, pretty wife Felicity. Chase asked some question of Philip. Kevin, however, gazed right down at his aunt.

"Richmond," he said. "You know that."

"She lives there now," Agnes said, cocking her head. "But I daresay she wasn't born there, were you, Miss Jameson?"

"I was born in Oxfordshire."

"Ah, yes, I can hear it now. Was your father in trade there?"

Briefly. Carefully. "He was a farmer."

"Was he indeed? How interesting."

"If not for our farmers, where would we be?" the duke said. "Not enjoying this fine meal, that is certain."

Lady Agnes looked at him as if he had challenged her. "That is true, Hollinburgh. However, her father must have wanted better for his children if she was apprenticed to a milliner."

Rosamund glanced quickly at Minerva, who was still chatting but who sent a sidelong glance that warned, *don't correct her.* Not that Rosamund intended to. No one at this table had a right to quiz her about her life. If she allowed that, who knew where it might lead? Possibly back to Mrs. Darling's brothel. Her time there would take some explaining, not that any explanation would save her from scorn.

"Do you have any family here in London?" Aunt Agnes asked.

"I don't. I have a younger sister. She is in school. Mrs. Parker's."

"I have heard of it. Was that where you were educated?"

"I was not that fortunate."

Aunt Agnes waited for the rest. Smiling. Watching. Rosamund just looked back at her.

"Most girls are not sent away, Aunt Agnes," Kevin said. "You weren't."

"With an army of tutors there was no need. Yet Dolores and I were well educated in our father's home."

"That is the schoolroom most girls know, isn't it? Instead of the past, let us speak of the present. Miss Jameson's millinery is much sought after," he said, changing the subject. "I would call it artistic."

"What would you know about that?" Philip said. "Do you now claim expertise in that as well as engines and moths?" He leaned forward so he could catch Rosamund's eye. "Have him show them to you someday. Moths. Not even butterflies."

"You are right, Philip. I would never dare to claim my taste in bonnets is informed. However, Minerva has seen Miss Jameson's creations. What did you think, Minerva?"

"They are superior. I think any woman at this table would be glad to be seen in one."

"Indeed," Lady Agnes said incredulously.

"Indeed," Minerva said evenly.

"The bonnet she was wearing in the park was hers, Aunt. It was nice enough," Felicity said in a condescending tone.

Across the table, Lady Dolores had been drinking some wine. Now she set down her glass with some force. "Oh, tosh. Bonnets and moths and farmers. Let us speak of what is on everyone's mind." She speared Rosamund with a sharp, dark stare. "What do you intend to do with our legacy? It really belongs to all of us, I'm sure you realize."

That ended all other conversation.

"Aunt Dolores," the duke admonished.

"Don't 'Aunt Dolores' me. She must know it was a mistake. A passing impulse. If my brother had not met an untimely demise, he would have fixed it soon enough."

"You don't know that," Chase said. "Nor does it signify, because that was the will when he passed. It has been a year now. You really must accept that."

"I won't. It is too unfair. Perverse. He had family to take care of. Instead this — this farmer's daughter hat maker inherits an obscene amount of money for someone of her station."

"That is enough," the duke said.

"Yes, quite enough," Walter echoed. "This is not the time or place."

"It isn't enough and there is no better time and place," Dolores said. "If she had any decency at all she would turn it back to the estate, or at least most of it. She has to know he never really intended her to have it all. If someone hadn't killed him —"

"Nicholas and Walter said enough and now I say it too. Must we all say it? You have forgotten yourself." Kevin spoke sharply, and loud enough to silence Dolores. "Aunt Agnes —"

"Yes," Lady Agnes said. "Dolores, you are not feeling well. I'm sure you would like some time alone."

"Oh, tosh. I didn't say anything the rest of you weren't thinking." Dolores stood and, with one last glare at Rosamund, strode from the dining room.

For a five count, everyone just looked at their plates. Then Kevin asked the duke about some horse he had seen race, and Minerva asked Douglas's wife about some party she had attended, and conversation resumed.

"My apologies," the duke murmured beside her.

"Not at all. I had no idea that the ton had such interesting dinners."

In truth, Rosamund was relieved to have the talk move around her instead of right at her. It had been an astonishing five minutes. She hoped she never saw the likes of it again. However, if one of them was that angry, maybe all of them were. Even Kevin.

She couldn't blame Dolores for being bitter, although she thought sisters of dukes did not act so rudely at dinner parties. Probably they didn't. Normally, at least. The difference was that this woman did not consider the target of her rudeness worthy of anything else. She could insult the *farmer's daughter hat maker,* just as she could scold a servant, to her mind. Politeness was reserved for polite society.

Still, it was useful to know the bad feelings about the legacy. She would keep that in mind in her future dealings with this family, along with the amazing bluntness with which Dolores had said the same thing as Felicity had in the park — That the last duke had been killed.

Not a single relative, not one, had disagreed with her.

Port was passed. Kevin poured himself a goodly amount. Sipping it kept him from succumbing to the urge to go upstairs, find Aunt Dolores, and — he wasn't sure what. He couldn't thrash her, which was what he felt like doing.

And the family claimed *he* was rude.

"That was quite a dinner," Philip said, throwing himself into his chair after finding a cigar. "To think I almost declined the invitation."

"It was beyond the pale," Walter said. "However . . ." He just let that hang in the air.

"Are you making excuses for her?" Kevin asked. He couldn't thrash Aunt Dolores, but Walter would do.

"Not at all. Her behavior was embarrassing, and an insult to Agnes and the rest of us. Yet it was understandable as well. Since that peculiar legacy affected you even more than the rest of us, I'm sure you will agree."

"Did she really expect Miss Jameson to say, *you are right, I shouldn't have it, Please, let me give it back so you can split it up?*" Nicholas said.

"I rather wish it had happened that way,"

Philip muttered.

"She would be an idiot to do that. Or a saint," Chase said. "Perhaps if she were weak, she might have been cowed by Dolores. Miss Jameson, however, didn't even flinch."

"No," Nicholas said. "Damned impressive."

She *had* been impressive. Kevin had felt obligated to protect her, but he doubted she needed his effort, or even that of Nicholas. He got the impression that if Dolores had continued much longer, Miss Jameson would have ceased her silence and given far better than she got, much as she had held her own with his father.

Nicholas began talking with Walter about one of the estates, and Philip availed himself of more port. Douglas sat quietly, as usual, observing.

Chase got up and came around to Kevin and sat down beside him.

"She will ask you about Uncle's death now. She didn't miss that slip Dolores made."

"She already has. Felicity was indiscreet in the park. I explained it. The basics, at least."

"If she is curious still, she may not ask *you* for more. It could be Minerva, or me."

160

"Whoever is asked can just tell her what the record supports, as I did. An accident."

"Do you think she will accept that after what Aunt Dolores said?"

"I don't know. She has other things to think about right now. It may not be something she finds intriguing or wants to learn about."

At the end of the table, Walter, who had assumed the head seat, was waxing idiotically about some bill being debated in Parliament. His musings probably sounded too much like a lecture to Nicholas, whose annoyed gaze did not match his amiable half smile.

"I think I will go and raise a different topic," Chase said, standing. "After Dolores's histrionics, we don't need fisticuffs too."

He strolled around the table and inserted himself between Walter and Nicholas. He brought up the subject of a different bill, one that Walter did not care about.

Kevin barely listened. He turned his attention inward and held a conversation with his own head. The topic was the enterprise, and a letter he had received from France in the morning post. That letter created a conundrum. It was a hell of a thing to have a door reopened when you still couldn't walk through it.

"Quite a scene, eh?"

The voice startled him. He turned his head to see Douglas sitting where Chase had just been. Only, from the sounds of the conversation down the table, Chase had left some time ago.

How long had Douglas been sitting there? It was easy to forget the man was around, but Kevin tried to at least be aware this cousin existed. At least he had since the day several years ago when he strode into a family meeting, sat down, and asked where Douglas was — only to discover Douglas was sitting right next to him and had been there first.

"Yes, it was a scene for the family legends." Kevin poured himself more port, then topped off Douglas's glass too.

"She didn't even blush, though. Miss Jameson. She held her own."

"She did indeed."

"I expect that quality doesn't make things any easier for you, what with her having half that business now. It isn't as if you can just dictate how things will go, I'd think."

"We get along quite well."

"Not the same thing, is it?"

He gave Douglas a good look. How someone could look so much like Nicholas but

162

be so . . . bland. These were the most words Douglas had spoken in Kevin's hearing in over a year. Even when the family reacted vociferously to the news of Uncle Frederick's will, Douglas had not joined in. His wife, Claudine, had spoken for them, as was her wont.

Now Douglas's impassive expression actually brightened a little. "She is a comely woman."

"She is at that."

"Rather startlingly so."

Kevin had to smile at this evidence that Douglas was not dead yet.

"So I was thinking," Douglas said.

Kevin waited. Who could guess that Douglas ever thought about anything?

"I expect that you will marry her. More famous scenes then, eh?"

"Excuse me?"

"It is understandable because it is the only way to ensure she doesn't sell out on you," he said. "And in terms of, well, you know — you could do worse. Far worse."

A ten count passed while Kevin accommodated that anyone had suggested such a thing, let alone Douglas of all people.

"Is this your wife's idea?"

"Goodness no. She will be appalled by it. Miss Jameson is little more than a peasant in her view." A smile barely formed. "I dare-say Claudine would be apoplectic."

Everyone would be. His father. His aunts. Maybe Nicholas. Quite likely Miss Jameson herself.

"Thank you for thinking," Kevin said. "Of me, I mean. I have no plans of that nature, but I'll ponder your suggestion."

Bland as ever, Douglas rose.

"If you are joining the others, move the other port decanter away from Philip," Kevin said. "He can barely sit up straight."

CHAPTER NINE

Dolores had removed herself not only from the dining room but from the evening, so Rosamund did not have to suffer her presence in the drawing room. She soon learned that did not mean she would be spared other probes into her life and character, however.

No sooner had they all settled themselves than Lady Agnes leaned forward and peered her way. "Did you make that headdress you are wearing tonight?"

"I did."

"Attractive. Perhaps a bit bold with your coloring. Why didn't you use a lighter-hued purple for the ribbons? Ones that matched your dress?"

"Because if they were lighter, they would not be bold."

Agnes veered back, as if astonished by any kind of boldness.

"It is what makes it distinctive, Agnes,"

Minerva said. "If the ribbons matched the dress, it would be predictable and bland. And, at the risk of speaking of the obvious, that hue of ribbon brings out the color of her eyes so nicely."

"I. *See.*" Agnes resettled herself on the divan, finding a queenlier pose. "From where did you say you hail, Miss Jameson? Oxfordshire?"

"Yes."

"I have many friends in that county. Perhaps I have heard of your family."

"That is unlikely."

"One never knows."

"I doubt my family had any contact with your friends, or your circle. As I said, my father was a farmer."

Agnes chortled. "See how wrong you might be, Miss Jameson. In the country it is not unheard of for members of good society to associate with neighbor yeoman farmers and their families. There are many county events where they might be introduced."

There was something to be said for getting this part out of the way.

"He was a tenant, Lady Agnes. I don't think they rubbed shoulders much."

Silence. Glances all around.

Rather suddenly, other conversations broke out. Walter's wife, Felicity, addressed

Minerva, launching into a description of some dress she had seen at the theater. Lady Agnes made it a point to talk to Douglas's wife, Claudine. Rosamund got the sense that everyone was embarrassed. Whether for her, or about her, she couldn't tell.

Minerva extracted herself from Felicity and came over to sit near Rosamund. "When they are all well engaged, we can slip out to the terrace. I have something to tell you."

Whatever it was would have to wait, because Felicity followed Minerva over and also sat close by for some private conversation.

"I expect Dolores's outburst at dinner surprised you," she said. "I did warn you."

"I knew there was unhappiness about the will. It is understandable."

"Not that part." Felicity lowered her voice. "The part about the last duke's death. He was pushed. Everyone thinks so, no matter what the official determination was. Someone . . ." She left the sentence unfinished and lowered her eyes, as if the words could not be spoken.

Minerva had been pretending not to hear, but now she turned in her chair so she could join them. "It is none of her concern, Felicity. Nor has that been proven."

"No thanks to Chase. He was supposed to prove it one way or another. With some of his discreet inquiries. Only he didn't. Even after I went to him and Nicholas and told them —"

"Enough of that nonsense," Minerva said through a firm smile. "Your revelation wasn't proof of anything."

"He wasn't in France as he said. Walter is shocked more inquiries were not made about that. One might think that perhaps . . ." Again, she stopped in the middle of a sentence. She pointed at Rosamund. "She has a right to know, if she is going to be —"

"Miss Jameson, if you desire to learn any more about this subject, please tell me and I'll have Chase explain it all," Minerva said pointedly. "It is hardly a topic for a dinner party."

Felicity gave Minerva a slit-eyed, belligerent glare. She rose. "I will leave it at that, except to say this, Miss Jameson. Whatever you do, do not make Kevin Radnor an heir to your new fortune." She strolled away, straight and proud.

"It was kind of you to interrupt and save me, Minerva. Although now I will have to ask for further explanations, won't I?"

"At least they will be accurate ones,"

168

Minerva said. "Come, let us take a turn on the terrace and speak of more interesting things."

The night air felt wonderfully refreshing. Nor did Rosamund mind leaving the Radnor women behind for a while.

She and Minerva strolled along the terrace balustrade, looking down on the small but neat garden. When they reached a spot as far from the drawing room doors as possible, Minerva stopped. "I have learned something more about that man you asked me to find for you."

Charles. She realized it had been a day or two since she had thought about him.

"Is he back in England?"

Minerva shook her head. "Nor is he expected." Minerva turned her gaze out over the garden, which meant she could not see Rosamund's expression.

Rosamund was grateful Minerva gave her that small privacy while she absorbed this news. Charles always had loved the Season, and she had assumed he would return for it. It had been a mistake to do that, or to allow her old dream to create a theater in her head, with scenes of reunion and romance.

Rather suddenly, her excitement about her new home dimmed. Her lessons appeared foolhardy. She could have found a house for one third the rent in a different neighborhood. A milliner did not need to live on Chapel Street.

"How did you learn this?" she asked so the silence would not turn too heavy, although a tiny bit of hope still burned. One that said Minerva could be wrong.

"We have had one of our agents strike up a friendship with one of the family's servants. When there was no evidence of this young man's return, our agent drew the information out of this servant."

"You went to a lot of trouble. I did not ask you to learn this for me."

"I thought you would want to know."

Minerva had guessed all of it if she thought that. What other reason could there be for wanting information about Charles other than an old tendre?

Inside the drawing room, someone began to play the pianoforte. The melody trickled out, muted by the closed doors, sounds that interrupted the night's silence.

"Thank you. It is good to know. I expect that Paris is much more interesting than London, even during the Season."

"I'm told it can be for some people." Minerva finally looked at her. No pity showed in her expression. A warm kindness did, however. "I think I'll return to the others. Why don't you enjoy the night air for a while?"

"I think I will do that."

Left alone, she released the disappointment building inside her. It flooded her so thoroughly that it left little room for anything else. Even the suspicion she had acted like a fool found no place in the dull ache growing thick and sad.

When she felt tears forming, she mentally slapped herself. *Enough of that.* Her plan still had value. For Lily's sake it did, at least. And someday, eventually, Charles would return. England was his home.

"Escaping them, are you?"

She startled at the voice and turned to see Kevin's cousin Philip coming up the stairs from the garden. The dining room had doors that opened onto another terrace down there. He appeared to be walking awkwardly, as if he did not trust his balance.

His face showed the remains of the boyishness that lingered in a man until well into his twenties. He wore an ugly waistcoat and a tight frock coat such as young bloods around Town might sport.

"I just needed some air," she said.

"I'm sure you did." He sauntered over.

"Have they been polite, at least? Or eager to demean you further?" He smiled so broadly she could see his teeth in the moonlight. "If Aunt Dolores did not hold back, I doubt the others did."

His proximity did not give her a way to avoid conversation. She wished he had not intruded. "They were polite enough. As for your Aunt Dolores, she did not join us."

"I expect not, after that spectacle. Just as well. She is the sort to ask rude questions of you because she thinks the social niceties do not apply to her inferiors."

There was nothing to say to that.

He cocked his head and considered her. "Odd that there were no more questions once the ladies had you alone. Hell knows the rest of us have some."

He kept shifting his weight and balance. Each time he did, it seemed he came a bit closer. He was foxed. Thoroughly drunk.

"There were a few questions. Not many."

"Negligent of them. That's their job, isn't it? To ferret out information?" He peered at her. "Maybe your appearance surprised them and put them off. You are not what was expected. Don't look like a poor trades-woman, do you?"

"Perhaps that is because I no longer be poor."

172

As soon as she said it, she knew it had been a mistake, and not just grammatically. A sneer absorbed his smile. "No, you aren't. A man half mad left you much of his fortune and let his own blood go without." His eyes brightened dangerously. "Seeing you tonight, I knew at once how it was. How you managed that."

"I managed nothing."

"Complete surprise, was it? Don't make me laugh." He leaned toward her, and she smelled the port and other spirits on his breath. "You must be very good. Hell, you are probably the most expensive whore in England, so your skill should be unsurpassed."

The urge to slap that leering face almost overcame her. She drew herself straight and took a step back. "You are too much into your cups and talking too freely. I will not stay here and be insulted by such as you." She turned on her heel, toward the drawing room doors.

A firm grip on her arm stopped her. "*Such as me?* Who in hell do you think you are, putting on airs? We both know what you are." He yanked her back and imprisoned her in his arms. "I've a mind to have a taste, to see what made him favor you so much."

She pushed against him, hard, but it did

173

not loosen his hold. She ordered him to stop. She squirmed so the kiss he aimed for her lips landed on her headdress. He grabbed at her breast and she kicked his legs, hoping he would go down. He let out a high-pitched, gloating laugh and grabbed the back of her head roughly with one hand. He tried to kiss her again.

She turned her head and bit that hand. He cursed, then swung a hard slap at her that snapped her head back. For a second, all she saw was the sky and stars while the shock of pain stunned her.

Then he was gone. She was free. She staggered and grabbed the balustrade. Philip was on his way down the stairs again, being dragged by the back of his collar and coat by another man.

Kevin.

She did not hear what was said, but the tones of their voices carried. Kevin's sounded crisp and angry. Philip's snarled, belligerent and nasty. She steadied herself against the balustrade. They did not go into the dining room when they reached the lower terrace. Instead, Kevin kept dragging Philip into the garden. Their dark forms disappeared amid the others down there, those of shrubbery and trees.

Then, with Philip's first howl of pain, four other men ran out of the dining room.

Kevin slammed his fist into Philip's face. Blood spurted, then flowed from his cheek. It did nothing to calm Kevin's anger. If anything, it fed his fury.

"How dare you impose on her like that, you worthless shit." He hit him again, and Philip fell.

"She's a whore," Philip gasped. "No harm done."

"I swear, if you say that again, I'll kill you." Kevin reached down and hauled Philip back to his feet and hit him in the stomach. Philip crumbled back down. "I'd make you apologize, but there is no apology for what I saw. No excuse." He lifted Philip again and started to swing once more.

Footsteps. Shouts. Firm arms imprisoned his own. He tried to shake them off so he could grab Philip.

"Calm yourself. Now." It was Nicholas issuing commands in his ear.

"The hell I will. He assaulted her." He strained against the hold, his mind darkening again.

"Is that true, Philip?" Nicholas asked.

Chase and Douglas were supporting Philip. Chase pressed a handkerchief against

Philip's face.

"What he said, did it happen?" Walter asked, repeating Nicholas as was his habit, while he stood aside like the great judge.

"I stole a kiss, is all."

Kevin struggled again to get free of Nicholas's hold. "Hell and damnation, you *forced* yourself on her, and when she resisted, *you hit her.* Let me finish the thrashing I started. The rest of you can make sure I don't go too far."

Chase stood back from Philip and gave him a hard stare. "Is that true? It wouldn't be the first time, Philip."

Walter looked from Kevin to Chase to Philip, then back again along all three. He puffed himself up. "Well, whatever happened it won't do to resort to fisticuffs in Aunt Agnes's garden, with the ladies nearby. Meet at a boxing club and have it out if you must."

"I'd rather meet him at dawn in a park," Kevin snarled.

Philip raised his head and looked down his bloody nose. "I don't duel over whores."

With one hard jerk, Kevin broke free of Nicholas and strode over. "I said I'd kill you and —"

Chase grabbed him and put his neck in a tight hold. Nicholas came to pin his arms again. "Get him out of here," Chase said. "Douglas, take your wife and Felicity home. Walter, get Philip into your carriage. Nicholas and I will deal with Kevin. Go now."

"My carriage?" Walter said. "He is bleeding."

Nicholas glared at him. Walter sighed. "Come along, Philip. Just try not to ruin the upholstery or my coats."

They all filed up the garden walk, leaving Kevin under the firm holds of Chase and Nicholas.

Sounds came from the dining room, then the upper terrace. Kevin pictured Rosamund up there, the object of either scorn or sympathy, depending upon the woman. He only counted on Minerva to offer the latter reaction to this scene.

The rage began leaking away with Philip's removal. The tightness in his body slowly unwound and his mind cleared. Neither of his cousins said a word. They just waited. Finally, they let him go.

"Did he really hit her?" Nicholas asked.

"Yes. Just as I came up the stairs. She had been fighting him and he slapped her in the face. It stunned her." He ran his fingers through his hair. "I'm sure there will be a mark. He hit her hard."

Chase shook his head. "I did not even

notice he had left the dining room. The last I saw, he was asleep in the corner. He must have woken and slipped out."

"I saw him leave but thought he was going into the garden to puke," Kevin said. "I only followed to escape Walter's endless political pronouncements. Then I heard something and noticed him up there with her." His mind saw it again and started down the same path it had upon realizing what Philip was doing.

"He must have been mad to importune a woman right there on the terrace," Nicholas said.

"He can be bold even when not drunk," Chase said. "Someone had begun to play the pianoforte, so he probably thought she would not be heard if she cried out. I don't doubt what Kevin describes, Nicholas. There was a near miss with Minerva once."

"Such behavior cannot be excused by drink or anything else," Nicholas said. "Let us get the poor woman home, Chase."

The three of them walked through the garden. Up on the higher terrace, two figures could be seen. The moonlight reflected off blond hair. The other woman was Minerva.

"Let me speak to her for a moment," Kevin said. "Wait for her in the reception hall, if you will. I'll bring her down."

Up on the terrace, Rosamund stood aside, at the far end of the balustrade. Minerva came over to them. "A bad business. She has not spoken," she whispered. "Agnes retired and the others are gone. What happened out here?"

"Come with me, darling, and I will explain all." Chase guided her to the doors. "You can wait for her down below and take her home in our carriage. Nicholas and I will find our own ways."

Once they had all left, Kevin turned to Rosamund. She did not face him, but he could see her posture fold in on itself as soon as the drawing room doors closed. He could *feel* her humiliation as surely as if he had been the one insulted.

He went over to her. "They have all left. You won't have to take your leave or anything like that. Only Minerva will bring you home."

"I did nothing wrong." Her voice came so quietly she might have breathed the thought.

"Of course not. No one —"

"They will have to choose between a relative and me who don't know me place, and I will be the one shamed."

"Not by anyone who matters." He doubted she took much consolation in that.

179

"Did he hurt you?"

Her hand went to her cheek. She nodded. "Did you hurt him?"

"Yes." He reached out and skimmed his fingertips down her cheek. Even with that light touch he could tell there was some swelling. That sent his mind back toward the fury. He only swallowed it because there was no Philip to take it out on now.

She faced him. "Thank you for stopping him. I should have myself. I should have guessed what he was about. I should have fought harder, or screamed, and not worried about where I was and who was in the drawing room. I should have —" She stopped, with a small sniff replacing the last words.

He held her head in his hands and gazed down at her troubled expression. "This is the last place any woman would expect such a thing to happen. Stop telling yourself that you should have anticipated his intentions or done this or that. The fault is all his. If you ever again meet my aunts or the wives, which I hope you never have to, because they are all insufferable, do so as you did tonight, proud and beautiful, and behave as if this never happened."

Tiny reflections multiplied in her eyes. Crystalline lights sparkled, beautiful even though tears created them. She looked so vulnerable.

He did not tell her not to cry. She had good reason to. She had been assaulted and struck and called a whore. She had been insulted by a man who assumed she deserved no courtesy because of her birth. After what she had suffered, the last thing she needed was another man telling her that her emotions were not warranted.

She also did not need another man imposing on her. When he gathered her into his arms, he did not think of it that way. It was a natural expression of his urge to comfort her.

She did not push away. She laid her head against his chest and allowed him to hold her. Then she turned up her head and gazed into his eyes. He suppressed the impulse to kiss her, but it was hard. She deserved better from him tonight of all nights.

She did not know why she allowed that long embrace. Perhaps it was the strength of his arms, so protective and careful. Or gratitude that he had thrashed Philip. No one had ever done something like that for her before.

She liked the intimacy. The warmth and very human touch. Liked it more than she expected to. It awoke something better in

181

her than what she had been feeling up here on this terrace. She experienced warmth and friendship and even some excitement.

She should not let it continue. It could be misunderstood. Men had a way of doing that. Philip was only the most recent in a long line of them, although none before had been so insistent or so ugly.

Proud and beautiful. He had not planned to flatter her any more than he had the first time they met. While he held her, she did feel proud and beautiful again, instead of used and demeaned and soiled the way she had just minutes before.

Their closeness did not stay that simple. He was a man. She sensed the arousal in him, like liquid beginning a low boil. The mood changed just enough to indicate he no longer merely comforted her. She tasted a new power coming from him, and noticed how her own body responded. She became very conscious of his hold on her. She lingered just long enough to give herself a small, distracting indulgence. Then she moved her head and leaned away.

He gazed down, his dark eyes still looking into hers, reflecting unfathomable thoughts as they so often did. His face, handsome and firm with its angles chiseled by moonlight, remained close enough to kiss her.

Instead, he released her. "Let us go find Minerva."

Chapter Ten

The summons came early. Kevin received it at once because he had barely slept. His fitful night left him in no mood for the message he read.

Whiteford House. Nine o'clock. Hollinburgh.

Nicholas used his title with the rest of the family, but never with Kevin or Chase. Seeing it now, and reading the terse command, turned Kevin's bad mood darker.

He did not have time to indulge Nicholas today. He had things to do, once the world was up. He was supposed to see Rosamund at ten o'clock unless she was too upset by last night to call. By then he needed to be past several decisions he faced, and already putting plans into place to execute them.

All the same, he rode to Whiteford House on Park Lane. As he handed his horse to a groom, Chase rode up.

"You too?" Chase said, dismounting. "If it couldn't wait for morning calls, it must be important."

"I hope so, if I am supposed to tug my forelock for him."

"I see your mood has not improved much from last night."

They followed the servant up to the ducal apartment, with Kevin thinking again about last night. The sorry episode had been on his mind a great deal during the last hours.

"Did Miss Jameson find some solace with Minerva?" he asked Chase.

"As I heard it, which means it may have been otherwise, she entered her home much composed. I think Minerva may have been more distressed than Miss Jameson by the time they parted. She certainly sounded both appalled and irate when she returned home."

"Filled your ears, did she?"

"She wants Philip drawn and quartered." He paused on one of the steps so the servant got farther ahead of them. "It was unfortunate the others were there. Otherwise, I would have stood aside and let you at him."

They reached the landing that led to the apartment. A forest of precious urns and vases stretched in front of them, placed on pedestals in rows that begged for accidents. "I thought he would sell these by now and get rid of this eccentric display that Uncle set out," Kevin said.

Chase began negotiating his broad shoulders through the fragile display. "He concluded that it discouraged Aunt Agnes from intruding on him, which normally she would feel free to do even if he sent down word he was not receiving. Her ample bosom is not happy among these rarities."

Kevin took a different path, one that brought him past a Chinese pot that he admired. They met up outside Nicholas's door. The servant opened it and ushered them in.

Nicholas waited in his dressing room. He had not changed it at all since he inherited Melton House. Still the same carved chair near the window, which Nicholas favored for reading. Still the blue upholstered divan and chairs in a circle, where he entertained friends and the relatives he could abide.

Now he greeted them from where he stood near a window, looking out on Park Lane. "Thank you both for coming."

"The hour is early," Kevin complained. "We both know Chase is up near dawn, and I am often not yet in bed if I am occupied, but what causes *Hollinburgh* to be awake and dressed?"

Nicholas's expression noted the emphasis on his title. "A matter of regarding the family's honor. Which means Hollinburgh's honor."

Kevin thought that odd, mostly because Nicholas had not been especially glad to find himself with the duties of being a duke.

"I have almost made a decision," Nicholas said. "I only need to know if either of you object."

"Oh hell, you are getting married," Kevin muttered. "Who is she?"

"You don't have to make it sound like it is a sorry fate," Chase said.

"Of course not. I am delighted for you, *Hollinburgh*. Who is the duchess-to-be?"

"Are you going to address me like that the whole time you are here?"

"I was summoned by Hollinburgh, so I am addressing him."

"I don't mean the title. I mean the sneering way you say it."

"I never sneer."

They both laughed. "You sneer so much, you don't even know it is a sneer anymore," Chase said. "Now, tell us what decision you are contemplating, Nicholas. I doubt it is marriage, because you have not expressed particular interest in any of the young ladies on the marriage mart this Season."

"Which doesn't mean one of them hasn't captured him," Kevin said.

"It has nothing to do with marriage." Nicholas stood a little straighter. "I have long believed that Philip would find a better path as he got older, but it hasn't happened. I made excuses for his wastrel ways and lack of honorable behavior, what with his father being a bad influence and his mother — well, all of that. However, after last night I have concluded that like many family trees, ours has a badly formed branch on it. I am inclined to saw it off the trunk."

Kevin did not hide his astonishment. Nicholas, who had taken on the role of duke with much reservation, now intended to wield that power in a way rarely seen.

"Are you sure?" Chase said.

"No. Which is why you are here."

That did not explain why Kevin was here, but he didn't press the point.

"I'm not sure I can help," Chase said.

"You can tell me what you meant last night when you said it wasn't the first time."

Chase did not look inclined to do that. After a long moment, he sighed. "Early on, during that family gathering that was held here after Uncle died, I came upon Philip importuning Minerva in the library. She had taken service so she could conduct a few discreet inquiries. He had backed her up near the fireplace and would not allow her to leave."

"You mean she was making inquiries into *us*," Kevin said. "Posing as a servant." He began searching his memory of that house party to see if he remembered her being there.

"The point is that Philip had blocked her way out and was —" Chase's jaw hardened and twitched, making him appear like the army officer he had once been. "He had grabbed her arm and was speaking of much more, and was telling her how no one would believe her if she complained. I stopped him, of course. Just as well."

"So he is the kind who will press his advantage with his inferiors," Nicholas said. "Not unusual, only he refuses to stand down when refused. He is too lazy even to seduce. He just assaults and uses his station in dishonorable ways. I daresay he has done worse than we know about."

Kevin's mind had settled on something else. "What did you mean, Chase, when you said *just as well*?"

"What he did not see was that she had found a poker behind her, with her other hand. One might say I saved Philip from Minerva, not the other way around."

"Too bad."

Chase ignored that. "What are your intentions, Nicholas?"

"I will no longer receive him. When I inform the rest of the family of this, they won't either."

"Which means almost no one will, once word gets out," Kevin said.

"I will also let it be known that he has no expectations from this family, least of all from me. My will shall be changed so he is in no way a beneficiary, should there be anything to be had by anyone, which at the moment seems unlikely. If one of the aunts decides to indulge him, either while she lives or after she passes, that is her business. The question for this morning is, do you think I am being too harsh?"

"You will ruin him socially and financially," Kevin said. "On the other hand, you will spare untold tradesmen a lot of misery."

"And perhaps the money lenders will give him wide berth, if it is known the family will not make good his debts," Chase added. "It could be a blessing of sorts."

"I don't care if it is or it isn't. I long ago gave up any belief that he would grow to understand that being a gentleman is not only about leisure and fashion. If my actions make him a better man, all to the good, but that is not my goal." A scowl marred his brow again. "I will tell him to write an apology to Miss Jameson, not that I expect he will do it."

"Someone should," Chase said. "Whatever Minerva said last night was hardly sufficient."

"I will," Kevin said. "She only suffered that because she had the misfortune to attract the family's attention due to our partnership."

"Her inheritance would have done so without that partnership," Chase said. "By rights, our aunt should apologize, as the hostess who had the poor judgment to inflict such a boor on the company."

Kevin could not picture Aunt Agnes ever apologizing to anyone, least of all the daughter of a tenant farmer.

Nicholas's expression dropped into one of resignation. "I suppose I can tell Agnes that I think that would be appropriate."

"I don't think a letter would influence her much," Chase said.

"You mean I should call on her." He shook his head. "Hell."

Rosamund set the metal stands on the

cabinet. She had bought the carved, mahogany cabinet already constructed. Far nicer than the counter she had intended to commission, it served the same purpose but appeared more impressive.

The metal stands would hold some hats and bonnets. A few more could go in the window. All she needed now were a few chairs and a small table on which to put the looking glass. Unlike the way she'd arranged her shop in Richmond, here she intended to have that out of view of other patrons, so there would be some privacy. Having her shop at street level might be a risk, so she wanted to provide a way for patrons to make purchases and have fittings without the world looking in.

She went to the window and looked out. Few people passed by at this hour, least of which the kind she wanted to attract to this shop. She did notice several women glance at her window while they passed on Oxford Street, though. Her conclusion that the shop would be visible on the cross street seemed to be correct.

She checked her pocket watch. Already quarter past nine. She hoped to keep her meeting with Kevin Radnor today, although it appeared she might be late. It all depended on when the wagon arrived.

Thinking of that meeting immediately brought Philip to mind again.

After parsing through her behavior last night, every moment of it, she could not think what she had done to invite such treatment. That didn't lift the pressing humiliation, however. Nor wipe from her memory what Philip had done and said.

She'd been glad Kevin thrashed him. Grateful. Relieved. Perhaps that meant at least he did not think she had somehow brought that on herself, although undoubtedly his family would blame her.

She thought again of Kevin seeking her out in the shadows on the terrace. Apologizing for his cousin. Once the others were gone, her ability to stand tall and proud had left her. She felt again his arms while he comforted her. That had been the sort of thing a friend would do.

It had been more than a friend's embrace, though. She could not lie to herself about that, although for hours last night she had tried to. Perhaps she shouldn't have allowed it, especially after what had happened with his cousin. But instead she had welcomed it, taken comfort in it.

Suddenly, her view was blocked by wooden panels. She ran to open the door.

"Mrs. Ingram, welcome!" she called to the

small, thin, gray-haired woman sitting next to the wagoner.

The wagoner jumped down, then helped Mrs. Ingram descend. Mrs. Ingram, sharp of features and sharper of eye, came forward to embrace Rosamund.

"You've an impressive spot here, right off a main shopping street."

"I've the first story too. You can live up there if you want. Or you can live at my house."

"Up there will suit me very well. Easier to walk to the shop, eh?" She chuckled. "Now, let me see the inside."

The wagoner followed them into the shop, toting a large wooden box.

"I have the bonnets you asked me to bring," Mrs. Ingram said. "They're in that box. There's plenty back in Richmond still. That new woman looks to know her business with a needle and such, so we won't be running out there."

"You are convinced Mrs. Hutton can manage the shop?" Mrs. Ingram would manage this new shop in London. That had meant finding someone suitable to take over the shop in Richmond.

"She seems more than fitting. Worked for a man in Bristol for five years who was too lazy to pay attention, so she did it all for him. At least he recognized her value and gave her a good reference that all but admitted it. I think we'll be fine with her." Mrs. Ingram lifted one of the iron stands and examined it. "You'll be going to see for yourself soon enough, I expect. If you are not content with her, we will find someone else. Lots who will be glad for the situation."

Two valises and another box were carried into the shop. Once he was gone, Mrs. Ingram opened one valise. It was full of caps.

"You didn't ask for them, but we've quite a few, so I brought these. Only a few plain ones. Most are the fancy ones, with lace and such."

"You have been thinking more clearly than me."

"In Richmond they always paid the lease. Maybe they will here too."

Mrs. Ingram straightened, then strolled to the back, peering around the wall.

"I'll be needing you to go to the warehouses, to purchase fabrics and ribbons and forms," Rosamund said. "I want to start as soon as we can."

"We'll be needing a girl."

"You may find one as you see fit. You chose the last apprentice, so I have confidence in your judgment."

Mrs. Ingram was of an age when fine lines had formed above her lip, like tiny, visual echoes of the ones on the sides of her eyes. She pursed her mouth and those lines exaggerated her expression. "Are you going to tell me how you got that bruise on your cheek? Seems that legacy should protect you, not cause you harm."

Rosamund's fingers went to her cheek. "Does it look very bad?"

"Bad enough." Mrs. Ingram opened the other valise and fished around in it. "You are not to tell anyone about this." She removed a small wooden box and opened it. "This salve will hide the worst of it. Come here and I'll dab some on."

It didn't look like salve. It looked like paint. Rosamund submitted to Mrs. Ingram's deft fingers. "You use this?"

"A bit here and there, vain fool that I am. Let's say that time is not kind and leave it at that." She stood back. "It will do. Best if you avoid strong light, though."

Rosamund fumbled for her pocket watch. It was almost ten o'clock. "Perhaps when you go to the warehouses, you will buy me some of that salve for tomorrow." She took a card from her reticule. "This is where I live. Have the bills made out to me and sent there. I have arranged accounts at most of the warehouses. Here is some money, to pay for hackney cabs."

Mrs. Ingram took the card and coins. "Accounts and transport, no less. I can see things will be a bit different here than what we knew in Richmond."

Kevin knew it was well past ten o'clock, but he checked his pocket watch anyway. From his position at a library window, he could see no activity on the street.

She probably would not come today. Not after last night. Still, he had prepared for her call, just in case. He suspected Miss Jameson was the sort of woman who did not miss appointments unless she sent word that she would.

He hoped she did come. There were decisions to make that should not be delayed.

He paced around the library, unable to sit and think, uncomfortable with his own body. If she did not show, he would go out and either fence or box. Some exercise should rid him of the agitation that made him so out of sorts.

He heard a carriage. He bolted to the window and strained to see it rolling down the street. When it slowed, he bounded out to the reception hall, sped past the servant on duty, and threw open the door. Miss

Jameson peered out the cab's window.

The servant nipped around him and handed her down. She smoothed her skirt before coming toward the door.

She had tried to hide a bruise on her face. Perhaps those who did not know it was there would not notice it, especially in the day's overcast light. He saw it right away, however. His anger at Philip had never fully receded, and now it spiked again.

He swallowed his reaction and greeted her. "Welcome. We have much to discuss."

"We do indeed. It is past time, I think, to show me the invention."

"Of course. However, I have had some coffee prepared, and the terrace is a fine spot from which to see the garden. Let us go there for a few minutes first."

"I do not need coffee. I have been busy since eight o'-clock. However, I suppose you are newly awake, so I will join you."

He ushered her through the house to the morning room. Breakfast awaited his father. He gestured toward it. "Would you like —"

"No, thank you. If you haven't eaten, however —"

"I too had an early morning." He pushed open the garden door.

A table had been set at the far end of the terrace, away from the morning room. He did not want his father's interference should the man rise before noon. He settled her down. A servant came to pour coffee.

He looked at her face. The overcast light evoked a special radiance from her skin, as if it penetrated deeply, then came back with subtle nuance. The result was a surface that appeared very white, with the vaguest shadows below her mouth and nose. Unpolished marble statues looked like that, with the material's crystals absorbing light instead of reflecting it.

Her hand went to the bruise. "I was given some paint to hide it. I don't suppose it worked if you keep staring at me."

"I was not noticing the bruise. I know it is there, but few others will."

"Then why are you looking at me so intently?"

"Because I have something very important to say to you, and I am wondering what you will think on hearing it."

Curiosity lit her eyes. "Have you decided you want to take on another partner?"

"Not at all. Why would you think so?"

She shrugged. "It has entered my mind that we could use one who has a factory."

What a nuisance of an idea. He swallowed his annoyance. That was for another day. "I have instead thought that we should reconsider our own partnership."

She looked at him blankly. So much so that it unnerved him more than he wanted to admit. The practical Miss Jameson had never seen the possibility that he had. She had never entertained the idea that he planned to broach.

Not once.

Mr. Radnor sat there, looking at her. She sensed surprise in him, but she could not imagine why.

She hoped he was not going to ask her to sign that stupid document again, the one that gave him all control of the enterprise. If he did, she would sell her share, even if they had now developed a friendship of sorts.

He was nothing if not a self-assured man, but right now she saw something else. Not lack of confidence in himself so much as in his idea.

"Perhaps you should explain what you have in mind," she said to encourage him to get on with it.

"Of course." He leaned forward. Closer. "When I say reconsider our partnership, I mean extend it."

"You have another enterprise?"

He smiled ruefully. In a blink, he became

more himself. "See here, we are bound to each other in this endeavor. Our lives are intertwined."

"Only if I don't sell," she reminded him.

A small glint of steel entered his eyes. Oh yes, very much himself again.

"It seems to me that because we are so bound, we should take the next step."

"The next step — ?"

"Yes. I think we should wed."

She heard the words, but the meaning of them took a moment to reach her mind. She stared at him while he looked back at her.

"It makes perfect sense if you think about it," he added.

Good heavens, he was serious.

She swallowed the nervous laughter that wanted to erupt. Whoever would have expected such a proposal? From this man of all men? And in such a manner? He might have been proposing a walk in the park, or something equally uneventful. He put this stunning suggestion on the table as casually as he set down his coffee cup.

"If this is because of last night, there is no need to propose marriage," she said.

"It is not to make amends for Philip, or for our brief embrace, although —" His gaze turned more intent in that way that discomforted her. "Our embrace was not purely one of comfort. Not entirely. Surely my suggestion does not come as a complete surprise to you."

She groped through her confusion to find some way to answer him. "The embrace was not a total surprise. This proposal is. Such as you don't marry such as me." That truth cleared her thinking. "They kiss such as me. But marriage? No."

"Yet I have proposed just that."

She did not know what to say. She could hardly explain that she had a dream, and it was not a life with *him,* no matter how interesting and compelling she found him at times. She wanted to see Charles again, and try to let that old love find its voice and future.

Other reasons not to agree flew through her mind. He had said he never became enthralled with women. His lack of such emotions hardly recommended him to a woman, no matter how convenient the match might be.

On the heels of those thoughts came memories about the dinner last night, and some of the peculiar things said by Felicity about the late duke's death. If those insinuations held any truth at all —

Then there were the things he did not

know about *her.* He had no idea just how inappropriate she would be as a wife. While she had been an inconspicuous servant at Mrs. Darling's, someone might eventually recognize her as a denizen of that house, no matter how fine she dressed or where she lived.

"You are doing this because you want control of my half of the enterprise. This is just like that document you wanted me to sign. That is your goal."

"That is one reason. The main one, yes."

How bluntly he said that. He was not even trying flattery. No declarations of affection or praise of her beauty to appeal to her emotions. Direct and honest, that was Kevin Radnor.

She began to resent that. "No doubt the rest of my inheritance is the other reason."

"In the long run, I have no need of your money. I may not have thousands in a bank now, but I am well situated. I am also my father's heir."

"He appeared hale and fit to me when I saw him. As for being his heir, if you marry such as me, he will probably disown you."

"There are parts he can't do that with. You don't have to worry that I have designs on your funds. If you want, we will execute a settlement that makes such a move on my part impossible."

"That goes without saying." She would never allow anyone to have that money. Even Charles would have to make such a settlement.

"I think you believe the benefits of this union would be all one-sided," he said.

"You would be sitting pretty and I would be much diminished. The benefits are all yours."

"You want to be a lady, for your own sake and that of your sister. I provide that immediately, to a degree few men can."

I want to be a lady so Charles will be able to marry me.

He did have a point about Lily, though. Damn him. She would not let him disarm her.

"Your own family castigates you for your interests," she said, triumphant when the idea came to her. "I'm not sure your reputation can provide what you offer."

"I am the grandson of a duke. Nothing changes my blood. The benefits are not all mine. You pride yourself on being practical. Well, this is very practical, for both of us."

"Perhaps too practical. You do not want to marry me. You want to marry my half of your enterprise. You are too conceited even to consider what would happen if your

204

grand scheme is not successful. Then you may find yourself encumbered with a practical marriage long after it has outlived its usefulness."

"Of course it will be successful."

"Not if my voice is silenced due to this marriage, which no doubt is another reason for this proposal."

He smiled, not kindly. "Do you truly believe that your judgment regarding this invention and its development is essential to the success of this enterprise? We are not talking about bonnets."

"We are not talking about brilliant inventions either. Not anymore. The true potential is in the making of this device, and its use, and I do believe that my judgment is necessary there."

"Zeus, but you are impossible."

He stood abruptly and walked away five paces. Hands on hips he looked to the sky, then down to the ground. She knew he was containing his temper. Since her own voice had raised, she was glad for the respite so she could collect herself too.

"You are being stubborn," he said. "Think of your intentions for your life, and for your sister's life. This enterprise is central to my future, but not to yours." She could not deny that this marriage would ensure Lily's future. He offered her his station and pedigree. His blood. There was no comparison between being the grandson and cousin of a duke and being a well-to-do gentleman like Charles. Even if most of society scorned her for *her* blood, a good number would probably still at least tolerate her, if only to get closer to Hollinburgh. She knew what most women in her position would do.

Most women would grab this chance and hope for the best. But Charles's face hovered in her mind, and she saw little else when she gazed inward. Her heart yearned to have its way. She did not want to bury her love and walk away from what still might be possible.

She spoke slowly so her confusion and astonishment did not trip up her language. "Your offer is very generous. I will acknowledge that. However, I think it would be better if we kept our partnership as it now stands. If we married, we would probably have numerous rows much like this one about the enterprise, especially because my voice would count for little after we spoke those vows. Thank you, however."

He did not respond to that. No request that she think about it more. No final arguments.

She stood. "Now, I would very much like to see the invention."

She had turned him down. Oh, she had been surprised, perhaps even shocked, but she had recovered soon enough. Her rejection had been damned articulate.

What was wrong with her? In truth the benefits would be more hers than his. Her change in station would last forever while, as she had so bluntly pointed out, his control of the enterprise might come to naught in the end.

Against all logic and her own self-interest, she had *turned him down.*

There was nothing to do but accept it and retreat with grace. He could hardly make promises of undying love, and admitting how his mind dwelled on her might even make her angrier. What could he say? *It would not be a love match, but I desire you fiercely. If you allow me to give you pleasure, you will never regret this marriage.*

He escorted her into the house just as his father entered the morning room.

"Ah, Miss Jameson," he exclaimed by way of welcome.

"Not now," Kevin said while he sped Miss Jameson through the chamber and along to the staircase.

"Thank you for that," she said.

"We've no time to entertain him." His father was the last person he wanted to see right now, after having proposed for the first time in his life to no avail. Rejected by the daughter of a tenant farmer, no less. A milliner. *I'll not be needing such as you, sir.*

He told himself to stop being a childish ass. In a day or so, his prickling resentment would pass. He might even find himself relieved by her choice.

He guided her up the stairs to the level where he lived, then across the landing to his door. "The engine is in my chambers. Had I known you wanted to see it today, I would have had it moved to the garden and fired it up for you."

"Would that help me understand the invention?"

"Demonstrations are useful, but I think you will understand my explanation."

The anteroom to the bedchamber served as his study. One window's drapes remained closed. He strode over and drew them so light fell on the table set a few feet from the glass panes.

When he turned back, Miss Jameson was gazing down at the miniature steam engine gleaming atop the table, her expression one of deep curiosity.

"Did you make this?"

"Some of it. I had the rest done to my requirements. It is to scale and constructed of the same materials as any other engine."

Her head angled this way and that while she studied it. "Does it work?"

"Yes. It is a simple design, such as those used to pump water out of mines." He joined her and pointed to the various parts as he explained. "Fuel burns here. Steam forms here and moves these rods, or pistons, up and down. That makes the pump here work. Steam has tremendous power when compressed the way it would be when contained."

"Which part is your invention?"

"It isn't there."

She took a step back and looked at him. "This is all fine and good, but do not expect me to be bedazzled to the point I forget what I have come to see."

The row on the terrace echoed behind her terse words. He opened a drawer on the table and removed a tiny, metal cylinder. He set it down. "There it is, to scale for this engine in front of us. Here it is in more normal size." He removed a much larger example and set it down too. "I was not attempting to keep it from you. I simply thought you should see the engine first."

She lifted the small version. "What does it do?"

"It permits the emission of steam to be regulated more precisely than is currently possible, by mapping it. It is called an indicator." He launched into an explanation of how it worked and the value it brought to engines. He rarely had the opportunity to explain the invention's workings, so this chance led him deeply into his preoccupation with its potential.

He never lost sight of his audience, however. The lovely Miss Jameson claimed a slice of his mind. That portion of his awareness admired her face and form and admitted some regret that she had not accepted his proposal. It also took in her interest and attention, and how her brow puckered when she did not understand some point he made.

When she did not yawn after five minutes, he delved deeper into the mechanics of the improvement.

Kevin Radnor might never be enthralled by women, but this machine obviously captivated him mind and soul. She had demanded a viewing and an explanation, and he gave her one. At length. She would say her presence became secondary, except she could tell he added little asides for her

210

benefit, lest she not comprehend his lesson.

Which she did. Mostly. At the least, he convinced her that the enterprise was not built on air. The peculiar piece of machinery he'd invented seemed capable of great things.

She kept one eye on him the whole time. Not that he noticed. She watched how talking about this endeavor enlivened him. She found that charming, and she experienced a kinship with him through it. She'd been just like this when she made her Richmond millinery shop a reality. Nothing else had mattered after she took the first step. She'd worked tirelessly to get it all done just right, and her first day of business had been one of triumph.

He had devoted himself to this invention. He had even proposed marriage because of it, to a most inappropriate woman. No one could say Kevin Radnor was not single-minded in his ambitions.

When his monologue finally waned, she jumped in before he found his second wind. "What is the enhancement you want to procure? How will it improve this?"

"It connects here and adds a valve that will allow pressure to also be read and mapped."

She dared not ask how it would do that. If

211

she did, she might be here all day. She strolled away from the table. "So it is indeed an enhancement, but not necessary."

"Not essential, no."

"I think that if you can't settle that in the next month, we should move ahead on our own."

Silence near the table. Utter stillness. He looked at the machine, not her. She braced herself for another row, one in which he mocked the opinion of a milliner on such important matters.

"We are in agreement," he finally said. "You are more generous than I am. I think two weeks is enough. One more try at it, then turn away and give it up."

He surprised her. From the way he looked at her, she suspected the reaction was mutual.

"To that end, I will go to France on Monday's packet," he said. "I'll meet with the other party and see if that part can be salvaged."

"France?" She suddenly felt light-headed. "Where in France does he live?"

"Paris."

Paris. Minerva had said that Charles lived in Paris.

She forced restraint on her exploding excitement. "You will need me to sign documents if an agreement is reached."

"I was going to bring them with me, already signed by you."

"What if some small change is made? The slightest one will make what you bring useless."

"I'll have new ones drawn up, signed, and return with them. After you sign here, we can post his copies back to him."

That would never do.

She pretended to be thinking hard. "It would be better if I went to Paris too, so it can be settled at once, if it is settled at all. We don't want to risk a change of mind once we have reached an agreement. I am coming with you."

His gaze sharpened. "What about your lessons? Your shop?"

"I will inform my tutors that my lessons must wait. Mrs. Ingram has come up from Richmond and can deal with the shop for a while."

"Traveling together — it isn't done, Miss Jameson."

"We will not travel together. We will travel at the same time, but independently. I can't object if you are on the same packet as I, or staying at a nearby inn."

His expression revealed misgivings — but also a vague amusement and — could it be calculation? "It would be more appropriate for you to travel with a companion or maid."

"Nonsense. I am not some girl. Besides, it is really not your decision. The timing is fortunate. I will be able to see the new styles in Paris and adapt them to my own hats and bonnets. I had intended to journey to Paris in the summer, but now will be more pleasant anyway, and I won't be totally on me — *my* own."

He shrugged. "It is not necessary, but . . . to avoid another row, I will allow it."

"To avoid another row, I will not say that it is not for you to allow or not allow." Relieved that he had not argued more, she gave the engine another good look, then eyed the invention. All the while she reveled in fantasies about her imminent reunion with Charles. She itched to be alone with her memories and plans.

"I should leave now. I have much to do before Monday," she said.

He escorted her out. They waited in the portico while a servant went to procure a hackney carriage.

"Hotel Le Meurice," he said. "That is where I will be staying. It is attuned to English tastes. There are others, of course. Minerva can probably advise you."

She pushed aside her daydreams and

considered the man standing beside her. He was behaving extraordinarily well, considering the way this visit had started. Her presence ever since had probably been a trial for him, yet he never showed that.

"I am sorry about how I reacted to your proposal. My response was not gracious."

His only answer was a slight nod of his head.

The hackney arrived. After the servant handed her in, she spoke to him through the window.

"I am curious about something, Mr. Radnor. You said that the enterprise was one reason for your proposal. What was the other?"

He stepped up to the carriage window. She found herself gazing into his eyes, unable to look away.

"Marriage was an honorable way to have you in my bed. Now I'm left with the alternative."

The carriage rolled just then, leaving her gaping at the open window.

CHAPTER ELEVEN

"What do you think?" Mrs. Ingram asked while she and Rosamund sorted through a delivery from one of the warehouses. This one consisted of ribbons and notions, along with some expensive silk flowers. Another included an assortment of ostrich and capon feathers. A sheet of paper waited nearby, for Rosamund to jot down anything that might be missing. Mrs. Ingram had chosen well, so that list remained very short.

"Put the ribbons on the shelf on the back wall here," she said. "The notions can go in the workroom."

Mrs. Ingram carried out the sack of notions while Rosamund looked around the shop. She had spent all of yesterday afternoon here, after leaving Mr. Radnor. Early this morning, she and Mrs. Ingram had returned to wait for a wagon that was bringing a bed and some furniture for the first story. For hours now, they had been readying the shop as best they could.

Because she would be out of the country for a week or two, Mrs. Ingram would now have to take command. Rosamund wanted to leave her with as little work as possible.

Some bonnets already decorated the window, high on their metal stands. A temporary sign on the door announced the location of Jameson's Millinery, and a sign maker had arrived an hour ago for the commission of installing a proper one. Rosamund had strewn some ribbons around those bonnets, and a few silk flowers, so they didn't look too lonely. Already she had spied some women peering in.

That heartened her, and confirmed her belief that making good use of a street-level window would benefit her. She had decided, however, to also take the front chamber up above for the shop, to have it available for anyone who did not want to be served down here.

Another wagon stopped outside.

"Hopefully, it is the hat forms and the buckram," Mrs. Ingram said as she came out to the front room. "No point in showing those plates if we don't have the materials to make the hats."

Two men came in the door, burdened with clumsy rolls and boxes. Mrs. Ingram directed them to the workroom in back.

"Once the Monday deliveries come, we should be in fine shape," she said approvingly while she watched the men disappear.

"With you here, I'm sure we will be."

"You make sure to keep an eye out while in Paris. Don't forget to make some drawings. Whatever they do there, we can do here."

"I'll stare rudely so I get all the details."

She looked down at her apron and the old dress beneath it. Both showed signs of the dusting and washing she had done today. She eyed Mrs. Ingram's dress, even older than her own. She would have a few new ones made for her. If Mrs. Ingram was going to greet patrons in a Mayfair shop, she needed better garments.

The men left, taking their wagon away. Rosamund set some caps in the window too, so any curious eyes had more to view. She unfurled an ostrich feather in front of it all. While she did that, a carriage pulled up on Oxford Street. She opened the shop door as Minerva stepped out and came toward her.

"I wrote that I would call on you tomorrow," Rosamund said.

"You also wrote that you could not do it today because of duties here, so I decided to visit and see your shop, if you will allow it."

"Of course, although it is not nearly finished."

Minerva's stride slowed as she neared. Her gaze went to Rosamund's cheek. So did Rosamund's fingertips. She had used some paint this morning, but the sun shone brightly and the "salve" barely helped.

"The rogue," Minerva said before embracing her. "Now, show me and tell me everything about it."

Rosamund introduced her to Mrs. Ingram, then gave her a tour. They ended it in the back workroom. Minerva looked over the materials and notions.

"Someday you must allow me to watch you create a masterpiece," she said. "I am envious of anyone with artistic sensibilities." She turned to face Rosamund. "You wrote that you needed my professional services again. How can I assist you?"

"Come with me." Rosamund led Minerva out of the shop, then up the stairs to the first story. She took her guest to the apartment in back that had been arranged for Mrs. Ingram to use. She invited Minerva to sit at the small table set near a back window.

"You told me that Charles lives in Paris. Do you know exactly where?"

Minerva opened her reticule. "I suspected you might want that information if you have engaged me again. I do know where he resides. Here is the street and number." She handed over a folded paper. "Have you decided to write to him?"

Rosamund fingered the paper. Just holding it made her heart quicken. "I have decided to make a journey to Paris. I intend to call on him while I am there."

"How fortunate of you, to visit that city. Perhaps when you arrive in Paris, you should write to him first, and not surprise him unawares."

She looked up from the paper, into Minerva's eyes. "Do you think it a mistake to do this?"

"I spend many hours finding past friends or lovers, or lost family members. The reunions that ensue do not always unfold the way my patrons envisioned. Time changes people. Are you traveling alone?"

Would time have changed Charles very much? Might he have forgotten about her? Her heart refused to believe it. Theirs had not been a common love, but one of astonishing depth.

"I will be making the journey independently, but Mr. Radnor is also going at the same time. He will be available to provide help if I need it, and I will be available to sign documents if he needs that."

Minerva's eyebrows rose a fraction. "Is your maid Jenny accompanying you?"

"I asked her to help Mrs. Ingram here, and she has agreed to. I expect I can hire a maid at the hotel. Mr. Radnor recommended the Hotelle Le Meurice. Do you know it?"

"It will certainly do. I will send you the names of a few others tomorrow. Chase and I visited there last autumn, and I will also jot down directions to some shops you may want to visit, and send along some letters of introduction to friends who live there, should you need help. When do you leave?"

"Monday."

"So soon? Have you recovered sufficiently from what transpired the other night . . . ?"

"I am not dwelling on it. There were things said, however, that I have been wondering about. Not said by Philip, but by others. About . . . our benefactor. Perhaps you can explain them. If they aren't part of secrets, I mean."

Minerva's face lost most of its expression, except for a firm, somewhat distant smile. "If I can in good conscience explain, I will try. He fell off a parapet at his country home. It was declared an accident."

"Yet some in the family don't think it was. Lady Dolores, for example."

"No. Some don't."

"Do they believe someone done him in?"

"Some do."

Rosamund swallowed hard. "Do some think I did that? What with the legacy, I had —"

"No one has cause to speculate about you. You were in Richmond, so you can pay all of the gossip no mind at all." Minerva smiled, as if that settled *that*. "Now, I will take my leave so you can finish whatever you need to do here. When you pack for this journey, remember to take along your best garments. You may want to attend the opera or theater, or dine in one of the special establishments there."

Rosamund led the way down and saw Minerva off. Then she returned to the shop to help Mrs. Ingram. Her conversation with Minerva kept going through her mind whenever she rested for a few minutes. Her new friend had ended their chat firmly, before any more questions about the late duke's death could be asked.

CHAPTER TWELVE

"Ooo. *C'est tres belle.*" Margarite smoothed her palm down the silk fabric of the pale, lilac dinner dress.

Rosamund had no idea what had been said by this young maid provided by the hotel.

"It . . . is beautiful," Margarite said in halting, careful English.

She spoke the way Rosamund assumed she herself sounded when she was trying to speak French.

Margarite continued to unpack the trunks. It would probably take some time. Never having traveled abroad before, and with Minerva's advice in mind, she ended up bringing all her new garments and a good number of her old ones.

Rosamund returned to the bedchamber. Although not large, she thought it luxurious. The long windows gave it good light, and the elegant high ceiling, with all its plaster decoration, created opulence.

Then again, perhaps she liked it so much because of the sitting room attached to it. Even better, the sitting room had a little terrace that overlooked a big park across the street.

She stepped out on that terrace to take in the view. People strolled much as they did in London's parks.

"Those are the Tuileries Gardens. It is where one goes to see and be seen."

She turned to see Kevin Radnor emerging from a chamber onto another terrace beside hers. She had not realized his quarters were next to her own. After he spoke with the hotel staff, she had been escorted by a formal gentleman to her door, while Kevin disappeared.

Now she pointed to his long windows. "Do you have an apartment too?"

He shook his head. "I don't need one."

"Nor do I."

"There may be evenings when you want to dine alone. The French are very liberal, and their restaurants are unsurpassed, but even they do not expect a woman to be seated alone. This way you can call for a meal in your suite but won't have to eat in the bedchamber."

"How thoughtful of you, to consider that.

I heard you in discussion with the gentleman downstairs but had no idea you were arranging this for me."

"One of us needed that extra chamber. If we require privacy, that is. Better you have it."

"Require privacy?" Her heart quickened a bit, in a combination of alarm touched by — excitement. The latter made no sense, but she could not deny its existence.

She had not forgotten his parting words when she left his family's house in London. Even as she rushed to prepare for this journey, it had remained in the back of her mind. When a man all but declared his intention to seduce a woman, that woman would be an idiot to ignore it. To then make a journey in that man's company was probably foolhardy. Even dangerous.

When that man was handsome and appealing, it was probably normal to experience these peculiar reactions to him. On their journey here, he often became absorbed in his thoughts. She could not resist examining him then, wondering if he had said those words to tease her, or in revenge for her rejection. On several occasions, however, that gaze had turned on her without mercy, as if he guessed what she contemplated and deliberately sought to fluster her.

She had remained on her guard the entire way to Dover as a result. His presence across from her in the carriage could not be ignored. She kept waiting for something inappropriate to occur. The truth was, the anticipation had titillated her without Mr. Radnor doing anything at all untoward.

A fine thing that was. Stupid and embarrassing. Whenever it happened, she had summoned Charles's image and concentrated on it. She had carried him in her mind on the packet, especially when Mr. Radnor on occasion stood by her side while they watched the sea from the deck. There was only one short spell, while they rode from the coast to Paris, when she sensed that an actual seduction was being contemplated by him.

Kevin had asked, while he arranged for transport, whether she wanted her own carriage. Being practical, it had seemed a stupid waste of money not to share one.

Within the first hour she had realized why it was not proper for women to travel alone with men. Even the most spacious carriage grew intimate over time. The space within might have accommodated shorter people better, but she was taller than most and his height meant his legs were always there, close to hers, intruding. In fact, after she had scooted over several times, it seemed to her that he deliberately sprawled in a way that imprisoned her against the window.

She might have suffered that as mere rudeness, but it was right then that he emerged from whatever thoughts had occupied him thus far and turned his intense attention on her. In the best of times that was disconcerting but cramped in that carriage his scrutiny felt relentless. It got much worse when he voiced his thoughts.

"How old are you?" he asked. "I'm guessing perhaps two and twenty."

"You guessed wrong. I am almost twenty-four."

She received a small frown for that. "Then you have been living independently for some years."

With that his curiosity became annoying. "I was in service up until fairly recently." She glared down at his legs. "I realize coaches are not built for men of your size, but you are taking more than your share of this one. Would you kindly move your knee?"

With a faint smile, he rearranged his limbs.

"How long until we reach Paris?" she asked.

"It will be evening when we arrive. . . . So

you were in service, then opened your shop in Richmond?"

She could all but hear him doing calculations. "In between, I worked for a milliner in the City."

"Then you have lived independently for two years or so."

If she had known that Paris was a whole day's journey from the coast, she might have hired her own conveyance so she could be spared this interrogation.

"Why are you asking me these questions? Are you still worried about some fortune hunter turning my head?"

"Fortune hunters will be interested no matter your age. You could be sixty and they would still dance attendance."

In that case, perhaps he was just bored. Apparently he had run out of brilliant ideas to contemplate. When he did not seem inclined to talk further, she retreated with relief into thoughts of Charles, and the anticipation of their reunion. After all these years, she tried to imagine seeing him again. He would look a bit older, of course, but she didn't expect any significant changes. He would greet her with a hard embrace and deep kiss, then laugh with happiness. She could imagine his broad smile and sparkling eyes while he looked at her running into his arms —

"I am trying to decide if you are an innocent."

His calm statement put an abrupt end to her fantasy. "If I am a — *Excuse me?*"

"You asked why I was asking about your independence. That is the reason." He looked over, as calm as could be. "And are you?"

"I can see why your family finds you so hard to bear. What a question to ask! Rude, inappropriate —"

"It is a very simple question." He settled his head against the back cushion. "The entire idea that there are topics a man can't discuss with a woman is ridiculous. One wonders who came up with these stupid rules. Probably women like my aunts."

"More likely women like me who find them far too personal."

"You only thought it too personal because you thought your answer would put you in a bad light, when in truth you merely confirmed my own conclusion, and in no way changed my opinion of you."

He closed his eyes and folded his arms then, presumably to return to whatever else filled his head this day.

"I have not confirmed your conclusion because I did not answer your question,"

Now, on the terrace, when she repeated his word "privacy," he looked back to the gardens, a slow smile forming on his lips. "We will meet with Monsieur Forestier soon. Hard decisions will have to be made then. Those conversations should not happen in public."

"Of course not. And I have many things I want to do here. I want to see the better shops, and observe the ladies' fashions. I don't suppose anyone speaks English?"

"The French assume that anyone who matters will learn their language."

"Which your sort do."

He not only spoke French, he spoke it in a long, unbroken, rapid, and incomprehensible melody.

"I am going to be helpless here, aren't I?" She folded her arms in front of her to warm herself a little. The sun was setting in the west, casting long shadows. Paris seemed colder to her than London. The breeze carried a bite when it flowed from the north.

"I will escort you wherever you need to go so you don't get lost."

She could hardly have him escort her when she sought out Charles. However, if she spent a day traversing the city first, she could probably learn enough to tell the hotel where she wanted to go, and have them find her a carriage.

"Why don't you visit the Palais-Royal tomorrow?" he suggested. "There are fine shops there, and you will also get a good look at current fashions in the garden. As for now, join me for dinner. I'll explain the food to you."

She agreed and returned to her chambers. The food needed explanations?

Miss Jameson insisted they were traveling independently, but of course they really weren't. Kevin saw to that.

As a gentleman, it was his duty to see her safely to Paris, after all. The best way to do that was to travel with her in the carriages and keep watch over her on the packet.

Now, considering her ignorance of the French language and habits, he was obligated to continue acting as her guardian.

He could have said something when he surmised that the hotel manager made inaccurate assumptions about their relationship. He could have made it clear that the two chambers need not be close to each other because Miss Jameson was merely a friend. It would have been possible to do that without saying a word.

But it suited him to allow the assumption to stand.

Dressed for dinner, he presented himself at her door. A maid opened it, a pretty, young one with dark curls and a very French nose. She stood aside so he could enter the sitting room. Rosamund waited there.

She looked ravishing in the lilac dinner dress that she had worn at Aunt Agnes's. A little headdress with a lively plume sat atop her blond hair. A few little tendrils hung around her face.

He offered his arm. "I thought tonight we would dine here in the hotel, if that suits you."

She nodded while she looked around the staircase and up to the ceiling as they strolled down. "Me thinks — *I think* this will not be like eating at a coaching inn."

"Nor like eating at my aunt's table. Although there are French cooks in London. My cousin Nicholas has one, for instance."

"Is the food that different?"

"Some of it is. Much of it is very familiar."

They were seated in the restaurant. Rosamund stared at the crystal and flowers and finally at the cutlery lined up at her place. She cocked her head and pointed to one eating implement. "What is that?"

"I'll show you soon."

It was not his goal to shock her, but he

decided that introducing her to new things might be wise. So he ordered champagne, and they laughed when the effervescence affected her nose. He called for shrimp and she enjoyed them. He had the kitchen send out snails.

She eyed them, then him. "What are these?" She poked her fork at one.

"You eat them with that odd little implement that confounded you."

"But what are they?"

"Gastropods. *Cornu aspersum.*" He popped one into his mouth. "The French call them escargot. We call them snails."

She made a face. "Back home we called them slugs, and we didn't eat them. We squished them or killed them with garlic water."

"These live in these shells they are lying in now. Slugs don't have shells."

"You *would* know the difference." It did not sound like praise. She kept poking at one with her fork, as if waiting to see it move.

"They have been eaten since Roman times. They are actually farmed. Try one. I promise there is no slime. They cultivate them so the ones they cook have been rid of that."

"Must I?"

"Of course not. It takes some courage the first time."

She used her implement to dig one out of its shell. She examined it. "If I shoot the cat, it will be all your fault for saying I would be a coward to refuse. Pour me more champagne so I can wash it down."

He did as she bid, then watched her gather her nerve. With one quick movement, she ate the snail, chewed three times, then reached for the champagne and took a good swallow.

"That was *not* pleasant. Other than the butter, it had little taste, and the texture was odd."

"It is an acquired taste."

Sole was served, which was more to her liking. "If you have acquired all these French tastes, you must visit frequently."

"Fairly often."

"Have you traveled to other places?"

"I came of age after Napoleon was defeated. I went on a tour of the Continent, like most young men." He realized how presumptuous that sounded. "At least most of those who are, as you would say, my sort."

"I've never even been many places in England. My home. London and Richmond. Brighton, once." She shrugged. "Just as well. *Your sort* speak all these languages.

I'm still learning me own." She grinned after she said that, as if to assure him that she had deliberately made the mistake.

"You do not need to know the languages to travel. Is traveling something you want to do?"

She appeared astonished by the question. "I've never thought about it. Such a thing was never possible before. But, yes, I think I would like that someday. It is interesting to see new things and habits. Even snails."

He wondered what it would be like to revisit the sites on his tour, only this time with Rosamund at his side. He pictured her basking in the warmth of Greece and Egypt, and walking the cobblestones of Florence. He imagined making love to her on a terrace in Positano, and swimming with her in Lake Como.

She set down her fork and knife. "I hope you did not tell them to bring more food. I am very done. In fact, I am so done that I need a walk."

"I will accompany you. We can take a turn down by the river."

He waited below while she went above to get a wrap. He had the hotel call for a carriage, then checked for any mail. One letter had arrived. He read it, then tucked it away just as Rosamund descended the stairs.

She looked lovely in the wide-brimmed bonnet she had donned. It flared around her face, its soft cream fabric pleated into a series of folds that acted like lines directing one to look at her eyes. Not that he needed instruction. It had taken true effort not to stare at her all through their meal.

She also wore a long, cream shawl that flowed all around her. Lightweight, it would provide little warmth. It could be chilly near the river.

"I could wear a pelisse," she said, fingering the shawl's edge, "but none of mine make an ensemble with this dress."

"That should be fine," he lied easily while he offered his arm.

Paris remained busy long into the night. That was Rosamund's first reaction when they began strolling along the Seine. They were not alone. Some people hurried past, but many walked slowly, taking the air.

"The river smells more than ours does," she said.

"It is a big city and the Seine runs right through it. It does not move as fast as the Thames either, or have a tide."

Although it was dark, she could see the buildings they passed. Streetlamps provided broad pools of illumination.

"They are still burning oil here," Kevin said. "These lamps have silver backing that reflects the light. Grows it. The light is superior, even if the mechanics are clumsy."

As they passed the next one, she peered up to see what he meant.

"This is much like the City," she observed. "Some grand buildings, like this one here, but right nearby, ancient, small ones."

"Very soon you will see very grand ones."

Across the river there loomed a large, castle-like structure with small windows and a tower on one side. She was so taken by it that she did not notice the cathedral until it rose in front of her, across a plaza.

"You may not have noticed, but we crossed a bridge and are on an island in the river," Kevin said. "It is the oldest part of Paris."

They viewed the cathedral, and he told her some of its history. Then they meandered down to the river again.

"I received a letter from Monsieur Forestier," he said while they stood on a bridge, gazing down the black ribbon of water. "He would like to meet tomorrow. An early dinner. You are invited."

"I won't understand anything that is said. What will I do there?"

"Look beautiful."

She glanced at his profile. They were not

near one of those streetlamps, so she could see little of his expression.

"Do you want me there to distract him, so he makes a bad bargain?"

"You are attending as a full partner whose agreement is needed. If for some reason your presence leaves him dizzy and irrational, it won't be your fault, or mine."

"I hardly think he will become irrational." She laughed. "Dizzy indeed. He is probably just like you, all science and machines and never distracted long by any woman."

A stillness opened beside her. She looked over and found his gaze on her. His eyes were dark pools in the dark night, but alive with tiny sparks.

"Is that what you think? I can see that I have been too subtle."

His tone, quiet in the night, unnerved her. "You were not subtle at all. You explicitly said that you were never enthralled."

"I suppose I did."

He seemed closer now, only he had not moved. His height dominated her, yet she did not feel threatened. Her heart beat harder. A delicious alarm pulsed in her. Not fear, but its friendlier cousin that teased with its caution.

Then his hand was on her face, and his gaze very close. The warmth of his palm flowed right into her.

Her thoughts scattered. Astonishment ruled her, and she barely breathed. Both of his hands cradled her face. His head dipped, then stopped, as if waiting for something. It lowered more and he kissed her.

That kiss had been waiting since they left London. Long anticipation made her respond with something akin to relief.

She had not expected that reaction. She had been on her guard for a reason, but all reason deserted her now. She accepted kisses warm and slow, then succumbed to others hard and passionate. His power seduced her. It had been so long since sensual excitement had overwhelmed her. Absorbed her. She had no weapons to resist, and she was glad that she didn't. His intensity turned physical, capturing her as surely as his gaze could at times.

Despite her blurred awareness, she noted details. The way his arms enclosed her. The scent of his garments and person. The artful way his tongue sent unbelievable thrills through her. The pressure of his hands splayed on her back and hips. His kisses sought her neck and she angled her head to permit it. Delicious shivers descended, tightening her breasts and womb. A wonderful madness beckoned.

Murmurs nearby. Her whole body cried for them to go away. Silence responded. Whoever had walked by paid them no mind. She was euphoric there had been no interruption because she wanted, desperately wanted — his hand rose and caressed her breast. Yes, yes, she wanted that.

She clung to him so he would not stop. He ceased kissing her and held her close, his lips pressed to her crown, while his hand explored. Careful caresses titillated her. Devilish fingers teased. He drew cries and moans from her and made her ache.

As if he knew, his hand went lower on her body. He pulled her closer and kissed her crown while he slid his hand between her thighs. Over dress and petticoat and chemise, he reached deeply between her legs, then pressed up against the exquisite agony that tortured her.

She hung on to him, mindless and gasping. She accepted what he offered. Not complete relief, but enough to keep her from dying. She bored down as best she could so that hollow craving might be removed. Only the pressure itself began to stir more profound hungers. It was then that he removed his hand and wrapped her in his arms.

They stayed like that, with her nestled

against him while she sought some composure and forced her body to give up hope of anything more. She became aware again of the river below, and the lights of the city and the balustrade behind her hips. Guilt began to whisper in her head, but she ignored it because she did not want to regret feeling this again. Not yet. She did not want to lose hold of the sensual glory that could exist between a woman and a man, but, moment by moment, it slipped away into the night anyway.

Kevin knew by the time they had walked to the end of the bridge that she would not have him tonight. So he did not propose that they continue this on a comfortable bed at the hotel, much as he wanted to.

He kissed her, then put her in a carriage and walked back alone. In less than a minute he was cursing himself for being so damned decent.

He should have followed his inclinations and taken her there on the bridge. She all but begged him to. No one in this city would have cared, should anyone notice. But no, he had to be an English gentleman about it. Lifting her skirts and her leg on a bridge would not be respectful. Not appropriate. *Not how it's done with a decent woman.*

Hell if he knew if that was even true. For all he knew, decent women gave themselves all over London in parks and on bridges. It wasn't as if he had tried to find out.

He walked on, taking a long, circular path, so that he gained some control on his body and mind. He summoned his well-known anger at how she was a nuisance. An interference. A stubborn woman who was nothing but trouble for him. Yet he also kept hearing her, and smelling her, and feeling her. He imagined her naked and accepting and desperate for more than he had dared tonight. It didn't help that she had been so passionate. Of course she was. Wanting her had been designed to be a special hell for him, so why not make the fires burn especially hot?

They certainly burned now. It took him almost an hour to escape the spell she had cast. He approached the hotel, looking up to the long windows behind her terrace, wondering if she still yearned for completion the way he did. No lamps burned in that suite, from what he could tell. The indomitable Miss Jameson had gone to bed.

One of them might as well get a good night's sleep. He certainly wouldn't.

243

CHAPTER THIRTEEN

Rosamund looked over the feathers spread out on a table in a back chamber of Monsieur Benoit's shop. Some of them had been dyed, and she was wondering if the ladies of London would want such brightly colored ostrich plumes come autumn and winter.

Monsieur Benoit, being a smart merchant, kept drifting by. Each time he did, he deposited some other interesting notion on the table. Old, wiry, and wizened, he smiled at her whenever their eyes met. She could tell he anticipated that her desires would overcome her hesitation.

She had found this shop by going to one of the dressmakers that Minerva had recommended and asking where such wares could be purchased. The modiste did not speak English, but they had communicated well enough. Five minutes later, she met Monsieur Benoit who, it turned out, supplied some of the most esteemed milliners in

Paris. He also spoke English.

That proved fortunate, because she was on her own today. Kevin left the hotel early, leaving a note saying he had appointments and would call for her at four o'clock to attend the dinner with Monsieur Forestier. She had been relieved that she did not have to face him right away, let alone spend hours with him. She doubted they could keep company that long and pretend last night had not happened.

She still accommodated it in her mind, even while she eyed those plumes. What had she been thinking? *There had been no thought to it, only feelings and pleasure.* That was what her inner voice said, the inconvenient one that spoke simple truths and did not attempt to make excuses or spin lies.

She had been too long alone, she decided. It had been years with no hands on her except her own. She had been vulnerable to Kevin's seduction due to being parched and desperate for rain. *Not so vulnerable. There have been others before him who you would not have.*

It seemed especially bad to have done that when she was going to see Charles soon. After all this time of being good, of saving herself, to have been so wanton just before their reunion seemed disgraceful. *And yet*

245

you did not think of Charles at all while on that bridge. The guilt only came on the ride back to the hotel.

She forced her thoughts back to the table. She set aside three colored plums. She reached over and fingered a lovely line of trim made up of tiny seed pearls. It would look wonderful on either a hat or a headpiece. She added it to the pile of trims she had already chosen.

Monsieur Benoit approached her again, ambling through from the front chamber carrying a flat box.

"I will take these, Monsieur."

"They are pretty, yes? Here, see what I have. It arrived yesterday. I normally do not sell fabric, but —" He made a little shrug.

The box contained a length of green silk. She fingered it, amazed at its tight weave and subtle sheen. It was possibly the finest gros de Naples she had ever seen. "What is the cost?"

He mentioned a price. She almost laughed. She could never sell a hat for enough to justify such a price.

He smiled along with her. His eyes sparkled. "For you, half that. Because you are *tres belle.* Perhaps you make a hat for yourself with some of it and wear it when you are again in Paris and visit my little shop."

"If I discover more shops as fine as yours, I will be sure to return."

"Ah. Then I must tell you of some others. The ones who have fine fabrics, perhaps. Not as fine as this, of course." He gestured to his silk.

"Of course."

She left Monsieur Benoit with a little list, and his assurance he would deliver her purchases to the hotel. She made her way to the garden of the Palais-Royal and found a bench on which to sit.

She opened her reticule and removed a pocket map of Paris. She turned to a page she had marked. She had penned a circle on one street.

Charles lived there. Tomorrow she would call on him. It was time to see him again.

Kevin drank some whiskey while he bided his time until he collected Rosamund for dinner. He sent his mind inward to review all he remembered about his prior conversations with Henri Forestier. There was little cause to think this one would end with a license when the others had not, but he could only try.

As agreed in London, if it could not be

arranged, he would move on without the enhancement.

The problem with going into his head was that Rosamund lived there now and had a way of taking his thoughts down the wrong paths. This time she beckoned him toward some scandalous fantasies. He trod along, even though discontent waited. Soon raw hunger grew, and his mind began having her, again and again. That threatened to have the predictable result, so he forced his eyes open, stood, and paced out his frustration.

He checked his pocket watch and realized he had been lost in erotic thoughts longer than he realized. He donned his frock coat. A few minutes later, he presented himself at the door of the chambers next to his.

A maid bid him enter, then left him to wait in the sitting room. Murmurs came from the dressing room. That door opened. The maid emerged. Rosamund followed.

The fantasies leaped into his mind again when he saw her. She wore the red silk dress she had commissioned that day at the modiste. The family joked that he never noticed fashion, but he paid enough attention to know this was of the latest style. The waist line — slightly lower than what was fashionable in London — flattered her full breasts. The broad, low neckline offered a décolleté that was tasteful but revealing. The skirt, cut in that new, conelike shape that broadened as it fell, flowed when she walked while so many other dresses like that rustled stiffly.

Also different to his eye was the lack of ornament. Women had taken to heavily embellished dinner dresses with lots of frills and lace and whatnot. Other than some lines of lace near the hem and neckline, the only thing adorning this dress was Rosamund herself.

The maid had piled her blond hair high on her crown. A headdress with tiny beads perched there.

She fussed with a reticule that also showed beads. "Won't it do? You warned that red could be risky, and you appear to disapprove."

Disapprove? He wanted to ravish her on the spot. "It is lovely. You are beautiful in it. I will probably be fighting Monsieur Forestier off with a sword."

She blushed. "As long as I won't embarrass you. I know you would prefer I didn't attend this dinner."

"That isn't true. A carriage should be waiting, so we should go down."

The maid draped a dark crimson silk

shawl over her shoulders. He offered his arm in escort. Down they went.

He wondered how he was going to manage this meeting with delicious Rosamund sitting right there.

The carriage took them past the Louvre and the Palais-Royal, then continued through the city to the river. They passed the bridge where they had walked the night before. Seeing it conjured up memories that Rosamund did not want to have at that moment.

"I found an excellent shop for millinery notions today," she said, lest Kevin's thoughts venture in that direction too. "It had the loveliest dyed plumes."

"Red?"

"Other colors too. The owner also agreed to sell me a special silk he had found. I am going to make Minerva a hat with it. She has been so generous with her time and advice, this will be a small way to thank her."

"Be sure it is a little dramatic. She said your hats are distinctive that way." His voice spoke almost absently. He looked out the window, and Rosamund could tell his mind dwelled elsewhere. Probably on Monsieur Forestier.

She hoped the evening went well, for Kevin's sake. If it didn't, at least this delay would be over. They could return to London and lay plans for making this business into something other than a young man's dream.

She glanced at him while the city unfolded, noting the small frown he wore, and that far-away expression. It surprised her when suddenly, his gaze swung over to her.

"I have a question," he said. "If I don't ask, it will drive me mad."

"Then ask."

"Last night, if upon returning to the hotel I had come to your door, would you have allowed me to enter?"

What a question. She fussed with her reticule to avoid looking back at him and finding that gaze trying to see through her. He waited her out. He expected a response.

She gave up any hope her silence would be her answer. "No."

It sounded so blunt. So unkind. "It was not because I did not — I mean, it was probably obvious that I —"

"Yes."

Goodness. That was equally blunt.

"When it is that obvious that a man and woman desire each other, they normally do something about it. Hence my question," he said.

He was better at talking about this than she was. Undoubtedly he had experience with such conversations. She had none at all.

She considered telling him about Charles, although that would not explain her behavior on the bridge. Even she could not make sense of it under the circumstances.

"But you did not come to my door, did you? Perhaps you did not for the same reason I would not have invited you in."

"What reason is that?"

"If I was not willing to be your wife, I probably was not willing to be your mistress."

"If only it were that simple."

The carriage began slowing. The setting sun streaked in the window. Kevin leaned forward, out of that harsh beam of light and into the shadow where she sat. "Should you ever come to my door, I promise that I would definitely allow you to enter, and it need not imply any formal agreement."

The door opened. The steps went down. She rearranged her shawl and, side by side, she and Kevin entered the restaurant.

Women ate with men in the good Parisian restaurants. Nevertheless, Monsieur Forestier had taken a private dining room for their meal. It had windows that looked out over the Île de la Cité and the apse end of

Notre Dame. Rosamund went to those windows immediately and stood in the golden light heralding the end of the day.

Monsieur Forestier joined her there. He pointed out this building and that. He smiled. He flattered. Kevin watched, deciding whether to mind or not.

He had introduced Rosamund as his partner in the enterprise. Forestier had looked as if lightning had struck him when he saw her. When Forestier gave him a sly, quizzical look, the meaning of which any man would know, he had given one back that was equally eloquent. *No, she is not my lover.* Damn, but he was more than decent, being honest like that. He had really wanted to send a dangerous glare that said *Touch her and we will duel at dawn.*

Now Forestier appeared to be cultivating the garden beyond the gate that had been left open. It didn't help that women probably found Forestier handsome. He was in his thirties, dark of hair and eye, and very Gallic.

Rosamund, to her credit, did not encourage it. Kevin wasn't convinced she even realized their host was flirting. Forestier spoke English, but haltingly, so his intentions might have been interpreted as nothing more than graciousness.

The restaurant owner arrived at the door. Their host went to speak with him. Rosamund sidled close to Kevin.

"I'm not sure what I expected, but not such a young man. He can't be more than thirty-five." Her gaze assessed Forestier from the distance. "I suppose he is handsome in a French sort of way. I wonder why he did not bring his wife this evening."

"I didn't realize he was married."

She nodded. "I asked him, indirectly. He pointed out a school, and I asked if his children attend it. He was obligated to say they attend one near the university."

"He teaches there." Not sure that she comprehended how things worked in France, he added, "Wives do not stop French men from pursuing women. It is commonplace to have a mistress here."

"As it is at home."

"Less discreet here."

"The discretion at home is recent, I've been told. Ah, here he comes. When will we talk about his enhancement?"

"When he chooses. After dinner, I expect."

The dinner was delicious. Rosamund tried everything without even asking what she ate. She gave Monsieur Forestier all her attention. It wasn't until the main course that Kevin realized she was plenty aware that

Forestier was flirting with her and permitting the man to think she found it flattering.

Perhaps she really did.

Jealousy had simmered all evening, but now it flared into something more. He regretted not responding to that silent male query differently.

When the plates were cleared and cognac was served, Forestier appeared content to drink on with a lovely woman and to hell with business. Kevin could tell that Rosamund grew impatient. Finally, she stood.

"I find that the wine has tired me. Mr. Radnor, perhaps you will bring me to the carriage. Then you can return and finish this fine meal." She gave Forestier a dazzling smile. "Your hospitality will long be remembered. It is one of the most wonderful experiences of my first visit to your city."

Forestier looked sad to see her go. Kevin escorted her down to the main salon, then out to the carriages.

"He would have talked about nothing all night if I remained," she said. "I am annoyed he will not discuss business in front of a woman, especially when it is *her* business, but better if I retreat so progress can be made."

He handed her into the carriage. "Tomorrow I will tell you what happened."

"Not until late afternoon. I have some place I intend to go earlier." She gave him a sharp glance. "I hope that you will come to an agreement with him tonight."

Rosamund sat in the hired carriage she had asked the hotel to procure for her. The street looked to be a fine one, much like the streets in Mayfair. The homes appeared of similar size to those in that neighborhood too, only they had a different style. They had very steep roofs, for one thing. The long windows appeared similar to the kind the hotel had, ones that swung out to open instead of rising up.

The coachman had asked her twice already if all was well because she had remained in the carriage so long after it stopped. She kept watching a door on one of the houses, wishing it would open and Charles would step out. How much easier this would be if she could simply come upon him while he walked along.

It was not to be. She steeled her courage and rapped on the little window. The coachman climbed down and came to help her out. She took stock of her ensemble and made sure her bonnet was not askew. Stomach churning with excitement and trepidation, she walked to that door.

An old man opened it. She handed him her card and asked to see Charles Copley. She imagined Charles's surprise when he saw the card, and not only because she had called. Charles would probably be astonished to see that she even had a card, let alone one with that street on it.

She waited for the rush of steps coming toward her and Charles bursting into this reception hall and his happy surprise in seeing her. She had seen this day in her mind many times, like a play unfolding on a stage. Now she was here, and she almost wept with her relief that the long wait was over.

Steps. Not rushing, but measured and slow. The older man reappeared. He gestured for her to follow him.

They walked through the house, past a dining room and a few other doors. In the back, the man took her outside. She found herself in a garden.

"There is a stone bench in the back," he said. "If you could wait there."

She strode the path to the back and found the bench. She sat and waited. She could not see the house well from here. After a few moments, she saw the crown of a dark head coming toward her. Slowly, the rest of that head came into view. The dark curls.

The gray eyes. The face she adored.

Charles.

She smiled and her eyes misted. She did not bother to wipe them. There was no shame in happiness.

He smiled back. She just looked at him, allowing his presence to fill in her memories. His face had grown firmer. Harder. Well, five years made a difference in a young man. He'd only been eighteen when she last saw him. She probably looked very different too. His dark hair had been dressed as fashionably unruly, and his long frock coat showed the fitted sleeves and broad lapels popular in Paris. His eyes — She remembered them full of joy and impish humor. Now their pale color looked opaque and . . . older.

"Rosamund."

It was only when he said her name that she realized he had been standing silently in front of her for some time.

"I expect you are surprised." She had to battle the urge to dance over to him.

"Stunned. What are you doing here?"

A slight misgiving wormed its way into her excitement. "I am visiting Paris and decided to call. It has been so long since I saw you."

He took a few steps towards her. "A very long time. I almost did not recognize you."

"Surely I haven't changed so much."

"Not very much. Still lovely." His gaze drifted down. "You have done well for yourself."

"I have, much to my surprise."

Again that long gaze, as if he calculated the cost of her ensemble. She could no longer ignore that he remained very reserved. Distant. Hardly delirious with joy.

He looked down, and she realized he held her card and was looking at the address.

"Is this your home now?"

"Yes, I have a house in London."

"Do you now." Not a question.

"Is this your house?" she asked, looking through the garden to the high-pitched roof.

"Only some chambers. They suit me, however."

"More than your parents' home in London?"

"Much more than that. We get on quite well now, with them there and me here."

"You plan to remain here? Forever?"

"Until my father passes, at least. I like Paris. Whether I will enjoy it as much when I am older —" He shrugged. "What did you do after they threw you out? I always felt guilty about that."

"I found service in another house."

"With no references?"

"There are always those willing to take on a girl if the pay is low enough."

He frowned at that. Once more, he assessed her. "And here I worried that you would fall victim to men who prey on pretty servant girls."

Something in his tone quelled her enthusiasm in a blink. A judgmental inflection suggested he had not worried at all, but now wondered. "You mean men like you, Charles?"

That took him aback. "I suppose I deserved that. But you were hardly unwilling."

"We were in love. That makes it different."

"Young men are always in love if the girl is pretty. You know that by now, I expect."

Her heart thickened. It was all she could do to hide how his words devastated her. How cruel she found them.

"Are you here with your sister?" he asked.

"No. Lily is in a school."

"You can't be traveling alone."

"Actually, I am."

"I doubt that."

She paced a bit closer to him. He had not moved much. He remained close to the end of the path, as if he needed to have the means of a quick escape. What had he worried about when he saw that card? That she had brought him a love child? That she wanted to demand payment of some kind? He certainly had not shouted with joy, if his manner now was any indication.

This was not the welcome she had expected. Not the man she thought she knew. While she stood there, watching him, seeing his caution and indifference, the dream disappeared.

It did not shatter or burst. It simply ceased to exist, and she was an old, forgotten lover who had intruded into a man's new life.

Young men are always in love if the girl is pretty.

Dear heaven, she had been a fool to come here. And a bigger one to have thought what they shared was love. She had merely been the convenient servant girl who was pretty enough.

Her heart hurt so much that it left her breathless. She wanted to crumble and fall to her knees and weep to relieve the pain. Instead, she held her composure. Somehow, her voice was clear when she spoke.

"I am traveling independently. However, my journey has been aided by a friend who is familiar with France and Paris, so I am not left completely adrift in a foreign country."

"A friend in Paris? Perhaps I know this friend."

"Not an inhabitant of the city. A friend from London." She hesitated, but wanted to let Charles know just how well she had done recently. "Mr. Kevin Radnor. He visits Paris often enough that perhaps you have met him all the same."

"Radnor?"

She took some solace in his surprise. His shock. It did nothing to ease the pain, but it helped her pride.

"That is Hollinburgh's family."

"His cousin. I have had the pleasure of meeting the duke. I know the family quite well."

He smiled broadly, and for one exquisitely painful moment looked just like the Charles she remembered. "You have done *very* well for yourself, Rosamund. Paris trips. Your sister in a school." He lifted the card. "A fine address. I thought perhaps you had come to castigate me for my indiscretions with you. Now I think you made this call to thank me."

"It is not what you think." *I made this call because I loved you and held the memories close for five long years.* She could not say that now. He had already let her know that her dream had been built on air, not anything real.

How had she lied to herself all this time? When they were lovers she had been ignorant, but she no longer was. She knew about men. He had not made any attempt to find her, and she was more easily discovered than he had been.

Stupid girl. Stupid, stupid girl.

"It is exactly what I think," he said with a vague sneer. "At least you are being kept, and it sounds as if you have a lucrative arrangement. You at least have spared me any concerns that men were taking you under bridges. I'm glad for your good fortune, Rosamund. Play your cards right and maybe next year it will be the duke himself."

His words shocked her like so many slaps. One after another they came, ugly and hurtful. She lost her hold on her emotions, and with them her pride.

It is not what you think, she cried. "There has been no one but you. No one. I waited for you all this time. You said you would come for me. That we would be together. I believed you. I looked for you. And all you can do now is insult me."

"Lower your voice and get hold of yourself. You had to know I could never come for you. That it was over from the moment when I got into the carriage that day. My family would never have accepted you. Even in your finery now, they wouldn't." He removed a handkerchief from his frock coat and gave it to her.

She dabbed at her tears. "You are horrid to say these things."

"I apologize. However, you are better off with this Radnor than with me, that is certain. I could never give you a house on that street."

He didn't believe her. He thought she was dressed like this because she was a man's mistress. He assumed Kevin was merely the last of a series of protectors.

She closed her eyes. She forced control over the anger building in her. She ignored for now the heavy, mourning heart in her chest. She gave him back the handkerchief. "You did not have to seduce me. You did not have to ruin me. Why did you, if you did not love me?"

"You are not an innocent, so you know why. You were lovely, fresh, and sweet, and I was randy as hell. Although —" He reached out and ran the backs of his fingers along her damp cheek. "The lovely girl has become a ravishing woman. If I had known you would grow into what you are today, I might well have looked for you. Before this Radnor found you."

His touch lured her, but his words insulted her again. *If I had known you were going to whore for a man, I might have considered having you whore for me.*

She stared at him, trying to remember the Charles of her memories. She doubted the man in front of her had ever felt the love and joy he had shown in her dream.

She did not trust herself to control how anger sent hot branches out of her pain. She needed to get away from him before fury made her a madwoman.

"I must go. Is there a garden portal in front? Yes? I will leave that way. I apologize for intruding."

As she walked away, she concentrated on keeping her expression calm and her back straight. She did not want him or anyone else to see just how humiliated she felt, or the desolation that threatened to engulf her.

CHAPTER FOURTEEN

The crash broke through his dream. He started, then stared at the wall. It had come from Rosamund's suite.

Another crash, and the tinkling sound of something falling. Glass, or china. Then nothing.

He rose from the chair where he had fallen asleep awaiting Rosamund's return, so he could tell her about the rest of his conversation with Forestier last night. The light filtering into his chamber told him it was late afternoon.

A deep moan came through the wall, low and long, like someone in pain. Alarmed, he strode to the door. Perhaps she had not returned in good time because she had been hurt.

He knocked on Rosamund's door. Silence. He waited, listening for footsteps. The silence gave up nothing.

He wondered if he had been mistaken.

Upon returning to his chamber, he stood still and listened again. When the barest noise penetrated the wall, he went to it and pressed his ear against the plaster.

He was close to concluding his abrupt awakening had left his senses befuddled when he heard something. A wrenching sob, muffled by the wall, followed by a curse.

She hadn't opened the door, so she must want privacy. Well, to hell to that.

He walked out to the terrace, climbed up onto the balustrade, and jumped the four feet to the one that surrounded Rosamund's balcony. He dropped down onto her terrace.

Through the glass, he could see her on the edge of the divan, her body folded so her face rested on both hands. The crown of her head hovered over her lap. No sounds came to him through the glass, but her body careened back and forth enough to alarm him.

He didn't knock this time. He turned the latch and entered.

Her body stilled. After a few sniffs, her hands fell to her lap. She did not straighten. She did not look at him.

"Are you unwell?" he asked. "Were you hurt in some way?"

She found enough composure to sit

erectly. She sniffed again and wiped her eyes with a crumpled handkerchief clutched in one hand. She still did not look at him.

She spoke quietly, just above a whisper. "I have not been physically harmed. There was no accident with the carriage, or a theft of my person." She smiled ruefully. "I am mourning someone — something. Do not be concerned."

She appeared so damned sad. Her eyes still glistened from her tears and her expression broke his heart. He ventured closer.

"Yet I *am* concerned. Did you receive bad news from home? Your sister? A friend?"

She shook her head. She looked at him, finally. Her gaze pierced right into him, as if she calculated what she had in him. Then she sat back on the divan, and her whole body heaved in a long sigh.

"I learned today that something I believed for a long time, something me heart counted on and trusted in, was a lie. So, you see —" She lifted the hand with the handkerchief and made a hopeless gesture with it.

He sat on the divan. "Then you are entitled to a good cry." He set his arm on the back of the divan, behind her head. "I've a shoulder if you need one."

She blinked once, twice. Then she slid over and made use of that shoulder, resting her head against it. She dabbed at her nose with the handkerchief. He fished out a clean one from his frock coat and gave it to her.

They didn't speak for a long while, just sat there with his arm embracing her shoulders and her sighs close to his ear. Outside, the late afternoon sun turned golden and the breeze coming in the long windows cooled.

"Thank you," she finally said. "It helps more than I expected."

His reputation for tact was not the best, but even he knew when to remain silent.

"When I first came up to London, I took service in the house of a gentleman. What references I had were rural, and not adequate for such a situation, so I was not paid the usual wage. I was glad for anything, though. I started in the kitchen; then, after a few months, was made a chambermaid. Such a grand house it seemed to me too. I thought I was lucky."

"You were probably worth twice what they paid you."

"I like to think I earned my keep at least. So there I was when I made a mistake. I fell in love with the son of the family. We became lovers."

Ah. "Did his parents discover that?"

She nodded.

"I suppose you were thrown out."

"In the middle of the night. No references."

"And the son?"

"He was sent on a long tour of the Continent." She settled in closer. Her voice had returned to normal now. "We had sworn our love. We would be together soon, he promised. I believed him."

"You were young."

"I wasn't young two days ago when I still believed him. Just stupid. Childish."

"I hope you are not blaming yourself. This man was a rogue."

"I do not blame meself — myself — for falling in love back then, or for believing in him. I blame myself for not seeing the truth of it for five long years. For holding on to a dream that had no substance. I should have known better long ago. I'm usually halfway clever at least."

Give me his name so I can go thrash him. It would serve no purpose, but he would enjoy it immensely. "Did you see him today? Is that why you were weeping?"

"I'm sorry to say I did. I had Minerva find him for me. I intruded on your journey here so I could have a reunion with him. Only — it was not what I expected." She laughed sadly. "Minerva warned me. I didn't listen.

I was so sure, you see."

He could tell her composure wobbled again. He ventured the smallest kiss on her cheek. "I'm sorry you were disappointed."

"That was the least of it." She turned in his arm and looked at him. "He saw my fine ensemble. He noted the street on my card. He learned you were a friend. He noticed my better speech now, and found it odd Lily was in a school. All the things I thought would make me worthy of him, he took as evidence that — that —"

"He said as much?"

She nodded, then dropped her head back on his shoulder.

"I do not know this man, but I already do not like him," he said, unable to remain silent now that it was clear she had been grievously insulted today. "Not only because he made you cry, although that is a big reason. Forgive my frankness if you still have feelings for him, but he is a scoundrel. He seduced an innocent who was in the care of his own family, turned her head, implied marriage would follow, then left her to make her own way after ruining her. He made no attempt to make amends later, or to ensure you had even survived. Then you turn up, still innocent in your own way, and he insults you."

She turned halfway through his tirade and watched him. It was her turn to place a little kiss on the cheek of someone who had lost their composure. "There is no reason for you to be angry with him," she said. "You don't know him."

"More's the pity. Give me his name."

"Why?"

"I'm going to call him out."

Her eyes widened. "You can't. That is dangerous."

"Not for me."

"You don't know that."

"Men like him are too conceited and lazy to practice enough. I, on the other hand, have spent many hours over many years perfecting my skill." He saw how alarmed she appeared. "Don't worry. I won't kill him. His name, now."

"No. No, no, *no.*" She smacked his shoulder with each denial. "I am touched that you want to fight for my honor, but it won't do. I regret now confiding in you, if you are going to even think of doing that. Turn your mind to something else immediately."

Her scold forced him to get hold of himself. He closed his eyes and did turn his mind to something else. Her.

"That's better." She almost sounded happy.

He kept his eyes closed and saw her in that red silk dress from last night. "Did you tell him about your inheritance?"

"No."

"Just as well. He would have lied to you, then, and pretended undying love if you had."

"And I would have believed him, because I wanted to. I didn't tell him because I was afraid he would assume the duke and I — and he assumed the same of me anyway."

He opened his eyes and looked down at her. "You are beautiful and desirable and far more than halfway clever, Rosamund. You are too good for him and are well rid of him."

She looked up at him. "Do you promise not to call him out?"

"If you insist." He pressed a kiss on her brow, in reassurance.

Surprise flexed over her expression. He wondered if she had returned to this hotel thinking herself unworthy of any man. If so, damn the blackguard.

He kissed her again, on the cheek, then the lips. He pulled her closer and held her head so the kiss could linger a short while.

Then, being such a good sort — a gentleman by Zeus — he stood and walked back to the terrace windows.

273

■ ■ ■ ■

Rosamund spent the rest of the evening alone in her chambers. She had a meal sent up and told the maid to leave her alone.

All kinds of thoughts ran through her mind. Perhaps she should see if Mr. Sanders could find a way out of her lease. She didn't need such a house now. She could probably tell those tutors she would not have lessons too. The whole plan had been about Charles, and now all of it seemed very foolish to her.

As night fell, she turned her mind to her shops and found solace in making plans for them. Even so, the shock of her meeting with Charles weighed on her. She no longer mourned, but she continued to feel adrift and ridiculous and — soiled. It reminded her of the night Philip Radnor had assaulted her, only today, Charles had done it with his words and manner.

That she had loved him, and had carried that love to the meeting, made it far worse than Philip.

She prepared for bed, then lay there unable to sleep. She realized that Charles had taken more than a girlish dream from her today. A big corner of her soul felt empty.

She was not sure that she knew herself anymore.

She wished she had never looked for Charles. Never sought him out. She could have continued as she was, believing what she chose. She could have pretended the inheritance might make her a lady and enjoyed Paris for the rest of this visit. She might have remained excited about all the new changes she was making in her life.

A sound came in the terrace window. She had left hers open to air out the sitting room. Now, she heard the mechanism on another window as a neighboring patron shut and locked his.

That would be Kevin, she guessed. He had been very kind. He had wasted a whole day on her, waiting for her return, then comforting her. It was not the sort of thing one expected of him. He always seemed so indifferent to social niceties. Even last night, during the dinner with Monsieur Forestier, while no more than pleasantries were exchanged, she could tell that Kevin grew impatient for more important conversation.

This afternoon, however, he had known just what to say. *You are beautiful and desirable and far more than halfway clever. You are too good for him.*

She believed he meant it because she

doubted he ever bothered to lie that way. At least he meant it when he said it. She had clung to that good opinion of her, to hold herself steady.

Now, lying in her bed, she did so again. She allowed herself to think about her experiences in this city. Last night's dinner, with Monsieur Forestier's flattery. Her discovery of those unusual notions for her shops. Kisses and pleasure on a dark bridge while streetlamps reflected from the ripples of the river below.

She had experienced such joy in those embraces. Pleasure too, but she mostly remembered a lightness of spirit and a glory in being herself. Walking away had not been easy, but to have continued would have betrayed Charles, or so she had believed.

She did not debate with herself long. She rose and donned an undressing gown. She unlatched the door to her chambers, slipped out, and knocked on another one nearby.

No more crying or moaning came through the walls, so Kevin decided to get some sleep. He would have a conversation with Rosamund about Forestier in the morning. Matters could not be delayed any longer.

He had spent hours today thinking about the critical stage of the enterprise. Little else had entered his awareness, other than Rosamund's long absence. Until he heard the glass breaking. Now, free to again mull over the problem, he found he had little interest in it.

His ears strained to hear what was happening in her suite. He hoped he had not left too soon. She seemed more herself, and after that kiss — He really did have to leave then, before he behaved like the worst scoundrel.

He was down to his shirt and trousers when he heard a light knock on his door. The man servant assigned to him had probably noticed the light in this chamber. He strode over to remind the fellow that he had said he would not need anything until morning.

No man stood there. It was Rosamund. She had changed into an undressing gown. Her hair tumbled around her head and shoulders, its long, loose curls hanging low over the frills cascading below her neck. His mouth dried at the sight of her in dishabille like this.

"You said you would open your door if I came to it," she said.

He stood aside so she could enter. She floated past him, and the light from his lamp made her hair glisten with gold.

She strolled aimlessly around the chamber, her long, slender fingers glossing over the furnishings. He could have watched her for hours, if this was what she wanted to do. Eventually he acknowledged that it probably wasn't.

"Are you too sad to sleep? Do you need some distraction?" He stayed by the door, leaning against it because he did not trust himself to get too close.

She shook her head. "I suppose I will be a little sad for a long time, but mostly now I am angry."

"That is a much better reaction. I trust you are angry with him and not yourself."

She stopped her movement near the terrace windows. "I think I am. Yes, definitely." She turned and faced him. "Even that, however — I don't plan to indulge in it. I have already wasted too much time on that childish dream."

The air grew thick with things unspoken, and with the tightening tethers of excitement that desire created. They just looked at each other. He dared not be the one to give voice to it. He could be very wrong.

She smiled tentatively. "I was wondering if perhaps we could kiss again."

That was all he needed to hear. He strode over to her, took her in his arms, and kissed her again. Both triumph and relief burst in him when their lips met.

He prolonged that kiss while his hands noted her body under his hold, and how she trembled with excitement and fear. His conscience waged a little battle and chose an easy truce.

He stopped kissing her. "I left after that kiss in your chambers so I would not take advantage of you. I cannot be that good if you stay here."

"I do not want you to be good."

He lifted her chin and studied her face in the dim moonlight filtering through the window. He wanted her so much he could devour her right now.

"Are you going to pretend I am your old lover?"

"I'm here because on the bridge I didn't think about him at all. Not once. Do you think you can do that again?"

"If you are sure that you want me to, I know that I can. Pleasure is one thing I know about."

She stretched up and kissed him. "I thought it might be. You are not given to half measures when a topic interests you."

He found the little buttons on her undressing gown and released one. "There will be no half measures tonight, just so you know."

When she did not object, he continued with the buttons.

She discovered that pleasure could obscure everything. Time and place. Fear and sorrow. Bit by bit, as his fingers released those buttons, one part of the world disappeared while excitement took its place.

When the undressing gown fell and she found herself in his embrace, warmth and care defeated the worst of the day's emotions. After that, she responded to his kisses as she had on the bridge, with joy.

She could tell he was being careful, as if he wasn't sure she knew her own mind. She pressed the back of his neck and kissed him so he might believe her. She used her tongue against his palate until he held her head and they shared dueling kisses that released their mutual passion. She felt the desire in him, controlled but hot.

His mouth moved to her neck while his hands explored her body with firm caresses. Each touch thrilled her and removed her further from the world. Glorious pleasure astonished her when he caressed her breast. Her nightdress offered little protection from his expert teases. Then the nightdress fell too, and she almost wept from how good it felt. No city now. No chamber. No walls and no world. Just a tightening space with him and her and incredible sensations.

Strong arms lifted her. She floated down gently and felt the linen beneath her nakedness. She saw her breasts, firm and high, their tips so hard that even the air titillated her. Beside the bed, a white shirt billowed. She looked over to see Kevin watching her while he undressed, his gaze full of hard lights and his expression firmed by desire.

He joined her and gathered her into his arms. A kiss, then he watched his hand make feather caresses on her breasts. He looked in her eyes. "It is charming that you do not realize just how beautiful you are."

His head dipped and his tongue flicked at one tight tip. Her breath caught at what that did to her, how a tremble moved down her body, carrying pleasure through her core. Again and again he made it happen. She exalted in her astonishing responses. The caresses began again, exploring, knowing, each one beckoning her further into their intimacy.

She came out of herself a little when his caresses lowered and he touched between her thighs. She knew it should not all go one way. When she reached down to caress him too, he took her hand and gathered the other and held them both above her head.

"Another time," he said.

Laid out like that, her body vulnerable and wanting, she could only accept. With his mouth and hands, he commanded her toward abandon. She went gladly, exalting in how pleasure and desire ruled all of her, even her awareness. Helpless to the slow, long climb in her arousal, she gave up control and kept wanting more.

Suddenly, every sense, every need, collected to one, small spot. He stroked her there and the intensity made her thrash. He stilled her legs with his own and soothed her with a kiss on her cheek, but still he forced the sharp pleasure higher. She almost wept with need, but just as she did, a wonderful burst of pleasure left her breathless and stunned.

He moved over her, starting to fill her. He released her hands and she grasped at him, the only reality where she dwelled. The feel of him in her was so right. Perfect. Her body and soul welcomed that fullness as a wonderful completion to what had happened in this bed.

"If you are cold, I can light a low fire."

The breeze coming from the terrace had chilled with the night. He could close the windows but enjoyed the fresh contrast on his warm skin.

Rosamund nestled closer, tucked under the coverlet. "This is fine. Pleasant."

He bundled her more, and pulled her under his arm.

"Do you want me to go?" she asked, her voice muffled against his body.

"I'd prefer you stay."

He would like to see her face a while longer, for one thing. She appeared peaceful and happy. Contented. That heartened him. He knew a lot about pleasure, but his partners had never been like Rosamund. His lessons came from the brothels of London and Paris. He realized that this was the first visit when he had not sought out the expertise found in Paris's best houses. That was a part of this city he normally looked forward to.

Rosamund's delight in the bed even now, luxuriating in how their bodies still touched and the pillows created a soft nest, made him wonder if this was new to her, along with several other things tonight. Perhaps that scoundrel had only taken her quickly, up against walls or on attic floors. As a servant, she could not show up at his chamber door, the way she had come to this one tonight. She would dare not dally in bed with him afterward.

She moved so she could prop her chin on his bare chest and look in his eyes. "You never told me about your conversation with Monsieur Forestier after I left the dinner."

"It can wait for the morning."

Her eyes narrowed. "You have never been good at dissembling. I can tell it is not good news just from looking in your eyes."

"Nonsense. This is not the moment for business, that is all."

She laughed softly and pecked a kiss on his chest. "You are charming in your own, odd way. You must know that if you want me to agree to something about that business, this is the most excellent moment."

"There is nothing to agree to. Hence —" He shrugged.

A frown puckered her brow.

He flipped her onto her back on the mound of pillows she had created. Propped along her side, he slid down the sheet so he could see her breasts. He caressed around their fullness and watched her frown disappear.

"It was much the same as before," he said. "Two changes, and not to my — *our* benefit."

"What are they?"

"It is up to ten thousand now. Also, there is someone else ready to pay it at week's end if we do not."

"The thief."

He glossed his palm over her tight nipples. "It is his invention. I think the door only remained open because he enjoyed your company. However, it can't be done. As agreed, we will go forward without it."

She seemed not to be listening now. Eyes closed, she enjoyed the pleasure he gave her. Her back arched so her breasts rose for more. He lowered his head and flicked his tongue lightly.

"How much do you have?" Her question came on a breathless murmur.

He had to forcibly divert his mind from where it now dwelled in order to find the answer. "Three thousand immediately. Five by June. That's when a trust pays out." He cast those words aside even as he spoke them. He didn't give a damn about that right now. He sucked at one breast while his fingers teased the other. Every sweet sigh she made caused him to get harder.

"I have the rest. We could do this."

Her response came as little more than sounds between begging moans. When he finally realized what she had said, he looked at her, astonished.

Her eyes remained closed, but a catlike smile formed. "Don't stop now. You promised no half measures."

He pulled her atop him and sat her up so he could see how she gave herself over to the sensations while he caressed her. Her lovely face, softened by her arousal and half obscured by her long hair, became an image of ecstasy. With lips parted and head lolling, her lids rose a tiny amount and glistening blue eyes looked down at what he was doing.

He resettled her and urged her down so her breasts hovered above his face. He used his hands and mouth until she trembled. He reached between her thighs and caressed her until cries of madness made his hunger raw. Lifting her hips, he entered slowly, and allowed the torture to turn exquisite.

She looked down at him, her expression dazed and a little confused. Then she nestled lower so he filled her, and shifted just enough to blind him for an instant.

She looked around at how they were joined. She moved again. "So it's my turn?"

"I'll help."

"How?"

"You'll see."

She rose, then slid back down. "It's different. It still feels wonderful, but also changed."

"They all are."

286

"All?"

"All the ways of doing this. Each feels different in its own way."

She rose again, but shifted when she came down so that he felt her distinctly, like a hard, velvet stroke.

"Oh, you liked that. I can tell. This is fun." Once again, she experimented.

He gritted his teeth so she could play longer if she wanted, but he was close to ending the game. Fortunately, her own desire made her quicken the pace. She closed her eyes and found her own pleasure by creating deep thrusts and wicked rubs. She rode him like a wild woman, throwing back her head and hair, gasping when a move sent her higher.

He slid his hand between their bodies, so he could touch her near where they joined. As soon as he did, she lost all control. She cried out again and again with increasingly desperate pleas. Then she squirmed against him hard and tensed as the desperation gave way to wonder.

He pulled her down on him and held her hips while he took over, thrusting hard and long while he climbed to a soul-splitting finish.

CHAPTER FIFTEEN

Rosamund descended the stairs, dressed for the day. She and Kevin had agreed to meet in the hotel garden for a *petit déjeuner.*

She had gone to sleep feeling like a new woman. She had awoken much herself, but still changed. As she sought out the garden, she acknowledged that she had not thought about Charles more than two or three times while she dressed. The dull ache that emerged with those memories passed soon enough too.

She didn't feel at all guilty for her inconstancy. Nor for her wantonness with Kevin. It had been fascinating, and highly pleasurable. She was lost, and he had helped her find her way. No one who had any kindness would think the worse of her for inviting that marvelous distraction.

The question was whether she should allow it again.

Small tables dotted the garden. Spring

blooms poured from vases and planters. Vines covered walls and arbors. She couldn't imagine a more beautiful place to have a meal.

Kevin already sat at one of the tables, drinking coffee. She paused. What does one say after such a night?

He saw her and stood, so she had to go to him before she had an answer to that question. He looked much the same, although maybe his smile appeared warmer than in the past. And his eyes — she could not ignore that awareness of their intimacy reflected in them.

A server came over and Kevin told him what to bring. Tea arrived for her almost immediately, along with a basket of rolls, breads, and little cakes.

"I suppose we should talk about Monsieur Forestier," she said. "You said we would in the morning."

"First, I think we should talk about last night."

"As I entered the garden, I was wondering what one said after — well, after."

"I expect it is customary to say thank you."

"Is it? Well, thank you, then."

She looked over her teacup to see he was almost laughing.

"It is customary for the *gentleman* to say

thank you, Rosamund. Not the lady."

"Oh."

"So, I thank you. I had a wonderful night. Incomparable."

She cleared her throat. "I thank you too, even if it is not customary to do so. After all, I barely gave you a choice."

"It was understandable that you required distraction. Did you find it?"

"I was thoroughly distracted."

"Should you ever need it again, I hope you will let me know."

He was asking for another night. Maybe many of them.

"I will do that. Now, should we discuss Monsieur Forestier? I meant it last night, about providing some funds. I am a partner. It is my obligation as much as it is yours, should we do this."

"You are very sure, in the clear light of day, that you still want to do that? Last night when you offered, you were disadvantaged."

"My, you are conceited, Kevin. Are you saying that I was not of sound mind?"

He leaned in. "I was licking your breast."

"Which was very nice. I was not so abandoned that I could not think, however. Indeed, learning at least the basic information about Forestier was necessary so that I would not be distracted by curiosity while I was being distracted by . . . other things."

He leaned back. "If you want to invest further, I am not going to complain. How do you see this being done?"

"We need ten thousand by the end of the week —"

"We don't have to carry ten thousand to him by then. Just sign the documents and reassure him of fast payment."

"What? You mean we don't have to hop a packet home, stuff a valise with gold, and hurry back?" She smacked her temple with her palm. "Thank goodness for that."

He eyed her cautiously. "I was only making sure that you understood."

She felt guilty for her little game. "It was good of you to do so. Anyway, it seems to me that when we return to London, I will provide seven thousand and you three. Then, come June, you can pay me back the two thousand, and we will remain equal partners." She sank her teeth into a little cake. "Or, if you prefer, you can keep the other two thousand and we will be slightly unequal partners."

A sweet scent came to her. She eyed the cake and wondered if they had included rose water in it. If so, that was unusual, but not unpleasant. Only as she finished the cake did she realize Kevin had not spoken.

She looked over to see him studying her. He had *that* look. The one that said he wasn't angry so much as exasperated.

"Rosamund," he said in his most Kevin Radnor voice. "If you think that I will allow you to be a majority partner in our enterprise, even by the slightest, tiny bit, even briefly, you are much mistaken."

"Have it your way. Now, you can go tell Monsieur Forestier of our choice, and I will go to the galleries at the Palais-Royal and fill my trunk."

"He may want to see you. He was much taken with you."

"He will see me when I sign the documents. If he refuses us, he will not." She allowed the server to pour her more tea and chose a bread that looked like a scroll. "What did you mean when you said 'incomparable'?"

"Excuse me?"

"You said last night was incomparable."

"That means without comparison."

"I *know* what the word 'incomparable' means, Kevin."

"Of course you do. I meant that —" He appeared uncomfortable, which for Kevin was unusual. "I suppose there is no harm in saying — I do not normally spend the night with a lover."

The roll was a revelation. Flaky and buttery. Pity she couldn't buy them in London. "Is it the spend-the-night part that is unusual or the lover part?"

The garden's appointments seemed to capture his attention. "Both."

"I suppose that is because no women enthrall you enough. I assume you prefer brothels. They would be better for your close study of carnal matters too."

He did not answer, which was eloquent in itself.

She wondered if tonight he would seek out one of the brothels in Paris. Word had it they were incomparable.

"Mademoiselle is not with you today?" Monsieur Forestier didn't mention Rosamund's absence until he had set out some wine in the study he used at the university.

"She decided to shop at the Palais-Royal this afternoon. She sends her regrets and asked me to tell you that she looks forward to seeing you when she signs our agreement."

"Have we then come to one?"

"We have. Ten thousand for the exclusive license, as you require."

They sat on two worn armchairs in front of a fireplace. Windows were open to the fair day, and scuffling students' feet could be heard outside. Forestier fiddled with a pen. A frown slowly formed.

"I did not think you would find the funds," he finally said. "I should have been more explicit at the dinner. But Mademoiselle, well, she, how do you say —" He shrugged and gave an apologetic smile.

"Flustered you." *Bedazzled you. Made you stupid.*

He should have insisted Rosamund accompany him today, so Forestier would be flustered again. He should tie them together until a bedazzled Forestier signed the damned agreement.

"You see, the other, the one I mentioned, offered more."

"How much?"

"Not more money. The same ten thousand."

"What kind of more?"

"A few shares in the company. They are of little value unless the business becomes very big." He smiled. "Perhaps you can offer the same? It has appeal, of course. A way for me to participate in that success if it comes."

Kevin barely controlled his annoyance. Forestier now was asking for part of the company.

Would Rosamund have the same reaction?

Or would she conclude this last-minute change was a small price to pay?

This was the problem with having an equal partner, something he had lost sight of because there seemed no way out. And because she bedazzled him and made *him* stupid. Here he was, trying to box against an unknown opponent while one hand was tied.

"I ask you to delay your decision by twenty-four hours," he said to Forestier. "I need to consider this additional change in our negotiations."

Rosamund strolled along the Galerie de Bois, admiring the luxuries displayed to the world, content with her shopping thus far. Some delicious fabrics and notions would arrive at her hotel this afternoon, along with a roll of buckram far superior to what she could easily buy in London. Even better, some interesting drawings rested in her reticule.

Sketching them had taken some doing. Kevin had warned that decent women did not sit in the cafés, so each time she saw a detail of interest she memorized it, then hurried to a park bench to draw it out before it faded from her memory. One bonnet with a very unique crown had almost defeated her skills with the pencil, but she finally recorded it correctly.

She paused in front of a shop that sold women's hats and shawls. Not daring to take out her pencil and paper to draw, she resorted to studying the hats while she memorized their smallest details.

The proprietor came to the window to re-arrange the shawls strewn among some birch branches propped amid the hats. He glanced her way several times, then more pointedly stared. He looked as if he thought she was stealing his designs.

What nonsense. He had his genius right there for anyone to see, so his styles were hardly secrets. His hats bedecked many crowns in the gardens and restaurants. How could he hope to keep them to himself and his clients? She never duplicated a hat she saw anyway. Not even the ones printed in the plates. She only borrowed bits and pieces of ideas at most.

His dagger gaze irritated her enough that she entered the shop. She looked at everything while the proprietor grew increasingly agitated. One hat had lovely, pale green silk covering its brim, pleated in a most unique manner. She wished the man would go away so she could examine how that pleating was done.

"I would like to try this on." She pointed to the hat, then her head, and looked hopeful.

Her English and her request appeared to reassure him. He invited her to sit and placed the hat on her head after she removed her bonnet. She admired herself in his looking glass. He said something in French.

"It is a little small. How soon can you make another that fits?" She tried some hand gestures to communicate what she meant.

He gave her a blank stare. She probably looked like that when someone addressed her in French.

She tried to figure out how to communicate her desire. She asked again. Very slowly. More blankness, plus a little shrug.

A male voice spoke right behind her. A long blur of French rolled over her head. She recognized the voice and looked back at Kevin. The proprietor rattled something back, and the two of them chatted around her.

"He said he can alter this one and deliver it to the hotel by this evening," Kevin said. "Is that even possible?"

"Yes, it can be done. That is fine. Please ask him the price."

More French. The proprietor's hand appeared in front of her with a slip of paper. Kevin bent over her shoulder. "That comes to around two pounds."

She took her pencil out of her reticule, crossed out the figure, and wrote another. "Tell him that if he alters it, he must stretch the underlying straw, so it is not worth as much."

Kevin gave the milliner that bad news.

The man examined her offer. Shock. Dismay. A lot of French. She did not look at him or Kevin, but squinted at the hat, giving it a very close scrutiny.

With more sighs and mumbles, the man scribbled on the paper and placed it firmly on the table in front of the looking glass. She did not need Kevin to translate.

She noted that the final figure was one quarter lower than the first. She removed the hat and handed it over with a smile and a nod.

Before she could take matters in hand, Kevin had paid and left the hotel's information. She tied on her bonnet and stepped out of the shop.

"Did I embarrass you?" she asked when Kevin joined her.

"Not too much."

"I suppose that isn't done in shops like that."

"France is still poor from the war. I don't think you are the first woman to demand a lower price. He probably hoped that because we are English, we would not quibble over ten shillings."

"I certainly hope your sort of English don't. Otherwise, why have my shop off Oxford Street?"

She gave the gallery structure more of her attention and realized why she had been drawn to these shops. "The windows are very large and look to be all of a piece. I wonder how they do that without mullions."

"It is one sheet. They make a long cylinder of glass, then cut it down its length and flatten it while it is reheated. It is exported and there are buildings in London where you can see it."

"You know such odd and interesting things. Could I have my windows like this?"

"It is very expensive, and I'm told it attracts mischief. Too expensive for a shop that you let, I would think." He gestured to her reticule. "Have you seen your full and jotted down your inspirations? Or do you want to continue?"

"I am finished, I think."

They hired a carriage to return them to

the hotel, then crossed over to the Tuileries and strolled under its budding trees. Kevin guided her to a bench.

"We need to talk."

"From your expression I think it did not go well with Mr. Forestier."

"He has one more demand."

"Not me, I hope."

He laughed. "You seemed so oblivious to his flirting. Gracious, but unaware."

"Oblivious seemed the wisest reaction. What other choices did I have? Flirt back or be very *ungracious.*" She shrugged. "I have learned that bland incomprehension is often the best response."

"You will be relieved to learn that you are not part of the payment he requires. He wants a few shares of the company. He wants to have the chance to participate in any success."

She thought about this unexpected turn in the negotiations. "I suppose that is understandable. It is something I would want if I were in his situation."

"It is also all but impossible, so we are once again faced with returning to London without the license and knowing someone else will get it. I would like to know who our competitor is, and to what purpose he will put it."

He descended into his distraction, probably to contemplate what other uses there might be for Forestier's enhancement. From the way his distance grew, she guessed he also tortured himself with notions that another person had duplicated his own invention.

She took the opportunity to tease out why Forestier's demand was impossible. "You think that if we give him even a small percent, he will have control."

"Yes."

"He would have the final decision, should you and I disagree. He would merely throw in with the side he prefers."

"That small percentage would carry an outsize influence."

"I see. As you said, impossible."

Only he had not said impossible. He had said *almost* impossible. She turned and gave him a good look. "Get out of your mind's pondering for a moment and explain what solution you saw. I know you devised one, even if you have not said so."

He emerged from his thoughts much like an object lifted out of a lake, shedding the private calculations like so much water. "His share would only carry that weight if we each gave up an equal amount. If it all came from one half, his influence would be nonexistent."

"Not true. Whoever gave up the percentage would be at the whim of whoever didn't, should Mr. Forestier be persuaded to that viewpoint."

"I suppose."

"You don't only suppose. You know. Let me guess. The *almost* impossible only exists if I am the one to relinquish some of my half."

"I certainly can't give up any of mine."

"I don't see why not."

"I would forever be at a disadvantage in any disagreement. He would be predisposed to throw in with you."

"You don't know that. It might not happen that way."

"Rosamund, *I'm* not the one he wants in his bed. He would probably agree to anything if he thought it brought him one inch closer to having you."

What a startling thing to say. "How dare you suggest that I would use that to win an argument about a decision regarding the enterprise. I do not employ feminine wiles that way."

His arm came around her shoulders. "I apologize. I probably could have said that better. Nor would you need to use any wiles. It would just happen. It would all come from him."

His discreet embrace felt very nice. She leaned toward him so he might be less careful. "If you are right, that would not be fair. So, we are back to impossible."

"It appears so."

He turned her and gave her a kiss. A very nice kiss. Most of her thoughts about Mr. Forestier disappeared.

"Unless . . ."

His kiss moved to her ear. "Unless?"

"What if we did not give him a tiny percentage of the enterprise? What if, instead, after we are successful, we gave him a tiny percentage of the profit? He would have no vote then. No ownership. Yet he would still participate in success."

He tucked her head against his shoulder and embraced her fully. "He would have to trust us to admit the correct profits. I doubt that he will."

"Then we need to think of a way to document that to his satisfaction."

They sat there in silence. She assumed Kevin was contemplating the problem for both of them. She just enjoyed the warmth of his arms and the fresh spring breeze.

"Something like piece work," he finally said. "In any given year, once we are profitable, he would receive a small amount of what we get each time the invention is used. I'll need to spend some time with calculations to come up with how much he gets, but I can do that tonight. I'm not sure he will accept your plan, but it is one way to do it."

She rather liked the way he called it her plan. "If you can find a way for it to work, I'm sure he will accept it."

"If you wear that red dress again, he probably will."

As soon as they returned to the hotel, Kevin procured some paper. When he entered his chamber, Rosamund saw him shedding his coats. He moved two lamps to a small writing table, set out the ink and pen, sat down, and disappeared into numbers. She closed the door because he had forgotten to.

At the dinner hour, she went to his door to see if he had plans to dine below. Just as she knocked, a servant arrived with a meal on a tray. At Kevin's call, the tray went in, not her.

She had her own dinner in her chamber, then went on her terrace to watch evening claim the city. Finally, she decided to see where all those calculations stood. She didn't even bother knocking this time.

He didn't notice. He just sat there in the

glow of the lamps, gazing down at a pile of papers covered in scribbles and numbers.

"Does it all fit? Have you found the possible?"

He looked over, surprised, then back at the papers. "I think so. I also think that we can use the agreement I brought with me and add this, like a codicil to a will. It does not change the basic agreement. It only expands it." He flipped through some pages. "I will have to write it out, of course. That should not take long. A few hours at most."

"I will see you in the morning, then."

He didn't respond. Already his mind was back in the figures.

She returned to her chambers, called for her maid, and asked that a bath be drawn. She needed one, and then a good night's sleep. She wondered if Kevin had been joking about the red dress. Surely he would want those papers signed tomorrow before evening.

She hoped Mr. Forestier did not balk at anything and accepted the solution they presented. She had enjoyed Paris, but it was time to return to London.

"Come and see this. Let me know if you would accept the proof regarding when the enterprise is profitable or not." Kevin waved the paper in Rosamund's direction. "As a gentleman, I of course assume my word would be enough, but I have devised documentation because he will probably expect some."

He waved the paper again, more insistently. When it remained in his fingers, he looked over at her.

Only she wasn't there. Where the devil had she gone?

He carried the paper to the door of his chamber. He wanted her opinion on this. It was critical to the entire plan.

Upon opening his door, he almost walked into a servant carrying two large pails of water. Three other men followed him. All of them had mastered this task so that no water sloshed out. They filed into Rosamund's suite, through a door held open by her maid.

What a time to call for a bath. She could be impossible at times, especially regarding the enterprise. Surely Rosamund understood that they had to settle this tonight, and that she might be needed. Especially regarding this particular part. He read the paragraph again, trying to put himself in her mind. If someone presented this to her, would her practical thinking find it sufficient to her interests?

It appeared good enough to him. And yet —

Hell, he didn't plan to wait all night to start on the final document. He strode to the door, threw it open, marched to hers, and entered.

"M'sieur!" The maid startled and jumped in front of Rosamund. Who was half undressed, as best he could see. Down to chemise and stockings. Her blue eyes peered over the maid's head. A copper tub stood in front of the fireplace.

"I need you to read this," he said, ignoring the way the maid rolled her eyes at his intrusion.

"It can wait, can't it?" Rosamund gestured to the tub.

"No."

She reached around the maid and took the paper. She bent and held it to the light of the fire. Which made her creamy shoulders visible, and the swell of her breasts and hip.

She straightened. "This is the best we can do. It is generous, because you allow him to have the accounts examined if he thinks we have cheated him."

"Would you sign it?"

"Me?"

"Yes. If you were he, would it allay your

misgivings?"

The maid tsked at the interference, turned, and began taking down Rosamund's hair. Strand upon strand of blond silk fell.

Rosamund handed back the paper around the maid's shoulders. "I would sign the document, but not because of this. I would do it because you have been honest thus far, so probably would be in the future. You did not steal his idea, did you? It seems to me that if someone is honest, documents are formalities. If someone is a thief, no document will protect me."

The maid dipped her hand into the tub, then gave him an annoyed look and a little gesture saying he should go.

He returned the same. *"Allez."*

"Mais, mam'selle —"

Rosamund looked over, curious. Her gaze met his. She touched the maid's shoulder. "Yes. Go, please."

"Do I get my bath?" she asked when the maid had left.

"Of course." He walked over and threw himself in a chair. "I'll watch."

She considered her extreme dishabille. She hardly needed help in removing what was left of her garments. Being watched while she did that . . . the notion dismayed her, but also stirred her.

She let down the rest of her hair, then propped one foot on the tub's edge to remove her hose.

"The rest first." His voice came to her in the silence, from the shadows away from the fire.

She hesitated while she contained the erotic reaction that provoked in her. Feeling both shy and bold, she let her chemise drop and stood naked except for her hose.

No more commands came. And it had been just that, not a request. A little wobbly from the shivers titillating her, she rested her foot on the tub again and peeled down her hose.

The other one required her to move. With her back facing him, she made short work of it, but before she had finished he was behind her, caressing her hips. He kept her like that, bent over her raised leg. His arm embraced the front of her shoulders in support while his hand explored her back and bottom, and his kisses thrilled her neck, shoulders, and spine.

He let her stand then, and embraced her from behind. His palms and fingertips aroused her breasts, skimming and flicking over the tips. Each touch sent an arrow of pleasure down her core. His mouth claimed her neck, making her tremble. Exciting sensations cascaded through her, and each one broke a thread of her control.

A new embrace, with one hand lower. Stroking. Probing. She lost hold of her balance and her mind. She leaned against him while torturous, relentless arousal pleasured and pained. Need began pulsing, absorbing all her thoughts and awareness. His touches left her groaning. Begging.

He bent her again. She found herself facedown on a cushion. The sofa's rolled arm pressed her stomach while her head lolled on its seat. Her hips rose high and her legs dangled.

Vision blurred, mind confused, she looked back over her shoulder. He stood behind her, his shirt gone now, his torso sculpted by the distant firelight. His gaze met hers.

"Like that," he said. "I want to see your face."

His words alone sent a sharp pleasure pulsing between her legs. She wanted him desperately. Only he did not take her then. Instead, he stroked her until he made her need excruciating. Her body shook from it. Her bottom rose higher.

She felt him right there, pressing, and cried out for him. He thrust hard and she moaned in relief. It felt so good. Different from the last time too. She clawed at the cushion and gasped for breath while he thrust again and again. Each new fullness brought her closer to a pleasure all encompassing. And then an unearthly, final tremor began.

"At least you didn't lie. I am getting my bath." Rosamund luxuriated in the tepid water while he washed her. "A very thorough one."

"It is difficult to keep my hands off you. This way they are useful." And still on her, even while he made good on his promise.

The sight of her half undressed had obliterated all thoughts of Forestier, the documents, even the enterprise. He had lost his mind when she bent to remove that stocking, and her back had dipped and her bottom curved round and high. He had almost grabbed her right then and thrown her over the sofa's arm. He was not sorry he'd waited, though. The pleasure she had finally experienced only increased his own.

The erotic memory of her watching him, waiting for him, impatient for him, would not be forgotten. So beautiful. So desirable.

She tucked a long, wet lock behind her ear. "The maid will have apoplexy when she sees what a mess you made with washing my hair. You should have let me do that part."

"I am here to serve, my lady." He lifted one of her legs and soaped down its length. Shapely. Even her feet were pretty. It was a wonder she had not married by now. That was because of her misplaced devotion to that scoundrel of course. He should probably send her seducer a gift of thanks.

Only that man was no longer available to make her unobtainable, was he?

"I expect that you have had a lot of men like Forestier," he said. "Men who pursued you."

She shrugged. "If so, I did not notice most of them. Only the bold ones."

"You were never tempted to give up on your lover and —"

"I don't think you understand how it is for my kind. I was working. Long hours. Even if a man was so bold that I noticed his interest, I hardly had the time to indulge in temptation."

He could be an idiot at times. She was not some lady of leisure who collected flatteries during the fashionable hour in the park. At least not in the past. Now she was, if she wanted to be.

That notion did not sit well with him. She was not just an heiress, but a very beautiful one. He couldn't keep an eye on her every day, all day. The last weeks had been spared those advances because she was settling in and setting up that shop and planning her grand reunion with that rogue. All of that would change, very soon.

He moved so he was behind her. He began washing her breasts and chest. "When we return to London, I would like this to continue."

She managed to look back at him. "You don't mean giving me baths, do you?"

"That too."

She untwisted herself and rested back. He lathered her breasts and watched the tips tighten.

"I see difficulties with that, don't you?" she asked.

"Not at all. It will require some discretion, of course."

"I have no experience in that kind of discretion. Do you?"

"How hard can it be?"

She laughed. "Spoken like Mr. Kevin Radnor. I doubt there are books on how to do it well, though."

"I'll ask. Nicholas and Chase will know where the lines have to be drawn."

She grew thoughtful. He decided that such contemplation would not benefit him.

Affairs like this rarely ended well for women, and she was smart enough to see that.

He set about rinsing her body and kissing her neck.

"See here," she said. "I don't think of myself that way. As a man's mistress."

"Heiresses are not mistresses. They are not kept women. They are lovers, if anything. Or wives." He angled around so he could kiss her fully. "I asked before. You declined, but I think the biggest reason was your old lover. Perhaps we should reconsider that idea."

She did not say no right away, but then, he kept her mouth too busy for that. Still, a quick refusal did not come.

"I will want to think about it," she said. "I also will want a frank discussion of what it means to both of us, and to the enterprise."

He stood and grabbed a big towel. "Think all you like. Now, up."

She stood, a Venus rising from the sea, all slick and creamy and more beautiful than she knew. He bundled her in the towel, then lifted her in his arms and carried her into the bedchamber.

She opened her eyes a slit and looked down her body and her position. She held her bent legs by the knees the way he had told her. It exposed her in a scandalous way.

He held up his own body on extended, taut arms in a position that left a gap between them. And so she could see how his long, hard cock was right above her, and how his head angled so he could watch himself. She could watch too.

He began entering, then stopped. She throbbed around him, aching. Wanting. He was good at doing that. Making her want him. She relinquished her pride when he brought her to this state of craving.

She could not even caress him while she held herself like this. She could only watch, noticing the way his hard body dominated her. Odd for a man so involved with his thoughts to have a body like that. It seemed he imposed the same discipline on his physical self as he did his mind.

He pressed further, then stopped again. He closed his eyes. She guessed whatever sensations they shared, he felt them more than she did. Not because he was a man and she a woman. Because he was a man who had mastered concentration.

He opened his eyes and looked in hers. Intense. Warm. Such depths his eyes contained. Captivating. As if nothing else mattered right now, and no other world existed except this bed with the two of them in it.

He joined them finally. Slowly. She discarded her impatience and accepted the delicious fulfillment for what it was. He withdrew and did it again, only she could not remain so calm this time. Nor the next, when she murmured encouragement, asking for more.

Harder, then. Deeper. So deep, she felt the thrusts touching her deepest essence. Desire and pleasure left her oblivious to her own words and sounds.

He finished hard. Almost violently. The power of it left her thrashing, reaching for him, for her own end, for that heaven just out of reach. Breath rasping hard, and his body still hovering over hers, he reached down and touched her. She arched in response to the intensity. Her whole body and mind screamed for release from the torture. He kissed her cheek and said something, and touched her differently, and suddenly she was screaming again, only in wonder.

"I suppose if I made this marriage of convenience you proposed, I know at least one part of it won't be horrible."

Her words, spoken softly into the night, roused Kevin from the sleep starting to claim him.

His reaction, unbidden and unexpected, surprised him. Triumph.

An odd reaction, once he had woken enough to think about it. The thing about practical marriages was that they had base reasons behind them. Financial ones, usually. This one would too. He would marry her so she could not marry someone else who might interfere with the enterprise. She would marry him to obtain a higher station. A match did not get more practical than that.

And yet, as he lay beside her after she opened that door again, he knew a contentment that had no name he recognized. He decided that it was merely the reaction of a man sated with pleasure happy to know he would be so sated again and again.

Only it wasn't just that. He could find that anywhere, or at least several somewheres. Better in a technical sense, because those women possessed expertise Rosamund obviously did not. Though they also lacked an element that he'd had with her, he had to admit.

"I can promise that much," he said, because it was long past time to answer her.

"I thought maybe you were asleep."

"No, no. I was enjoying having you in my arms."

"Did I send you into deep thoughts with my small observation? Or perhaps you were already there and didn't hear me."

"I was deciding what to say that wouldn't scare you off."

She snuggled closer. Her hair teased at his nose. "I haven't actually agreed to this."

"I'm aware of that."

"I'm only agreed that we might consider it. Then, after a spell, we will make a decision. You may conclude it is not really in your best interests. And I won't do it unless my interests are protected."

"How so?"

"I must keep full control over my inheritance, including my share of the enterprise. If you don't accept that, there is no point in talking about it at all."

She clearly didn't know anything about marriage law. Of course he would control it. She would retain ownership, but her husband would have use of the share.

"I intend to talk to Mr. Sanders to see about an agreement on that," she said. "One where you will accept that peculiarity in our marriage."

Hell. The familiar old annoyance began worming into his head. Rosamund had a stubborn side to her, especially when it came to *his* invention.

318

"You can't have so much control that you can sell it without my permission, Rosamund. If you can still do that, this marriage of convenience will be most inconvenient to me."

She shrugged. "I expect Mr. Sanders will know how to fit in that part." He felt her yawn against his chest. "Your family will be horrified. Once they make that clear, you may change your mind about the entire notion."

"I am accustomed to their being horrified. That will change nothing."

"There are some relatives you like, though. When they voice objections, you may think differently."

He only liked Chase and Nicholas. They would see how this benefited him. Nor were either the sort to harp about Rosamund's common birth or poor background.

"As long as we are setting some demands, I should express one of mine," he said. "In marriages like this, it is common for both parties to seek out others after a while. I won't stand for that."

She sat up and looked down at him. "Are you saying I can't take lovers?"

"I am."

"Is it common for your sort to do so when they have practical unions?"

"It is. I'll not have some man influencing you, however."

She smiled. "You think a lover will use pleasure to sway my thinking, do you?"

Hell yes. After all, he'd used it that way, apparently.

She leaned down so her face hovered mere inches from his. "It is not common among my sort. Not at all. I assume that if this is how it will be for me, it is how it will be for you too. Right? I wouldn't want a lover swaying your thinking either."

That had not been his meaning at all. He sought a way to make a distinction. "I've already told you that women do not influence my thinking. You are in no danger of that."

"Never enthralled, you said. Still, there is always a first time. And fair is fair."

"Fine. I accept that I also will not have lovers."

"Nor mistresses or impulsive liaisons."

"Agreed."

"Nor courtesans or whores."

He just looked at her. She met his gaze with very knowing eyes.

"I expect, if you remain agreeable and willing, I could accept that," he said.

She returned to his embrace and yawned again. "We can talk about what agreeable and willing means later."

He decided that later would be a good idea. He still didn't want to scare her off.

CHAPTER SIXTEEN

Rosamund hopped out of the carriage, too excited to wait for the carriage man's help. She strode to the window of her shop and examined the display. Then she stepped back and admired the new sign that had been raised in her absence. She hoped the color, a violet gray similar to her pasteboard boxes, held up to the sunlight.

She entered to find Mrs. Ingram sewing some silk flowers onto a cream-and-rose bonnet. At her footstep, Mrs. Ingram hurried over to embrace her. "You are back. I'm so glad. We have been far busier than I expected. Once the sign went up, women decided we were open."

Rosamund strolled over to the counter where the hat in progress rested. "A commission, or something for display?"

"A commission, I'm proud to say. For a young chit enjoying her first Season. From the sound of things, she only wears hers once and must have new ones every week. If she likes this, maybe there will be more." Mrs. Ingram handed over the bonnet, then stood back and eyed Rosamund's own headdress. "Did you buy that in Paris?"

"I did. The pleating intrigued me. I couldn't study it in the shop, so I bought one to have here." She unpinned the hat and set it down. Together, they poked around the pleating to see how it was sewn. "We can do this. I think it is very handsome. Now, see my drawings."

The carriage man brought in a trunk. After he left, they spent the better part of an hour discussing the drawings, sharing ideas on how to implement them.

"Did you find a girl?" Rosamund asked.

"She starts on Monday. You can examine her then. She sews well but has no experience, so she will be an apprentice. She wore a nice bonnet that she had made herself, though, so I think she may have the makings of a good one."

Rosamund toured the whole shop, now set up for production and sales. Mrs. Ingram had not disappointed her, and trailed along, informing her of the state of things in Richmond. Finally, they sat in the back room.

"Tell me about Paris."

Rosamund described the city, the food, the gardens, the buildings. Mrs. Ingram peppered her with questions. When the topic waned, Mrs. Ingram reached across the worktable for a little stack of cards.

"Now, allow me to inform you of matters here."

"You said they were going well."

"They are indeed. There has been a peculiar interest in this shop, however." She set the cards on the table between them. "We have had some visitors who came not to examine our wares, but to welcome you. Some left their cards. I think doing that is an invitation for you to call on them."

Rosamund flipped through the three calling cards. "People are being extremely friendly. I know none of these names. I wonder why they seek a friendship with me."

"Forgive me for being suspicious, but those are all men. Two of them have shops in this area." She set them out and pointed at each in turn. "Haberdasher two doors down. The jeweler around the corner. Unmarried, both of them."

Rosamund set the cards aside to take home. "You are very suspicious. I don't think they are doing more than being friendly."

"Perhaps, but think about being friendly

in turn. You may decide you want to make a pursuit of your own later."

"If I do, it will be in the hopes that their relatives buy lots of expensive hats from us."

"You might see if one is of any interest. It can't hurt. You are still young."

"I don't think so. There are many reasons to ignore those cards. Most importantly, I began a liaison with Mr. Radnor while in Paris."

Mrs. Ingram's face fell in surprise. "I confess that I worried about you, what with traveling with him, but in my years of knowing you there has never been any interest on your part for . . . that. Not for lack of men with ideas, or even suitors. You just never seemed to notice them."

Mrs. Ingram knew nothing about Charles, and Rosamund did not want to be explaining that long, sad mistake. She just shrugged and smiled. "And yet, here I am."

"Are you going to marry him?"

"We have talked about that. It might be useful to solidify our partnership in that business of his that I inherited. It would be a practical union. The biggest benefit to me is his station, of course. It would mean a different life for my sister Lily, to be associated with that family."

Mrs. Ingram's mouth pursed, drawing

those tiny lines down to her lip. "It would not be the first time such as he traded his position for a beautiful woman."

"It isn't a beautiful woman he wants. There are plenty of those among his own kind. He wants to be sure I don't go selling my share, or having my head turned by some other man, or losing control to a husband. All he thinks about is that enterprise, I promise you."

"Just as well you began this liaison, then."

"How so?"

"You need to know how that part of it will be, seems to me. Can you imagine marrying like this, only to discover the fellow didn't know what he was about in the marriage bed?" Mrs. Ingram placed a hand on Rosamund's arm and leaned in. "He *does* know what he is about, I trust?"

Rosamund felt her face getting hot. "I would say so."

"I'm relieved to hear it. Now, let's see what is in that trunk you brought back with you."

The morning after his return to London, Kevin made it a point to have breakfast at the same time as his father. He suffered a conversation that centered on how his father had managed to break the swan automaton and needed Kevin to fix it immediately. He in turn told his father about which English lords he had seen walking in the Tuileries, and what little he had learned about current French politics.

Having done his filial duty for what he hoped would be a fortnight, he stood. "I have to go and make some arrangements with the bank. It is good to see you are doing well." He turned to stride off, then paused. "Oh, I probably should tell you that I am going to marry Miss Jameson."

He left without looking back, claimed his horse, and rode to the City to arrange matters regarding Forestier's money.

On his way back from the bank he stopped off at Angelo's to fence. Refreshed by the physical activity, he finally returned to the house in early afternoon. He went in to spend the afternoon planning the next stage of the enterprise.

To his surprise, the servant at the door made a faint, pointing gesture. "They want you in the library, sir."

They?

He opened the library doors and faced a phalanx of family members. His father sat muttering. Aunt Agnes posed like a queen. Aunt Dolores drank tea. Nicholas looked bored.

"There you are. Finally," Aunt Agnes intoned. "Do come in."

He stayed in the doorway. "How good of you and Aunt Dolores to call on Father. It has been some time. I would love to visit, but I am very busy, and —"

"I said *come in.*" Agnes's ample bosom swelled. An imperious glint entered her eyes.

"You'd better join us," Nicholas said. "It won't do to put this off."

Kevin entered and found a chair on the outer perimeter, next to his father. His father harrumphed and glared at him.

Kevin glared back. "Did you summon them? If so, do not expect that stupid swan to be fixed for a very, very long time."

"Of course I sent for them. You can't throw out such an outrageous revelation and march off, as if it is of no account. The family must be consulted. In the least, Hollinburgh must be."

Kevin caught Nicholas's eye. Nicholas returned an apologetic look.

"I don't see why anyone needs to be consulted. I thought it was generous of me to inform *you.* Clearly that was a mistake. I won't let sentiment rule me again."

"Oh, tosh," Aunt Dolores said. "We only need to know one thing. Are you engaged to this woman already?"

Four pair of eyes bored into him, too curious. For the love of —

"Not yet."

"Thank heavens." Aunt Agnes all but swooned with relief. "All is not lost, then."

"I expect we will be engaged by week's end, however."

"No, you will not be. It is out of the question. I understand that she is pretty enough, but —"

"She is more than pretty enough, Aunt Agnes," Nicholas said. "Give the devil her due. She is stunningly beautiful."

"You are not helping, Hollinburgh." Agnes scolded.

"What the hell do you mean, 'give the devil her due'?" Kevin snapped.

Nicholas leaned back, out of the onslaught. "It is just a phrase. I didn't mean she is a devil in the literal sense. I —"

"I think she is," Dolores said. "She has bewitched you. Ensnared you. Used her wiles to make you besotted. I knew the first time I saw her that she was not to be trusted and would lead you to ruin, and she is well on the way to doing so." She twisted her hands together. "If only my brother had given some thought to his will and not been so capricious. Now look what he has done."

"Let us calm down," Agnes said, although

her chest heaved in a manner to suggest she was not calm at all. "Kevin, your déclassé interests in mechanics and whatnot are one thing. Your ridiculous preoccupation with this invention of yours, your befriending men of industry — your reputation, and the family's, can survive all that. However, if you marry the daughter of a *tenant farmer* —" On saying the words she faltered, looked to the ceiling, and fanned herself.

"Are you going to faint?" Nicholas asked, concerned.

"She's not going to faint," Kevin said. "She never does. She only threatens to, for effect."

Agnes recovered at once. She speared him with a malicious glare. "You know nothing about her. Other than that she is *pretty enough,* and now wealthy enough."

"The two most important qualities my father taught me to look for in a wife. Right, Father?"

His father almost sent a nod in his direction, but Agnes's hand landed in a firm slap on the cushion of the divan where she sat.

"I assumed he would know that good blood was necessary too. Who needs to explain that?" His father asked the question of Agnes beseechingly.

"You have been neglectful in raising him,"

Dolores said. "Careless. You were probably so busy playing with your toys that you didn't even notice how he was straying, and now see the mess you have made."

His father looked dismayed.

"Didn't expect them to devour you along with me, did you?" Kevin muttered to him.

"Kevin is not stupid, Sister," Agnes said. "He knows this is beyond the pale. Don't you, Kevin? Is this your idea of a perverse joke on all of us? Revenge for all the slights and criticisms? If so, it will not do. You must break this off, whatever it is, and inform Miss Jameson that you were not thinking with the head on your shoulders, but with another further down."

"Aunt Agnes!" Nicholas said.

"She always had a bawdy streak in her," his father said to Nicholas.

"Oh, tosh. We all know what happened. She seduced him, and he thinks he has to do right by her now. Well, you don't. Not with such as she." Agnes took a deep breath and exhaled, as if to indicate that was that, and all was settled.

Kevin gazed around his own little star chamber. "You have that wrong, Aunt Agnes. I seduced her, and she refused my first proposal. However, she is honest, and good, and I could do much worse. Uncle liked her; otherwise he would not have left her that legacy, and his judgment of people far surpassed yours. So if she will have me, after the theatrics end, I will be marrying her."

"She'll not live in this house," his father exclaimed. "I'll not have her here."

"I would never subject a woman to this house, so that is of no account."

"I'll disown you!"

"You can't. Your estate is entailed."

"Not all of it."

"You mean if I marry her, I won't inherit your automatons? Well, damn, that is a bother. I'll have to rethink everything now."

Nicholas bit back a smile. Aunt Agnes noticed.

"Hollinburgh, it is up to you. Tell him this is unacceptable and you don't approve. Tell him he risks his place in the family."

"I will tell him nothing of the kind."

"You must do *something*," Aunt Dolores cried.

"I must indeed." Nicholas stood. "Taking my leave seems an excellent something to do. Uncle, the next time you send me a message that reads 'Disaster has struck and Kevin's life is at risk,' please have it be about a matter of significance."

"I demand that you accept your duty in

this," Aunt Agnes said, her voice now close to a screech. "If he does this, he deserves no better than Philip. Tell him that and he will come to his senses."

"I have no intention of threatening Kevin with losing my friendship over this. He wants to marry a woman. It is a simple thing, and an honorable one. Now, good day to you."

With that, Nicholas strode forth and left the library. Kevin wasted no time in following in his wake, ignoring his aunt's call that he stay with them until all was sorted out.

Outside in the street, Nicholas waited impatiently for his horse to be brought around. He kept glancing over his shoulder, as if he expected the harpies to come flying out to grab him.

"Hell of a thing," he muttered. "You could have warned me."

"I only returned yesterday evening."

"I will not issue threats or talk sense to you. I will say, however, that I would feel better if I believed this was about more than her share of your business." Nicholas sent him a sidelong, quizzical look. "I would also be more at ease if I had any idea how that mind of yours worked, and that you could separate good sense from enthusiastic impulse. Since I don't begin to understand how you think, other than that it is not like normal men, I'll merely wish you well."

The horse arrived and Nicholas mounted. He looked at the house. "Living here will be hell now. You are welcome to chambers in Whiteford House if you want some peace."

"I'll see if my father resorts to silent disapproval or hounds me through the halls."

"If he called for a high council meeting, he may throw you out. I know you probably only stayed here for his sake, but you will be leaving when you wed, so you may as well depart now."

"I'll consider it."

"Chase is coming for dinner tonight. Why don't you join us and tell him about this, lest he hear from someone else?"

Kevin agreed to do that. He needed to talk to Chase on another matter anyway. Aunt Agnes had actually said something of interest amid all her indignation. Something that piqued his curiosity in ways it should have been jabbed weeks ago.

Mr. Sanders pondered the problem Rosamund had laid before him. His fingers formed a little steeple on his desk while he frowned and considered. She waited for his judgment. She had begged for an audience in a letter sent early that morning and arrived mid-afternoon when he wrote back that he could see her.

She had spent the entire journey back from France considering this marriage she had all but agreed to. Before this went any further, she wanted to make sure that she could actually have the agreement she had demanded of Kevin.

"Marriage is a contract," Mr. Sanders finally said. "However, there are traditions and there are laws that come into play. A married woman loses much of her independence and personhood, so to speak. You cannot make a contract after you are wed, for example. Your debts are in reality your husband's debts. That sort of thing."

"So I can't do this."

"Anything can in theory be done. One contract can affect another. Are you very sure you do not want to tell me the name of this gentleman? I confess that I am concerned. You only recently inherited, and there are those who might —"

"I would rather not at this time. I just want to know if I can reserve my inheritance to myself, no matter what traditions and laws say."

"You can have a contract with him that

does that. However, should he not honor it, and you go to court to enforce it, I can't promise the courts will support you."

That was not good news.

"If this gentleman is honorable, he will abide by anything he agrees to." Mr. Sanders tried a little smile. "Is he, to your belief, honorable."

"Yes. I believe he is."

"Then perhaps all will be well."

It all came down to trust. She wondered if her thoughts about that could be trusted in turn. After all, she had begun reconsidering this proposal after entering into a liaison with Kevin. Their conversation had been held while she remained befuddled by pleasure.

Did she really think marriage would be a good idea, or did she only want to preserve their dalliance?

Memories flooded her from their nights together. She felt his hands on her again, and arousal began flowing like an incoming tide. She realized that a bit of time had passed since Mr. Sanders spoke. She startled herself out of the reverie, to find him watching her.

"I was thinking about your question regarding honor. Giving it some hard examination."

He just smiled back.

"I'd like you to write the contract. The other one we would have to sign. I'll let you know the name once we are engaged. If we are ever engaged."

She left the solicitor's chambers and made her way outside. She did think Kevin was honorable. However, she also did not put it beyond him to use his sensual abilities to make her amenable to his notions. He had not asked her to provide money for Forestier, for example. However, floating as she was in sated bliss, she had only seen the bright side of any situation. If they married, would he continue doing that? Had he planned it at all?

All of which reminded her that she didn't really know much about him. She knew he could be rude, and she knew his family were astonishing. She knew he spent most of his time on this enterprise. Or keeping watch over her. Or, presumably, at brothels.

Other than that, she possessed no picture of his life. He knew far more about her than she did about him. More, but not everything. She should rectify that. Quite likely when she did, he would conclude he didn't even want this marriage.

She returned to the shop, making a little list in her mind of things to learn. She would ask him about some of them. Others she would discover on her own.

"What in hell are you doing out there?"

Nicholas's voice came from a window in Whiteford House. It drew Kevin out of his contemplations.

"I am feeling the lay of the land," he called back.

"You haven't moved. You have merely stood there for close to an hour."

He had not been checking the lay of the land in this garden. His mind had been pacing through the land at Melton Park. Specifically, the land between the lake and the manor house. It would not do to try and explain that to Nicholas. The entire idea was a mere seed at this point. He could not answer questions about it even if Nicholas could understand the answers, which was doubtful.

"Come in now. Chase has arrived," Nicholas called.

Kevin walked toward the house. "Did you tell him that I am marrying Miss Jameson?"

"I did. If you had not wandered away and meditated in my garden you would have been here for it."

"Was he shocked?"

"Only by the marrying part. Not the Miss

Jameson part. Meet us in the dining room and we can talk about it."

He didn't want to talk about it. That usually meant someone intended to tell him that his behavior was unacceptable, that he was not thinking clearly, that society would be appalled, etcetera, etcetera.

He drew up under the window. "I want to go to Melton Park later this summer, if you are agreeable."

"I thought the country bored you."

"It does. I still want to go."

Nicholas shrugged. "Go whenever you want. Now, go directly to the dining room. Don't get lost in either the house or your thoughts."

"Congratulations." Chase raised his glass.

"It has not been settled, as I said."

"I can't imagine she would not agree."

They sat in Nicholas's library. Nicholas had claimed he needed to attend to something about the estate after dinner and left them alone.

"One never knows," Kevin said. "Paris is one thing. London is another. As I learned this afternoon, to my endless irritation."

"You can hardly be surprised. Agnes was willing to receive her for a family dinner so everyone could look her over. She will never

339

accept Miss Jameson as your bride. It is not her decision, though. It is yours."

"Nicholas thinks it is only about her inheritance. He left us alone, so he has probably expressed reservations on that. He wants you to do a discreet inquiry now, doesn't he?"

"He had a pressing matter to attend. However, since you mentioned it — Is this about her inheriting half your enterprise?"

Was it? Mostly. But, Kevin realized, not entirely.

"If tomorrow a codicil to the will were discovered that transferred that share to you and she no longer owned it, would you still marry her?" Chase asked ever so casually, as if a challenge was not being posed.

"If there had been such a codicil, I never would have met her. If you don't hold her birth against her, I don't see why you would have any concerns. It isn't as if such marriages aren't normal. This year or next, Nicholas will make a good, practical marriage too. *Your* marriage is the one that is unusual."

Chase smiled with some chagrin. "Forgive me. I have developed the odd notion that my good friends should know happiness too."

Kevin watched how the lamplight played

on the inky red of his port. "I think I have a fair chance at happiness. However, during the inquisition I faced this afternoon, Aunt Agnes said something that does cause me the slightest pause."

"You were listening? I send my mind elsewhere when she goes on."

"She said I knew nothing about her. That is not true. I know quite a bit, but — when I line up what I know, there are gaps."

"Gaps?"

"Mmm. The whole way Uncle met her, for example. I know why she says he gave her some money. Because she nursed some-one he knew, she said. But when and how? There are empty spots in her history like that."

"Perhaps you should ask her about them."

"I thought you might already know. You are the one who found her."

"You found her."

"I gave you a name and a town. You did the rest."

"Minerva did the rest. I left it all to her."

Chase was good at dissembling, but Kevin had known him long enough to spot when it was happening. "And your wife said not a word to you about it? I find that hard to believe."

Chase was also good at hiding discomfort,

but Kevin knew the signs of that too. So when Chase rose to fill his glass, and drank some before returning to his chair, Kevin fully expected the impassive expression turned in his direction.

"As I said, you should ask Miss Jameson."

"I'm asking you."

"You are indeed." Chase showed irritation. He drank another swallow. "Damn. Fine, what gaps do you see? I'll fill them if I can. Minerva told me much, but not everything. Which is why Miss Jameson, or Minerva herself, would be the better person to question."

He would rather not question Rosamund, and he would never face Minerva over this. "She came up to Town when she was maybe seventeen. She was in service for a while. How long?"

"Approximately a year and a half."

"Then she left."

"Yes."

"Do you know why she left?"

"No."

Chase was lying. Kevin let it pass, since he already had that information.

"Where did she go then? Not to that milliner who taught her. That was later. So this is the gap. The biggest one."

"As I understand it, she took service in

another house."

Chase appeared resolute. Definitive. It had not been a lie. Rosamund had implied the same thing while they journeyed to Paris.

"What family?"

Chase's expression cracked just enough to be notable. A vague pulsing started on his jaw. A determined hardening of his gaze created a shield. "I don't know."

"I think you do."

"Ask *her.*"

"I would rather not. It may not be anything important and I don't want her thinking —"

"Thinking that you are suspicious of her? Hell, you are, so you may at least say so. This is a damnable way to make a marriage, Kevin. All this time and you have only now come out of your head enough to notice that you have these *gaps* in your knowledge of her."

Kevin waited while Chase's annoyance dimmed. He had nothing to say for himself. He had been stupidly oblivious to what he did not know about Rosamund. But then he had not needed to know much, except that he desired her.

"Was she some man's mistress during that time?"

Chase looked over, surprised. "Not that I

know of. As I said, she took service again."

"Yet you won't tell me the family. That is very odd."

Chase sank back in his chair. "I swear, I will kill Nicholas. The coward, leaving this to me alone." He sighed deeply. "I did not say she took service with a family, Kevin. I said she took service *in a house.*" He turned his head and looked Kevin right in the eye.

Kevin looked back, perplexed. Then clouds parted and light flowed. Of course. He had been an idiot not to see it before.

Just then the door opened and Nicholas strode in. He came over and looked at the two of them. His expression fell. He sent a questioning glance to Chase, who merely nodded.

"Welcome back, Nicholas," Kevin said. "Just in time to be spared the moment when Chase told me my intended was a whore."

"I should have seen it at once. After all, it is where I learned her name. At Mrs. Darling's." Kevin mused over the revelation while Nicholas sat down. "I assumed they only bought bonnets from her. Not that she had lived there. Yet it would have been an excellent place for Uncle to have met her, because it was one of his haunts."

"You are taking this awfully well," Nicholas said. "It must be a shock."

"Not too much of a shock. It does fill the gap neatly."

"But to learn — That is, to discover —"

"Better now than later," Chase said.

"So you said this afternoon," Nicholas said. "I told him your intentions and he turned green. I got it out of him. We decided we should tell you. Better now than later, he said."

"*You* decided *I* should tell him, as I recall," Chase snapped.

"I feared a big Kevin scene. Cursing. Rudeness. Nasty sarcasm. Only look, he is being a real soldier despite the destruction of his plans."

"That is because this doesn't affect my plans."

They both peered at him. Nicholas looked dismayed. "Damnation, I knew it. Practical marriage hell. He is enthralled by her, Chase. He'll do this even now that he knows."

"I'm never enthralled. I'm sure, however, that while she may have taken service in that house, she was not one of the ladies *of* the house."

"You can't be sure," Chase said.

"Mrs. Darling would never employ a woman as ignorant as this one is. That house is famous for an elevated level of expertise."

It took a five count for them to comprehend what he had said.

Chase looked relieved, probably because he would not have to explain to Minerva how he had ruined Miss Jameson's possible engagement. "Tell me, if you didn't know with such certainty that she could not have worked there as a soiled dove, would you still become engaged to her?"

"Yes." It surprised Kevin that he knew the answer right away.

"Good. Because it is inevitable that men probably saw her there. One day one of them may say something. You might start practicing with pistols as well as swords."

CHAPTER SEVENTEEN

Rosamund did not see Kevin for two days after their return. After spending the second one with her morning tutor, then setting her house in order, she donned a bonnet and walked to Minerva's house in the afternoon. As she handed over her card, she realized it was the first time she had paid a social call like this, in her new role of wealthy heiress.

She wondered if Minerva knew about her liaison with Kevin. It entered her mind that her friend might disapprove, and not receive her.

While she waited for the verdict, she pictured what it would be like to be rebuffed. It would happen eventually. Perhaps not with Minerva, but some other woman. She might think she had started a friendship only to arrive like this and be turned away. A husband or father might interfere, or her new friend might prove not to be a

347

friend at all.

Kevin would spare her much of that, but there was only so much he could do. She had not lived in society, but she knew it could be cruel. The more people learned about her, the less they would want her in their circles. Daughter of a tenant farmer might be the least of it. If word ever was spread about her time working at Mrs. Darling's brothel, she doubted anyone would talk to her again.

Not for the first time during the last few days, she weighed the likelihood of that happening. She had been a servant, and they are rarely noticed. In that white cap and shapeless sack dress, she was hardly impressive. Nor did she spend much time among the women once their trade began. She completed her duties prior to that, and only attended one of them if there was a special need for more fuel or something else.

And yet, she had not been invisible, had she? Who knew if one day some man who had indeed noticed her saw her in the park and recognized her? It could happen. She dared not assume it couldn't.

The servant did not come for her. Minerva did. She descended the staircase, her dark hair a little disheveled and her ensemble quite plain. "Forgive me for having you

348

wait. I was just back from an investigation."

She brought Rosamund into the library and sent for some tea.

"I look odd, I know. Unkempt. Had it been anyone but you, I would have begged off, so I wouldn't be seen. I knew you would understand, though." Minerva poked some errant locks back into her hair while she spoke.

"Do you often go off on investigations?"

"Usually I have agents who do it at my direction. But today's assignment needed a woman of a certain age and manner, so I decided I should go myself. I'm supposed to be a reformer with good breeding but little concern for her appearance. Did I succeed in the ruse?"

Rosamund took in the hair and the boring brown dress and half boots. "I would believe it."

"Fortunately, the family in question did as well. I confirmed what I had suspected and can report to my patron in full."

"Is it an interesting problem?"

The tea arrived and Minerva poured them both some. "A unique one. My patron suspected her husband has an entire second family. I learned today that indeed he does."

"Right here in London? That is bold."

"Many men assume that a quiet wife is a

349

stupid wife. Unfortunately for this man, his quiet wife is as sharp as a sword and missed nothing. She turned a blind eye for years, and would have continued to do so, except she suspected he had taken a final step that was unexpected. One that would change everything."

Rosamund pondered what that could have been. A final step — "Did he marry the other woman too?"

"Very good. I will have to watch myself around you, lest my indiscretions tell you more than I intended. I have no idea why he did it, although I have a few theories. All that matters is that when my patron confronts him with this, she will have knowledge that will ensure he listens very carefully to her for the first time in their marriage."

"How interesting your life is."

"Not as interesting as one that hops packets to France. Tell me about your journey."

Rosamund had come for other conversation. She did not want to be rude, so she described some of what she had seen.

"Did Kevin behave himself?" Minerva asked.

Rosamund felt her face getting hot. "What do you mean?"

"Did he avoid being rude to this Forestier

man you mentioned? To you? To the hotel servants and packet crew?"

"He wasn't rude, that I saw. I can't swear what happened while I was shopping and he was about on his own."

Minerva glanced over, then looked more directly. Her head angled back and her lids lowered. Rosamund fussed with her teacup.

Another cup clattered when it was set down. "The rogue."

Rosamund's mouth dried. "Why would you say that? I explained he was not rude."

"He seduced you. I can see it in your eyes. He seduced you to make you pliable to his demands about that invention." Her eyes flared with hot lights. "Chase knows. He had dinner with Kevin last night and was very odd when he returned and I asked about the journey's success. Very vague. He didn't tell me about you two because he knows that I will —"

"Please. I was not — I hardly resisted much. Not at all, to be honest. However, it has made me wonder about some things. We are thinking of getting married, you see, and now I need to know more about him."

"*Married?* Kevin?" Minerva sank back on the cushion, astonished. "What happened to that man you had me investigate? That Charles fellow?"

"I met with him. It was not the same."

Minerva's expression grew serious. "It is not wise to turn immediately to another when one person disappoints you. Least of all to Kevin Radnor."

"I am still deciding. However, for me such a match is fairly wise, I think. Nothing else will change who I am quite so thoroughly."

"Ah. Yes, of course. How unkind of me to imply you have not considered this fully. You are being far wiser than I am, it appears. And more practical." She lifted the teapot to pour again. "What do you want to learn about him? I daresay you may know him better than I do now."

"I want to know about the late duke's death."

"I told you that it was determined to be an accident."

"You also said the family did not agree with that. Is an accident what you and Chase decided?"

Minerva hesitated. "No. We are convinced it was not."

"And Kevin?"

"I never spoke with him about it, but Chase did. Kevin was there, at the estate. He says it was the day before the duke died, and that he had left by the time it happened. He admitted that the two of them had a row. It did not help that he claimed to be in France then. Only he had returned for a few days."

"Hopped a packet."

"Yes. We learned about it on our own, but another member of the family also saw him in Town."

"Felicity."

Minerva's gaze hardened. "She couldn't wait to tell you, it seems."

"Yet despite all that, it was determined to be an accident. Was that to protect him?"

"Not at all. Chase presented what he knew to the authorities. There were other possible culprits. I was one. He included all of us. They called it an accident anyway."

"Wouldn't Kevin's father know if he had been in Town the actual day the duke died?"

Minerva hesitated. "I only tell you all this because you are considering such an important step. He was not at his family's house in Town while he was back. There is no proof he was not at the estate that day."

"Do you think he did this, Minerva? I need to know if you do."

Minerva took her time thinking about that, her expression one of a person who had been cornered and didn't like her position.

"He has a temper. I expect he would

control it with a woman. Yet it flared with Philip that night at the dinner, so you have seen it. If the other cousins had not intervened, he would have done Philip serious harm," she said. "And he is devoted to that project of his. It consumes him. The will had recently been changed to give the duke's half of that enterprise to you. The will's changes were not commonly known in the family, but Kevin may have learned of it and been angry. He said the row was over the money for that man he visited in Paris with you, but —" She let all that sit there, all but damning Kevin.

It would have been enough to convict most men. Normal men. Men who weren't grandsons of dukes. For some reason, someone had decided not to accuse Kevin. But what if that someone changed his mind? She realized Kevin lived with that as a possibility. Whether innocent or guilty, that would be horrible.

Minerva reached over and took Rosamund's hand. "You asked what I think. I don't believe he was responsible. I have no facts to support my estimation, only my observations of people. I have met men who are capable of such things, and he is not one of them, in my opinion. However, the question is not if I think so, Rosamund. It is whether you do."

She didn't know what to think. The man who had comforted her after her meeting with Charles would not do such a thing. The man who stayed in his family home so his father would not be completely bereft of companionship would not either. But she had seen how his intensity could alter his whole manner, and how this invention had become the center of his world.

"I expect the family knows about your intention to become engaged," Minerva said, lifting them out of the topic. "Be prepared."

"I know they will not approve. That is why we are not engaged yet. So they can change his mind, if it is changeable."

Minerva laughed. "Kevin bow to the family's preferences? I don't think so."

"Possibly not. It was only fair to let them try."

"If this marriage happens, it will be good for him. That is not a happy house he has lived in all these years. Chase told me that Kevin's father never forgave him for the death of his mother. It had been a love match, it seems. Deeply passionate. The man was lost when she did not survive her lying-in. Devastated. The last duke stayed in the house for a month to make sure his brother did not do something rash. Then Kevin was raised there, with a father who barely acknowledged he was alive."

Minerva's explanation made Rosamund sad. Sad not only for Kevin, but for his father, who had escaped grief through eccentric pastimes instead of treasuring the child left behind with him. She thought it a tragic choice.

A love match, Minerva said. Deeply passionate. The man had been enthralled, and it left him mourning forever.

Kevin folded a sheet of paper and tucked it into his frock coat. He went down to the morning room for coffee and flipped through the mail waiting there. One of the letters joined the paper.

He was finishing his breakfast when he sensed a presence in the room. He looked up to find his father standing across the table from him.

"Are you going out?" his father asked.

"I am."

"To see her?"

"Yes. We have business to discuss."

"That's a pretty word for it."

"It is an accurate word. She is still my partner."

His father caught the eye of the attending

servant. The servant left.

"You have decided to disobey me, then."

"We are past such things. I am almost thirty years old."

"Old enough to scorn your family, it appears. Allow me to make it plain, lest you think your aunts spoke only for themselves. I forbid this marriage."

Kevin stood and faced him over the polished wood surface. "I understand that. It is my decision, not yours, however."

"So be it. If you have decided to make this marriage, all for the sake of your machines or whatever they are, if you are prepared to embarrass me in this way, I don't want to see you. Do not come back today, or ever."

The command summoned more relief than concern, although he experienced some of the latter for the man facing him now. His father's expression appeared stern, but a lot of dismay reflected in his eyes too.

"As you wish. I'll send for my things once I'm settled."

His father looked surprised, as if he really had expected capitulation. Kevin collected his mail, then strode from the morning room.

I will call at two o'clock to take you to the bank.

The note arrived early morning. At two o'clock, Rosamund waited for Kevin in her library.

She had not seen him since they returned. That was not such a long time, yet this outing made her nervous and excited. Paris had receded into the past already. She wondered if they would see each other differently here at home. As less interesting. Less desirable.

She distracted herself by staring at her empty bookshelves. She needed to do something about them. They shouted that she was new to this home, and this life.

Kevin entered the library right after the hour. She heard his boot step and turned around on the divan so she could see him. His warm smile made her core twinge, like an echo of stronger sensations she had experienced with him.

She hopped up. He strode over, pulled her into his arms, and kissed her. "It seemed forever," he said. "Only now it is like no time at all has passed."

She couldn't keep from smiling and laughing. He kissed her again, deeply, and she began to fly.

"We have to go." He set her away from

himself.

She went out with him and got into the carriage. She noticed it was a hired one.

"Have you found all well at your shop?" he asked.

She regaled him with the progress and the commissions coming in. "Matters seem well in hand in Richmond too. I think I may be able to keep both of them. And you? What has happened with you?"

"Nothing much, other than planning the next steps. I spent some time with Nicholas. I arranged the documents we need to send funds to France. Oh, and I told my father about us."

He said it all casually, as if he barely paid attention to his own words. He might have been saying he ate his dinner, read a book, and by the bye, took a walk.

"What did he think of that news?"

He looked out the window, his lids lowered against the sunlight that sculpted his fine face into their aristocratic planes. "He did not like the idea, but we expected that."

"Was there a row?"

"Not at all. Although he insisted Nicholas and the aunts come to weigh in. A minor irritation, that. And he told me this morning that he never wants to see me again. Hence the hired carriage you are in." He smiled at her. "All of which I anticipated, and none of which signifies."

"He closed his home to you? That's terrible."

"Had I been sure it would happen, I might have found an inappropriate match years ago."

"Where will you go?"

"I'll stay at Whiteford House for several days, then find chambers. Don't look so distraught. I don't mind, so you shouldn't."

He acted as if his family's rejection of him would not bother him, but he wasn't indifferent to all of them.

"Did the duke also —"

"The aunts wanted him to, but he refused. He was not happy to be dragged into the fray. I don't think Chase cares either. The rest can go to hell."

"I told Minerva, and she did not seem shocked."

"She wasn't disapproving at all?"

"Not about you having a liaison with me, or about your perhaps marrying me. She was very surprised, but not disapproving."

"Was she shocked that *you* would consider marrying *me*?"

She bit her lower lip, but a giggle found its way out. "Maybe a little?"

He laughed. "More than a little is my

guess. She doesn't like me much." He bent and looked out the window. "We are just starting down the Strand." He pulled the curtains, then reached for her. "That means I have enough time to kiss you properly before we reach the bank."

Kevin dealt with his own draft first, then allowed the clerk to handle Rosamund's. With blotting paper at the ready, she dipped the pen and signed her name. She then requested some additional funds for her use.

"Those drafts will go in the mail to Forestier's bank. It should only take a few days," he explained while they emerged from the building. "We should receive confirmation by return post."

"Then it is done, and I have some banknotes in my reticule and none too soon. The journey to Paris used what was left from my first withdrawal." She took his arm and they strolled down the street. "I have a dinner being cooked for us. You can explain our next steps then."

"We have a few hours to spare. What would you like to do?"

"I want to buy some books. The library still looks very sad."

"Books it will be. Do you know which shop you want to visit?"

"I have never been in one. They always looked forbidding. Any shop you choose should be good enough."

The shops could be forbidding. He knew one that was not, however. He told the carriage man to take them to Finsbury Square.

"This is one of the largest. It is called Temple of the Muses." He explained about the muses while guiding Rosamund inside. "It can't be too forbidding if it dubs itself the cheapest bookstore in the world. No credit, but we should have enough on us to purchase a good number of books."

She entered, gazing around. "It is very large. Look, there is a dome."

"Even this level is huge, and there are four stories in all. When it first opened, a mail coach and four drove inside around the center here."

"I don't know where to start with walls of books to choose from. I want some proper ones, though. The kind Lily should read." She made a crooked, little smile. "Me too, if I'm to improve myself."

"They buy up whole libraries. Let's see if any have come in that are good." He brought her to the circular counter and asked to speak with Mr. Lackington, the owner, about the recent acquisitions.

They were sent to an office the next level

up. There, a white-haired Mr. George Lackington received them. Upon hearing Rosamund's interest in shelves of books, he ushered them to a large nook. "We still acquire and sell libraries. I think what you want will be here. These are all leather bound and very handsome. This group here includes the usual poets and philosophers, along with a nice selection of more recent writings."

He removed one mahogany-hued tome and placed it in Rosamund's hands. She did not pay much attention to the fine leather binding or the perfectly worked letters on the spine. She opened it reverently, paused a long time at the engraved frontispiece, then turned a few pages.

She asked the price.

"These are only sold together." Mr. Lackington eyed the shelves. "Just over fifty titles, in matching custom bindings of superior quality. Let us say twenty-five pounds. We do not dither, so I request no less be offered. Our prices are indeed as cheap as we say. Purchasing these same books at auction would be at least twice as much."

Kevin had spent the time perusing the titles. Rosamund caught his eye with a question in hers. He nodded.

"I will have them," she said. "Can they be delivered?"

"Of course." Mr. Lackington slipped her banknotes into his waistcoat pocket, then placed a little card on the shelves. "They will arrive early tomorrow. It has been my pleasure to make your acquaintance."

"I don't see why he assumed I would offer less," she said after she and Kevin took their leave.

"Because he thought you were about to. Were you?"

"Yes, but he couldn't know that for certain."

"He was not treating you any differently than he would treat me. Everyone haggles in bookshops. It is commonplace. Hence he reminds his patrons of his policy before they try."

"They are very impressive books, I will admit. Even the paper was beautiful. I may just sit with one on my lap, even if I am not in the mood to read. Although the one he handed me was full of poems, and I think I'll try a few of those."

They had returned to the street level. "Are we finished here?"

She strolled away. "Perhaps a few novels . . ."

"I may have overdone it." Rosamund voiced her misgivings while removing her bonnet in the reception hall of her house. "Do I have to have all the other books I bought bound to match that set of them?"

Kevin was watching her movements with the bonnet, as if the simple act was a revelation to him.

"If you want to, any bindery can do it. If you don't want to, just shelve them as they are. In the future, you can purchase new ones with no binding, and have them bound however you choose."

She led him into the library. "You must think me unbearably ignorant, not to know such simple things."

He took her hand and drew her closer. "You are very worldly in those things you know about. However, you are refreshingly honest regarding what you don't know. I think that is charming." He gave her a small kiss. "Adorable." He gave her a fuller one. "It is a type of innocence. I also find that I enjoy teaching you."

"I don't think you are talking about books now."

"How suspicious you are." He began to

embrace her, but the sound of the door opening had her jumping back.

Her lone footman presented himself and informed her that dinner would be at six o'clock. She sent him away. Kevin pulled out his pocket watch.

"I suppose you want that dinner," he said.

"It was a special request on my part."

He accepted that, but she guessed he could think of better things to do. He ambled around the library, but paused at the writing table. "When did these calling cards come?" His fingers spread them out.

"There were some when I returned from Paris. Two more were left yesterday. I feared I would be cut if I moved here, but instead, my neighbors are being very accepting. I suppose I should call on some of those ladies, to be polite."

"Some are not neighbors, or even ladies."

"A few men who have shops near mine have been calling at mine to welcome me."

"One of them has a shop on The Strand. He came quite a way to welcome you. The pursuits have begun."

"What do you mean?"

"It is a useful ruse for these men. No need for a relative to first make your acquaintance, then provide an introduction. In the name of business, they can introduce themselves."

"Perhaps they just wanted to be friendly."

"If I were a haberdasher on Oxford Street, I would want to be very friendly with a beautiful heiress who opened a shop nearby." He tapped those cards. "You will discover that none of these men are married."

She wanted to accuse him of being suspicious, but he was probably right. Mrs. Ingram had said much the same thing. Only "beautiful" had nothing to do with it. Her fortune made her attractive enough. Those ladies had probably called on her for the same reason. She was not appropriate for their male relatives, but if word of her inheritance had become known, some would swallow their pride and take the necessary steps.

Unless the women were in Kevin's family.

"I think you should come sit with me," she said. "A few more kisses before dinner would be nice. I thought about little else all day."

He tasted little of the meal. His plate filled and emptied and his fork moved to his mouth, but he barely noticed. His attention remained on Rosamund instead.

Their kisses in the library had aroused him to the point of making dinner a chore. He watched her eat, and every bite, every chew and nibble, carried erotic implications. He imagined her naked on this table, amid her new china, and taking her in multiple ways, half of which would undoubtedly shock her.

"You mentioned next steps," she said. "Twice I have asked what you meant, only to have you ignore my questions. Don't you plan on telling me what they are?"

Had she asked about that during dinner? He vaguely recalled a light string of small talk that he barely heard.

She delicately spooned some custard into her pursed mouth. He watched the spoon penetrate her lips, and her mouth slide down its small bowl, then back up. Her tongue flicked at a bit that had remained on the spoon.

"I assume you are now plotting how to finally make the invention pay," she prodded. "Steps toward manufacturing are probably in order now."

Damnation. She was going to insist on this conversation. He forced his gaze from her so he might get hold of his thoughts.

"The ideal way to do it is to build a factory," he said.

"That would take a huge amount of money, wouldn't it?"

"The second-best way is to sign a contract with another factory to do it for us. Also a goodly amount of money and the design would be in another's hands."

"You still worry about it being stolen. Once it is made, that will be a danger anyway, won't it?"

"It isn't easy to understand how it works unless you are making it yourself. Once it is in use, it won't even be visible on an engine."

She finished her custard. He was sorry to see the servant remove the dish. She lowered her lids and turned thoughtful. "Perhaps we should not make it at all. Maybe we should allow those who build steam engines to make it, along with their engines."

"We could not control the quality then."

"If someone is building a machine, he would want it to work. Why improve it with this invention, only to make a mess of the whole thing?"

"This is a precision instrument. It must be exact."

"I'm sure there are many factories that can make it exact enough. Such a business made the sample you showed me, after all. Is that foundry near London? Maybe we should strike a bargain with them."

"You would be amazed at how careless many factories are. Foundries in particular. Unless they work iron for decorative use, they have standards that can never be considered precise."

"And yet you found one that was different. Probably several, knowing you. If we go back to that little list, it will save —" She had been looking at him, and suddenly, she stopped talking, leaned forward, and peered intently. Her gaze bored right through him.

An expression of disbelief flexed across her face. "You did use a foundry to make that sample, didn't you?"

He would crawl through broken glass to kiss her, but she could be a true nuisance sometimes. Such as right now. He wished his uncle had left that half of the business to a stupid woman, if he was going to saddle him with a partner at all.

"Didn't you?"

The answer was already in her head and reflected in her eyes.

"I made it myself."

"You worked the iron yourself? How?"

"It wasn't hard. I watched it being done for several weeks, then gave it a go. After a while, I learned well enough."

"Better than well enough, knowing you.

Especially because you insist it has to be made with precision. You probably did nothing else for six months. Where?"

"I have a small building across the river where I do — did it."

"I should have known as soon as I saw the sample that you had not trusted another person to make it. Do you intend to make all of them?"

"If we have any success to speak of, that will not be practical."

She smiled at that. Then her smile got broader, and she began to laugh. She dabbed her eyes with her handkerchief and tried to stop, but she couldn't.

"Forgive me. I am not laughing at you." She got the words out before another outburst interrupted. "I am picturing the look on your aunt Agnes's face if she ever saw you at your forge. I see her walking in and you are there, stripped to the waist in front of a hot fire, casting iron."

"I think she would drop dead on the spot."

She drew herself up straight and angled out her chest. She lowered her chin and pursed her lips. " 'This is beyond the pale, Kevin,' " she trilled, imitating Aunt Agnes. " 'Bad enough for you to be in trade, but to actually perform labor — It is not to be borne. You are humiliating the family.' "

"You have her voice and her words exactly correct," he said, laughing along with her. "I'm glad you are not shocked too. There was the chance you would be."

Her gaze turned sultry. "Such as me aren't shocked by a man using his strength to forge a dream, Kevin. That is not the word for what I am feeling now."

He looked in her eyes. He quickly considered and discarded using the table, wall, or floor. "Come with me. Now."

Out of the dining room he sped her. Up the stairs, all but carrying her, his arm supporting her beside him so he could move her along. At the landing he paused. "Where is your chamber?"

She pointed, and he strode in that direction. He threw open the door, dragged her inside, and slammed it shut. He held her head with his hands and claimed her with a fevered, impatient kiss.

Her own longing had simmered all day and only grown at dinner, and now it flooded her. She lost herself in the escalating madness they shared, joining him in clutching holds and hard caresses. His hands and mouth were everywhere, as if he could not get enough of her. She pressed against his chest with her hands, but his garments obscured his body too much. She wanted to see him as she had in her mind, naked and hard.

A small sound came from the dressing room. She glanced at that door.

"Your maid won't come in," he said while he began releasing her dress. "She knows I am here."

The notion that the servants would know what she was doing dismayed her. Then her dress fell down to her hips, and Kevin's kisses bit against her neck, and her stays loosened. There was no room in her mind for servants after that.

Frantic now, her outpouring of passion matching his, she tore at his cravat and fumbled with the buttons on his waistcoat. In a whirlwind of hunger, they shed their clothes until they embraced body to body and skin to skin. She held her breath in wonder of how good that felt, and she throbbed, sensitive and wet, in expectation of what was coming.

She found herself on the bed. He kneeled over her and used his mouth. Kisses, licks, and bites covered her body, each one arousing, each one demanding. He moved lower, then lower yet. She guessed what he was going to do. Shocked, she instinctively covered herself with her hand.

He kissed her hand. "Move it."

She hesitated.

"Move it now, Rosamund."

She obeyed and closed her eyes. He pleasured her with his hand until she surrendered to abandon. She was beyond shock when she felt his tongue begin a devastating tease. Soon, all was darkness and sensation, and cries of need screamed in her head. She felt him lift her legs.

She looked down her body. He stood beside the bed, holding her knees to his hips, thrusting into her. The sight of him aroused her more. He brought his intensity to everything he chose to do, even this, and it thrilled her to see his face hardened by passion, and his hair hanging about his brow and face, and his mouth and jaw so firm.

That special tightening began in reaction to it all, shimmering around his fullness this time, building into waves through her body that grew more violent. Her peak now centered where they joined. The release was so long and encompassing that she truly lost hold of the world while she cried out at the blissful freedom flooding her.

When her senses returned, he was laying in her arms, with his hard breaths feathering her ear.

"I was going mad without you," he murmured.

She tightened her embrace and floated in perfect peace. Not only pleasure created this mood. A special intimacy absorbed her now, as if their essences touched as well as their bodies. That had become part of the desire and pleasure, and even of their easy friendship. She didn't want to lose any of that.

Perhaps she would wait a day or so to let him know just how unacceptable she would be as a wife, and to ask him about the duke's death.

"I suppose all the servants now know."

Rosamund said that simply. He lay on his back and had her bundled into an embrace in his arms. He had been taking notice of the chamber's appointments. She had done some redecorating and the place looked much nicer than when they had toured it with the agent.

Her reference to the servants returned his mind to a reckoning that he had started a few minutes earlier but quickly discarded for a while. The truth was, he had not taken much care with her reputation tonight, and the servants were the least of it.

He had no idea how to manage an affair, because he had never really done so before.

There had been a short-lived debauch that might be called a liaison by the generous-minded, but otherwise his carnal appetites found the most practical solutions. Presumably there were standards for carrying on a liaison for any period of time. This one might be lengthy if she chose not to marry. He didn't intend to give her up just because of that decision if she went in that direction.

"If they are good servants, they will be discreet. Nor will they ever let you know what they think they know. Don't mention it and your maid won't. If you want to pretend we discussed the enterprise, tell her that." He trusted he had this much right. That was how servants behaved in his experience about other matters that required privacy and discretion.

"I'll see if I can be sophisticated, or if I want to start explaining away your presence in my bedchamber this long. I doubt she will think we needed to come here to talk about the enterprise, though. I have a whole house for that."

His mind walked through the house and its various chambers. If he ended up living here, he could see a notable deficiency. The house lacked a good-sized study where he could sequester himself when he pursued his interests. There would need to be a place for the business to be managed too.

"I think I will let chambers," he said. "You can always visit me there, if my coming here is awkward for you."

"That would be more scandalous."

She was probably right.

One thing he did know. He could not stay here all night. Eventually, maybe, when she knew her servants better and if she was very sure of them. But not tonight. Marriage would be much more convenient, that was certain.

He set her away, then sat. "I'll make sure no one sees me leave."

Her hand caressed his back. He turned, bent, and kissed her.

"Tomorrow next," she said. "I'll decide by then."

CHAPTER EIGHTEEN

Kevin punched toward Nicholas's body. Nicholas danced out of range, then stepped forward and punched back. The impact on his torso almost took Kevin's breath away.

Nicholas stepped back again. "I refuse to go on. You are not paying attention. Much more of this and I will hurt you. I'm going to wash."

"My apologies," Kevin said while he followed him toward the dressing room. "I have no excuse."

"I shouldn't have encouraged you. You came down to breakfast half asleep." Nicholas stripped off his shirt while the attendant poured warm water into two basins. "Are you announcing that engagement soon?"

Kevin dealt with his own washing. "That will be decided soon. She may well decline. She is smart enough to know what she will lose in the marriage. I may have to content myself with the way matters now stand."

"It is odd for a woman to choose a liaison over marriage."

"I'm wondering how to do that, if it goes that way." Kevin wiped his face. "How do you do it?"

Nicholas's motions stilled. Kevin kept washing.

"Are you asking me how to conduct an affair?"

"Only the practical strategies. I assume you know all about maintaining discretion and such. I am a novice at that."

Nicholas proceeded to dress. "The first thing you need to know is that discretion is something of a joke. You need to go through the inconvenience of being discreet, but everyone will still know what is going on. They will pretend they don't if you make the effort, however."

"Why bother if there will still be gossip?"

"It buys you quiet gossip, instead of insults-at-your-club and doors-closing-in-your-face gossip. As for the lady, efforts at discretion will protect her reputation in a public sense, but there will still be talk. Just not getting-called-out-and-killed talk." Nicholas checked his cravat. "Come with me if you expect more."

Kevin joined Nicholas in wandering the

streets until they found a tavern near the river.

"You have grown fond of democratic drinking establishments," Kevin said, joining him at a rough table. The men around them bore the garments and speech of workers from the docks.

Nicholas called for two pints. "The ale is good and there isn't a single member of the ton present to eye me like a chicken to be had for dinner."

"The Season isn't going well?"

"The fathers are as bad as the mothers. I lately embarked on a very indiscreet liaison in the hopes of discouraging them all, to no avail." He shook his head.

"You were about to tell me about the discreet kinds, however."

"You would see the steps if you turned that mind of yours to it. You go to her house, not she to yours. You arrive very late and leave before the street has risen."

"I have figured out that much."

"Even in the house, you avoid being seen by the servants, although they will all know you are there. If you arrive by coach, you get out two streets away and walk the rest. If you ride your horse, you use a stable in a distant mews. If you truly want to be discreet, you do not enter by the front door, but through the garden."

"Must I climb up to her window?"

"I'm glad you find this amusing. No need to climb in windows because, as I said, no one really is being fooled."

"Thank you. I'm sure this will help —"

"There is more. This part involves society, so you are sure to get it wrong without help. You —"

"I think I'm insulted."

Nicholas ignored him. "You are allowed to encounter each other in the park on occasion and walk a short while, but you do not arrive together, least of all in a closed carriage. You are permitted one dance, no more, at a ball or party. You do not attend the theater together, or any other entertainment, and if you meet at a dinner party you bore each other when you converse. If you give her a gift, have the shopkeeper bring a selection to your home and choose there, so no one else can identify the gift as coming from you." Nicholas drank some of the ale.

"Is that all, or are you only taking a breath?"

"There is more if she is married."

"She isn't, of course."

"Not yet."

"Nor will she be. If she declines me, it is

because she wants to control her inheritance."

"She may fall in love. There is no telling what a woman will do when that happens. Not only men become stupid when they fall in love."

Kevin wanted to say Rosamund would still want to preserve her independence then, but he couldn't count on it. She had waited years for that scoundrel in the name of love, hadn't she? It had been one notable exception to her clear thinking and practical nature.

"In the least you need to remember this. If she does marry, it is over as soon as she is engaged. Done. Any revival of the affair after her marriage is completely up to her. Should there be such a revival, come to me and I'll tell you how to manage that."

"I had no idea you had such expertise. I'm glad I asked you instead of Chase."

"You go to Chase if you ever need to know how to be utterly sly. He uncovers such subterfuge all the time. The kind you need to use if a husband is unaccepting, suspicious, and keeps his dueling pistols clean. Although only a besotted fool would continue an affair then, and I assume you will never be one of those."

"It is probably very complicated if it

requires someone like Chase to uncover the deceptions. Your lesson alone comes close to making the entire idea of a liaison boring."

"Eventually, it is. You know it is over when the notion of arranging the assignation and stealing in like a thief makes you choose gambling at your club instead."

Kevin left soon after. Nicholas had described a situation that held little appeal. Visiting a brothel was much simpler. Not that a woman in a brothel could replace Rosamund.

It was a peculiar thought to have jump into his head. He pondered its emergence while he crossed the river and aimed toward Southwark.

Rosamund climbed out of the hackney cab. What she wanted to do required she be on foot. She asked the man to wait for her return, then paced down the street.

It had taken some doing to find these factories south of the river. This was not an area frequented by women much. In fact, she saw not a one for a block. Men entered and left the buildings, though. Laborers from the looks of them. A few others merely lounged against the outside walls. Noise came from one of the taverns she passed.

Most of the factories had been built of brick. None of them were very large. She plucked a piece of paper out of her reticule. The hackney driver said this was the street. Now she only had to find the correct establishment.

She had wanted to do this ever since she saw all those automatons. It seemed to her that they were simply large, elaborate toys for grown men. Wouldn't it be fun to have a small, less elaborate one that was for a child? She had an idea of the one she wanted, as a gift for Lily.

The street was narrow and she kept crossing it to avoid horses. It surprised her, then, when one of the horses came up right beside her, all but crowding her against a brick wall.

"What are you doing here?"

She looked up. Kevin looked down. She smiled and held up her paper. "I'm looking for this factory."

He dismounted, tied up his horse, took her arm, and guided her firmly to the corner. There he took the paper and read it.

"What are *you* doing here?" she asked while he looked at the address.

"That forge is nearby." He sounded distracted.

"Are you going to cast something? Can I watch?"

His gaze rose. He did not look distracted anymore. His expression was hard and tight. He lifted the paper. "Why are you looking for this factory?"

"I was told they make brass machine parts, and I wanted —"

"And you wanted to hold a conversation with them? Without telling me?" He became the picture of a man barely controlling his temper. "First, they will not talk to you because you are a woman. Then, you have nothing to tell them because you don't really understand what we need done. Finally, you lack the ability to determine if they can fulfill our requirements in terms of quality."

She had been glad to see him, but she really did not like either his tone or his assumptions. "My guess is they will talk to anyone who can pay."

"You think so, do you? Look at the men here. See how they find your presence odd. It is a good thing I chanced on you or you might have gotten into trouble, instead of only being troublesome to me." Exasperated, he looked around. "How did you get here?"

"My hackney is down the street."

He took her arm by the elbow and began moving her again. "I will escort you there."

She dug in her heels. "I am not done here. Stay with me if you are worried, but do not presume to command me to leave at your whim."

"Whim? This is no whim. I refuse to allow you to begin discussions about manufacturing the invention at this time, let alone without me. You can be willful and stubborn, Rosamund, enough so to drive me mad. You need to accept that there are ways to do this that you don't understand, and that your impatience will only risk whatever future the enterprise may have. We aren't talking about making a damned hat."

She thought her head would burst, it throbbed with so much anger by the time he finished. She glared at him. "Unhand me, Kevin, unless you want me to start screaming for help."

For a moment she thought he might not release her. Their gazes remained locked in a hot, furious connection. Then he did let her go.

"It is inexcusable for you to begin a row with me on a public street," she hissed. "I don't care how rough these men are, me thinks they know better than to do such a thing. But perhaps you think your good blood allows you to break every rule ever made." She snatched the paper out of his hand. "As for this, it has nothing to do with your precious invention. Unlike you, I have other interests too."

With that, she strode away, making it a point to look up at every building's sign that she came to.

Boot steps fell in beside her. "I ask you again, what are you doing here?" he asked tightly.

"Seeking out a man who can make an automaton."

"Zeus, not you too."

She lost her patience and smacked his upper arm. "Go away if you are going to glare and moan. It isn't for me. It is for Lily. A toy that moves, that is all. It is a wonder no one has thought of making them for children before."

She had to suffer one of his exasperated sighs. "They would be too expensive. There are hundreds of parts, intricately connected. The craftsmanship would be even harder in a small version."

"I am aware of that. Which is why I first asked at watch and clock makers. I assume it is much the same sort of craft."

They paced on in silence. "Similar," he finally said.

"One clock maker gave me this address and said this man might be willing to try it." She waved her paper in front of his face. "I don't need something like that swan. Just a woman who puts on a hat. Simple. Arm up, hat on, arm down. Although even the mechanical man in a smaller size would be a fine toy. If he was small, it would not matter if he rammed into things."

More silence. Then — "Even simple, they would be too costly for parents to buy for children."

"My sort, for certain. But not your sort. Your sort indulges their children. Which is why some of your sort have *no manners.*"

Having spied the sign she wanted, she broke away and strode across the street. He caught up at once. "I will accompany you."

"No. Don't you dare."

"Then I'll wait outside."

"I can't stop you. Do as you wish." She turned the latch and entered the building.

A half hour later she stepped back onto the street. Kevin pushed away from the wall. "It must have gone well. At least you are smiling."

"No thanks to you." She was very pleased with herself, so she could not scold much longer than that. "He will do it. I sketched out enough of the woman for him to have an idea. The notion of making it charmed him. He mostly makes clock parts for others to use, so using them himself for this other purpose intrigued him."

"Then you saw success. Come, I'll walk you to your hackney. You should not be alone on this street. Promise you will not venture here again unprotected."

She allowed him to walk with her.

"My apologies," he said. "Can you forget our argument?"

"I'm not sure that I can. With no cause, you assumed betrayal on my part. If you don't trust me, there is really no purpose in our having anything more than a business partnership."

"I will admit that I behaved badly. I made assumptions when I should have first learned your intentions. I do trust you, Rosamund. I don't think I would have been like that if I didn't."

She stopped and looked up at him. "I know how important this is to you. I understand that. I may not always agree with you, but I would never do anything to endanger your plans. It was hurtful of you to say I would."

He looked very contrite now, as well he should. "I know that."

"If you really do, then I can forgive you."

He smiled. "Since I am so inexcusable as to have a row on the street, I think I can be inexcusable enough to kiss you on the street."

He leaned in to do so. She turned her head. "Not here. Not now. Tonight, maybe, if you promise to be very nice to me."

Bursts of light filled the sky with thousands of tiny flames. Again and again the booms crackled as the fireworks shot up.

Rosamund had asked to go to Vauxhall Gardens two nights after their row, and Kevin had agreed.

"I've been before," she had said. "But I want to do it up right."

They had sat in one of the pavilions and eaten the proprietor's ham, and later strolled the gardens while music played. Now, as the night deepened, she knew it was time to tell him the truth.

She had said she would decide about a marriage today. Yet here they were, on that day, and she had avoided the subject because another one needed to be discussed first. She did not think she would need to make a decision about marriage after that.

The booms stopped. Only stars now lit the sky. The onlookers dispersed, to return to other pleasures and entertainment.

"Let us walk on the secluded paths," she said, turning toward the wooded copse at the western end of the gardens. "I never have before. Everyone warned it was not safe for a woman alone."

"More misunderstood than not safe."

"Misunderstandings can be the worst kind of danger." She examined the passersby. "It was busier when I came in the past. More of your sort too."

"The pleasure gardens have become less fashionable. Also, there was a big ball tonight. The kind that all the ladies would insist on attending."

"Yet you are not there. Were you invited, or had you offended the hostess?"

He made one of those rueful, slightly crooked smiles that she loved. "I may not be considered the best of company, but I'm not avoided, no matter what my relatives say. I was invited. I chose not to go. I much prefer spending time with you to dancing with a list of boring women."

"I'm sure they are not all boring."

"A good many are."

He really did not know that. He assumed it because big, noisy balls probably did not suit him.

"Do you think you will still be invited if we marry?"

391

They had arrived at the entrance to the wooded path. He guided her in.

"I can't see why not."

"Can't you? Even if I do not play a visible role in the shops, I will still be a milliner. They are mine, after all. I have decided I don't want to give them up. If we marry, that is. I may not assist patrons, but I'll still design the hats."

The trees allowed little light to penetrate to the paths, although some of the gardens' lamps sent a few beams and twinkles through the branches. Sounds of voices and low laughs said they were not alone. They passed a shadow several feet from the path that moved enough to reveal it was a couple embracing.

"You have been thinking of the practicalities," he said.

"One of us has to."

"I am just happy that you have been thinking about it at all."

She stopped walking and stepped to the side of the path, under the canopy of branches. "I said I would, and that I would tell you today what I concluded."

He waited to hear it. Instead, she took his hand and raised it to her lips.

"There are things I want to talk about before we make this bargain. Things you need to know, and things I want to know."

The mood between them had been light and joyful all night, but now a heavy seriousness quaked between them. She had guessed saying what she had just said would provoke no matter what came next, but she couldn't avoid it.

"You never asked about my past," she said. "It would be dishonest to allow you to take this step not knowing." She peered up through the dark at his face. "I spent close to two years working in Mrs. Darling's house. I think you know which one I mean."

To her surprise, he eased her into an embrace. "I know that."

"You do?"

"You took service there after you were thrown out by your lover's family."

She laid her head against his chest. He had known and had never asked. He would have gone forward, never asking, if she had lacked the courage to do the right thing. He still was not asking.

She could leave it at that. She could simply trust him to believe the best. She imagined the long years of marriage, with that open question standing silently between them.

"Don't you wonder what I did there? It would be normal for you to be curious."

393

"Why don't you tell me, if you want to."

She nodded. "I could find no respectable work. I had no reference. I was reduced to sleeping in doorways and begging for food. I had decided to try to make my way back home because at least there I might find work, but I had no money for the journey. On the streets, men would . . . I was offered money." She paused a long while. "I considered it."

"No one can blame you for that, in your situation."

"That is good of you to say, but you don't understand." She stretched up and kissed him. "I did more than just consider."

Did she only imagine that his embrace altered a little? Tightened? She could not see his face well.

"I made a most practical decision. A desperate one. Then I thought, if I'm going to do that, I may as well get a roof over my head for the doing. I went to the park and watched until I saw a group of women who looked to be whores of a better sort. They were playing together like children. That made me feel better somehow. I followed them when they left. They went to a house near Portman Square."

He said nothing, but she sensed his concentration on her and her story.

"I presented myself to the owner, Mrs. Darling. She asked me some embarrassing questions. Then she told me I would not do." She laughed at the memory, then sighed. "I was shocked. I never thought I would be turned down. All that thinking and anguish for nothing. I wanted to laugh at myself, and also cry. Goodness, to be turned down even for *that* —"

"Did she say why?"

"She said that I was too inexperienced, and not of good character for the trade. 'Barely willing won't do,' was how she put it. However, they needed a servant to serve as a chambermaid and to help with laundry. So I took that work, and lived there."

"I'm glad Mrs. Darling recognized desperation when she saw it and offered you other employment. The owner of the next door you knocked on probably would not have turned you down. One look at your face and avarice would have won out over any decent sentiments."

"For almost two years it was my home. I still have some friends there. I would be very discreet about them, if we — That is, if you still think you want to —"

"How did you meet the duke if you were a servant? I assume you met him while you were there."

He didn't sound suspicious. Only curious. "He was a patron on occasion. I ate with the women, and they spoke of him, and one of them pointed him out. He and I met when one of the women he favored became very ill. Marie, her name was. Mrs. Darling believed it was cholera, so she put her in a chamber and said no one was to go in there, only leave food by the door. I disobeyed her and took care of her and prayed I wouldn't get sick too. I told Mrs. Darling she needed a physician, but none was sent for."

"I am liking Mrs. Darling less now. Avarice won anyway. She did not want her house known as a place where there had been disease."

"One night, while I was tending to Marie, the duke came in as if he didn't worry about getting sick. Maybe dukes are special that way too."

"Hardly. He was not very careful with his health, however."

"He sent for a physician, and while we waited for the man to come, we talked a bit. When it was all done, he paid the fee, then left me a small purse too. Ten guineas. I had never seen so much before. Not in my whole life."

He continued embracing her under the trees while the sounds of the gardens came to them, distant but joyful.

"It was good of you to care for this woman. Dangerous, though. Did she survive?"

She nodded. "Once she was better, she left." She slipped out of his embrace and faced him. "There it is. I needed you to know."

They continued strolling the path. They passed a lantern and she looked over at him. His fine profile had set itself into an expression she knew well. He contemplated something. Her, most likely. The rash proposal he had made.

"If you worked there, you were probably seen," he said. "Most servants would not be noticed, but I doubt that was how it was with you."

He had seen the problem, and why it mattered as much as it did.

"Were there misunderstandings, on the part of the patrons?"

"That is a nice way to say it, Kevin. There were a few. Two men asked Mrs. Darling about me. It was a good amount of money, but I said no. Another man saw me as I tended a chamber and he did not bother going to Mrs. Darling. I called out, and two of the women came and set him to rights. If there were others, I did not learn about it."

She stopped in her tracks and faced him. "I did not whore, even once, if that is what you are asking."

"I wasn't."

"It sounded as if you were. I don't mind. You would need to know."

"I did need to know, but not for the reason you think."

They had arrived back at the entrance to the path. Darkness on one side of them, and lamps and lanterns on the other. He looked down at her. "You are uncommonly brave and honest to have told me this."

"You already knew."

"You didn't know that I knew. What was the question you had for me?"

She hesitated. He had accepted her at face value, so to speak. He trusted that her time at that house had been as she said. He believed her. She did not doubt that during his intense contemplation while they strolled, he had considered every complication her past might cause to him and his life.

To now ask him if he'd killed his uncle would be the worst insult. A betrayal. What would be gained by it? If he was the sort to do such a thing, he was the sort to lie about it.

It all came down to what she believed.

What she trusted. Whether she accepted what she thought he was, as she had come to know him.

She hoped her better sense was not deserting her, the way it had with Charles. "I only wanted to ask if you still thought this marriage of convenience a good idea."

He lifted her hand and bent to kiss it. "I think it is an excellent idea."

"We should do it then, before one of us realizes we are insane."

CHAPTER NINETEEN

They married a week later, in a quiet ceremony at St. George's. Rosamund wore a cream dress she had ordered upon her return from Paris.

Attendance was sparse. Minerva, Chase, and Hollinburgh were there, along with Rosamund's maid, Jenny. No one else from Kevin's family came, not even his father.

When Rosamund turned after saying the vows, she saw Beatrice at the back of the church. She had worried that her friend would not like this marriage, but Beatrice gave a little wave and a smile before immediately slipping out. Rosamund wondered if Kevin had noticed her.

Rosamund's only regret was that Lily could not be with her. She had written with the news, however, and received a response in which her sister expressed excitement for her. Lily probably was relieved that her older sister had not ended up a fallen woman.

Minerva hosted the wedding breakfast out in her garden. The weather held, and a lot of joy and good wishes surrounded that table. Finally, she and Kevin rode back to her house to start this marriage they had chosen.

She was up in her chamber when Kevin entered. Jenny slipped out at once.

He took her in his arms and gave her a much better kiss than the discreet one after the ceremony. "So here we are."

"Do you feel strange? I do."

"Most strange. Forever is a long time."

"I was thinking the same thing during the ceremony."

Jenny had started undressing her. Now Kevin turned her around to complete the task of unfastening her dress. "I saw one of the women from Mrs. Darling's house at the church. Did you invite her?"

"She never would have come if I hadn't." She suddenly realized why he had asked. "She was not there for you, if you were worried that she was."

His fingers stilled on her back, then continued. "Then you know about that."

"I do. She and I remain friends."

"I thought they only bought bonnets from you."

"She was very kind to me when I was there. She was probably the only friend I had in London at the time."

"I will not be seeing her again, in case you wondered. Even if I ever break my promise to you, it will not be with her."

He slid down the dress. She stepped out and faced him. "I know. She would not have you now, even if you did go there. She may be a whore, but she understands friendship." She looked down at his fingers unlacing her half stays. "She gave you the highest recommendation, though. She said you knew what you were about."

He gave her a charming half smile. "Did she now? How generous."

"Of course, I already knew that."

"Actually, you don't know the half of it, darling." The stays fell to the floor.

"Perhaps you should be another of my tutors and teach me at least half of it."

His fingertips skimmed over her freed breasts, drawing lines on the chemise that covered them still. "That is a splendid idea. Today we will have lesson one."

The caller was announced ten days later. After breakfast, Kevin had gone to the small study attached to the library. A footman later interrupted to deliver a card. Annoyed that he had been disturbed on the first day he could concentrate in over a week, Kevin set aside the sketches he was toying with and went up to the drawing room.

Rosamund was there, along with the man whose card he held, Mr. Theodore Lovelace.

The man's back was to him, but he garnered what he could from that view. Ginger-haired. Big. He had the looks of a laborer to him, with his broad shoulders and thick form. One visible hand showed calluses and scars. His coats were of high quality, however.

"Here he is," Rosamund said. "This is Mr. Kevin Radnor, whom you asked to see."

Kevin positioned himself to welcome Mr. Lovelace and get a full view. Rough-hewn. Craggy face. Gray eyes. But a smile broke out, and those eyes twinkled as he stood to make a greeting.

"Mr. Lovelace has a mutual friend with us," Rosamund said.

"Who might that be?"

Lovelace beamed. "Mr. Forestier. In Paris."

"Forestier? Are you saying he gave you my name?"

"He did indeed, sir."

"How do you know him?"

"Met him, I did. Was in Paris myself. It was a holiday, but men talk, and his name was mentioned as someone with good knowledge of machines and such. That's my trade. I've a factory in Shropshire and a smaller works out farther on the Thames here."

"What kinds of machines?"

"All kinds. I've a knack with them. Some we make for others. Some I devise myself. I've a new one I'm making, to be used in textile factories, but it has a little problem, and I called on Forestier to see if he might have some solution."

"How did my name enter the conversation?"

"He said you were a man with similar interests and such. He said you might have an idea for the problem, what with your experience." He reached in his pocket and withdrew a long paper. "I've a drawing here that —"

"Did Forestier say anything else about me?"

Lovelace blanched at the tone of that question. Rosamund sent Kevin a disapproving look. Kevin forced some control over his suspicions and tried a more congenial voice. "I'm just curious what he said that convinced you to seek me out."

Lovelace smiled again. "He said you were an inventor, so you might think of the way a solution required."

"That is all?"

"Well, he might've said that perhaps we could do some business together. What with your inventions and my foundry works."

Kevin barely saw Lovelace now, his head had gone so hot. "Among the machines you make, do you construct engines?"

The man misunderstood. He grinned. "I do at that. Here I mostly make the molds for the casting of iron, as required for them and other machines. Shropshire is where I make the engines whole."

Kevin thought his mind would explode. "I'm sorry. I can't help you. Good day." He strode out of the drawing room, ready to kill someone. Forestier preferably, but the scoundrel was in Paris.

Light footsteps hurried up behind him and caught him at the stairs.

"What is wrong with you?" Rosamund hissed. "That was rude to the point of cruelty."

"He is the competitor who cost us two thousand, not to mention a percentage of profits."

"You don't know that."

"Don't I? I wonder what Forestier told him about what we have."

"Do not be so fast to assume betrayal, Kevin. It sounded to me as if Forestier truly thought you might see a solution where he did not, and that he also thought Mr. Lovelace might be of use in our own enterprise."

He shook off the hand she had on his arm. "I'm not interested."

"It can't hurt to listen. It may come to nothing, but we should at least —"

"Damnation, *no.*"

She narrowed her eyes. She backed up two paces. Then she turned and strode back to the drawing room.

That night, when he retired to his chambers, he found a long sheet of paper propped on the dressing table. He stared at it while his valet helped him undress.

"Mrs. Radnor brought that, sir," Morris said while he set aside the waistcoat.

Kevin picked it up and held it to the light. It looked like the drawing Lovelace had taken from his pocket.

He had not seen Rosamund since she marched back into the drawing room. She had spent the afternoon at her shop, and had had dinner sent up to her apartment. He had spent the time immersed in thoughts on an idea he had for a new invention. Even so, he had not missed the brittle silence that permeated the house.

Now he examined the paper. There was no note with it, but he read her message all the same.

Cursing, he threw himself onto the divan and held up the damned paper so the lamp on the table beside him illuminated the drawings. Thus did women win their battles. Weaker sex, hell. Men didn't stand a chance.

Rosamund turned on her bed and snuggled against her pillow. No, not a pillow.

An arm moved to surround her.

No wonder her fitful sleep had turned peaceful. "You're here," she murmured.

"Do you mind?"

She shook her head and drifted in the peace his embrace always gave her. She was so glad he had come. She had spent the evening full of self-righteous anger, but by the time she retired, she had worried that he wouldn't even care about the distance she had imposed. More likely he would find her pique irritating and boring.

Perhaps he had. Maybe he had not even noticed her absence. Right now, she didn't care because his embrace made her heart so happy for their special friendship.

Not friendship, her heart's voice said. *Call it love, because that is what you feel.*

"The problem with his machine is simple to fix once you give it some thought. I will send him the solution I propose."

Machine? Solution? Oh yes. Mr. Lovelace. "That is nice of you."

She felt him kiss the top of her head. "Think nothing of it."

Rosamund walked to her shop, eager to do something besides practice elocution or manners. Her tutors had a habit of congratulating her, but it always sounded as if they praised themselves instead. She had improved much in the month of lessons, and they saw her as one of their creations, much as the new hat she was finishing was one of hers.

Upon arriving at the shop, she immediately went to the workroom. The apprentice, Sally, labored over trimming a headpiece. Rosamund checked her work, then sat to finish her own.

The hat used some of the ideas she had carried back from Paris in her reticule. The brim was uneven, and deeper on one side than the other. The larger side curved up, and she had split the brim there in three places. That allowed the plumes on the crown to show through to the front, and also gave the hat a different flair.

Covering those split sections had been a challenge. She carefully picked out the stitches on one of them and began to redo it.

Mrs. Ingram entered. "There's someone asking for you in front."

"Not a local businessman, I trust. My marriage was announced."

"Nothing like that. Mr. Walter Radnor and his wife."

Surprised, Rosamund set aside her trimming and made her way to the front of the shop.

Felicity waited there, dressed very fashionably and wearing a hat Jameson's had not made. Walter hovered near her, looking pompous and vaguely uncomfortable. Felicity saw her and fluttered over.

"What a charming shop. Such interesting hats."

Rosamund welcomed them, then waited with curiosity. When they both kept ambling around her establishment, she moved in and forced the question. "How can I help you? Have you come to commission something, Mrs. Radnor?"

"I think that you can address me as Felicity now, because we are related."

"How generous of you."

Felicity glanced at her husband.

He offered a hearty, bland smile. "We want you to know that we have accommodated ourselves to the marriage. What's done is done."

"How good of you."

"Yes, well, about that, however." He glanced around, his gaze returning repeatedly to the window. "Is there somewhere we can talk alone?"

"Come with me." She led the way up to the first story and the space in front that the shop used. She had installed a divan and some chairs there, along with the necessities for fitting headwear.

"We called at your home, but were told you were here," Felicity said after sitting on the divan.

Rosamund wondered who had told them that.

"Do you think this is wise?" Walter asked. "Continuing in trade now that you are wed is neither necessary nor appropriate."

"Did the family send you to instruct me? If my husband does not mind, why should you?"

"Kevin has never been careful about social expectations," Felicity said soothingly. "Walter is only trying to help you. Isn't that right, darling?"

Walter nodded.

"Then you have done your duty." Rosamund stood. "Now, I have a full day and —"

"Actually, we wanted to talk about something else," Walter said while he half-rose himself.

Rosamund sat back down.

"Your marriage settlement — How did that address this enterprise of Kevin's?" Walter asked.

"That is more private than I want to discuss."

"Did you leave it that he is your heir?" Felicity asked. "I did tell you not to do that."

"My dear, please don't divert the conversation," Walter said. "That is neither here nor there to our purposes."

"Perhaps you will explain what *is* here or there," Rosamund said.

Walter shifted how he sat. "Here is the thing. When almost a year had passed and you were not found, we assumed you would not be. That you were . . ."

"Dead?"

"Or had moved abroad. America," Felicity added quickly.

"It was a fair conclusion," Walter said. "I took it upon myself on behalf of the family to find out what that enterprise might be worth, should the legacy be divided up. I was surprised that while the details of Kevin's invention are not known, there are those whose estimation of my cousin's mind is quite high and who would purchase a share of something they knew nothing about, simply because it was his idea."

Rosamund had been ready to usher them out, but now she was glad she hadn't. What a stunning thing to hear. "This was a recent discovery, you said."

"Recent enough." Walter's face tinged pink for an instant.

"Perhaps you looked into this earlier. When you thought Kevin might be arrested."

Walter looked shocked, but not at her accusation. At her guessing what he had done.

"It was a reasonable thing to do," Felicity said, with unctuous sweetness touched with enough beseeching plea to be irritating.

"Whenever it was done, I don't see why you need to talk to me about it."

They looked at each other, then at her, then at each other again. Felicity turned a big smile on Rosamund. "We want you to turn the company back to the estate. Not the money, just the company. Our share of that is far less than the money, but it is something."

"It would benefit Kevin, because he really is not experienced in business and would be wise to have investors who are," Walter added.

"I would think it would benefit your marriage too, to remove that partnership from it. It can't be a good thing to have that between you." Felicity's expression turned sly. "And if that was why he married you, well, he is well caught now anyway."

"Yet you just told me it has value, even without being fully realized yet."

"Quite small compared to the rest you have," Walter hastened to say. "It is like a puddle is to an ocean."

Rosamund forced her mind to step away five paces, so she might see this peculiar visit for what it might really be about. Once she viewed it fully, the oddness started making sense.

"Tell me something. Upon learning about its value, and assuming I would not be found, did you trade on your expectations?"

"What do you mean?" Walter asked.

"Did you sell your share before you had it in hand? I can think of no other reason why twice now I have been encouraged by one or both of you to turn my half back to the estate. As you say, its loss to the rest of you is like a puddle. Were you so confident it would be yours that you sold it in advance of receiving it?"

Walter's expression revealed the truth. Felicity tried to mask her surprise with hauteur.

"How awkward for you," Rosamund said. "I'm thinking that is illegal. You should probably give back the money."

Like most men, Walter preferred anger to embarrassment. "I told you she would not listen to reason," he snapped to his wife. He began to stand. "I'll not be subjected to this by a common hat maker."

"Wait!" Felicity cried, grabbing blindly for his arm. She turned wide, frightened eyes on Rosamund. "We can't give it back. It is gone."

Gone. Spent. Rosamund looked more closely at Felicity's ensemble. New and fashionable. She wondered how much this woman spent in a year. Probably a lot. Walter's fortune might be much like Kevin's, but it could not support a woman who wanted to live like a duchess.

Walter stood. Red-faced, he walked to the door. "Good day to you."

Rosamund waited for his boot steps to stop sounding on the stairs. Felicity dabbed at her eyes with her handkerchief.

"How much?" Rosamund asked.

"Three thousand. A trust pays out in June, but the man who purchased this grows impatient. Even if we can convince him to wait, should we give him that, there will be nothing left for us."

If it was a trust like Kevin's, it paid out twice a year, so five or six thousand in all. That was a huge income.

She should not pity Felicity for her current situation. Yet she did. The idea of her husband possibly being arrested for fraudulent business dealings hopefully mattered more than the loss of a new wardrobe this autumn.

"I think I can find a way to help you," she said. "First, however, I want to talk about something else."

Having heard the hint of a reprieve, Felicity calmed. She nodded and waited.

"You told me you had seen Kevin in London in the days after the duke's death. What days and where did you see him?"

Felicity thought before speaking. "It was the next day. He was riding his horse. He did not notice me. He had that expression he gets when he is not paying attention to anything but his own thoughts."

"Do you know where he was going?"

Felicity shrugged. "It was not far from

Grosvenor Square. I assumed he was going to visit Lady Greenough. She is a widow, and very wealthy. There were quiet rumors about the two of them that winter. That was only notable for it being Kevin. He was not known for such flirtations."

Rosamund battled to keep her surprise from her expression. She hated that jealousy rose fast and hot into her heart.

"I will help you out of your situation," she said after collecting herself. "I want something in return, however."

"I will receive you, if it is that. I will encourage the family to as well."

"That would be nice, but it isn't that. When you leave this chamber, you are to forget that you saw him in London that day. On considering it, you realized that you never saw that rider's face, and made unwarranted assumptions. Because you question your own memories now, you will never again, to anyone, insinuate that Kevin had something to do with his uncle's death. You will tell your husband that you made an unfortunate mistake, so he does not continue suspecting Kevin unfairly."

Felicity nodded without hesitation.

Rosamund stood. "Have your husband send me the name of the man from whom he accepted the money, and the exact amount he owes. I will have a draft drawn and left with Mr. Sanders. Matters can be resolved in his office. You will have to sign loan documents for it that say the amount will be due immediately if either of you ever again gossips about my husband."

CHAPTER TWENTY

"What is that?" Chase asked Kevin.

The two of them were in the library of Chase's chambers on Bury Street. Chase had lived here prior to his marriage.

Kevin continued unwrapping his bundle. "It is a small steam engine. I stopped by the house on my way here and spirited it out."

"I hope you don't intend to fire it up in here."

"It is perfectly safe. Even if there is a mishap, it won't do more than take down some plaster. I need it for demonstrations."

Chase appeared skeptical. "You had better explain that to Brigsby, and warn him whenever you intend to demonstrate."

Kevin stood back and eyed the placement of the engine on the library table. "It is good of you to lend him, as well as allow me to let these chambers from you."

Chase reached for the brandy decanter, then poured into two glasses. "You are doing me a favor on both accounts. Brigsby has been without a proper situation since my marriage. It has created complications. He refuses to be a mere valet but is not suited to manage an entire household. Due to his long history with me, he considers himself first among equals with the servants, much to the annoyance of the butler and housekeeper. You have your own valet at your house now, but taking care of this part of your life will keep Brigsby occupied. The suggestion he serve you here delighted him. He now has his own kingdom again."

"I thought he served as one of your agents now."

Chase sank into a chair. "Sometimes." He looked to the door, then lowered his voice. "He is too notable to be useful most of the time. A more anonymous look and manner is often required. He has —"

The door opened just then, and the man in question entered. He carried a tray with coffee and cups and swept it over to a low table. He deftly poured and handed over the results, then beamed with pride at his own job well done.

There was nothing anonymous-looking about Brigsby, that was certain. Of middling height and slight of build, he exuded a self-confidence that often got servants sacked.

His collar had been ironed to such perfection that its edge could be a weapon. Pomade slicked his sparse black hair to his skull. His expression stayed just shy of impertinent. He clearly was the kind of man servant who saw his charge as someone who needed help in the most rudimentary exercises in living.

"The coffee is very good," Kevin felt obligated to say, because Brigsby appeared to be waiting for praise. Or something.

"I am pleased if you are pleased, sir." He pivoted slightly so he faced Chase. "I was wondering if we might have a brief talk regarding my duties here, so I am able to execute them properly."

"Certainly." Chase turned an amused, expectant expression on Kevin.

"I expect they are the same as they were when you were here with Chase," Kevin said, not really knowing what that meant.

"If I may say, sir — You have another home, so am I correct that you won't be living here?"

"Not in the normal way."

"Ah. I am an excellent cook. Far better than most households employ." A quick, sidelong glance aimed at Chase. "Will you on occasion want meals here?"

"I suppose that is possible, if I am here late."

"Very good, sir. Other than linens and such, will you need laundry done?"

"I doubt it."

"I see. That will spare me much time. Because I will not be required to perform some duties, would you mind if I on occasion continue my employment in the inquiries, when I am needed?"

Out of the corner of his eye, Kevin saw Chase's thin smile. "Let me think about that and see how things go here first."

"Very good, sir. I do not want to be presumptuous, but it would perhaps be best if we also discussed my requirements."

"What would those be?"

Brigsby smiled a smile that managed to appear both subservient and superior. "I prefer to receive my wages every fortnight. I know it is not the normal way to do things, but it suits me. And if you anticipate having a guest for meals, notice by that morning at the latest is necessary so I can procure the necessities."

"That is very sensible."

"Thank you, sir. Oh, there is one more thing. If you intend to have a lady stay the night, I ask that you remove the door pull that hangs off the latch to the cellar. I wouldn't want to intrude by mistake."

"I don't expect to be doing that, but it is good to know the custom."

With a gracious bow, Brigsby left the library.

"What have you done to me?" Kevin asked.

"He is an excellent manservant. He can even do your accounts if you want. Once that enterprise starts showing sales and profit, you might consider using him." Chase drank the rest of his coffee, then set the cup aside and picked up his brandy. "You are lucky to have him."

"I'll let you know if I agree after a month or so." He stood and examined the library. Most of the books had been removed to the house Chase now shared with Minerva. It reminded him of the empty shelves that so distressed Rosamund when she bought her house. That library now overflowed with Kevin's books. Maybe he would move some here, so she could continue buying the ones she preferred.

He had come upon her yesterday, reading one of the custom-bound volumes she had bought. The pages turned slowly, but she had kept at it. Twice while he was in the library she rose and went to the dictionary she had left open on a writing table.

"Does domestic life suit you?" Chase asked.

"Very much." Kevin continued his perusal of the chamber.

"Your deciding to take separate chambers within a month of marriage implied otherwise."

"They are not separate. They are extra. There is a difference."

"If you say so."

Kevin knew that tone of voice. It was Chase's it-is-not-for-me-to-question tone that had ten questions waiting behind it.

"I'm not regretting my marriage, if that is what you think."

"I don't think anything except that this is odd." Chase gestured with his glass around the library.

"If you think so, why did you offer this apartment?"

"You said you were going to do it, and this was available and well situated. It isn't for me to make your decisions."

"Yet it is for you to question them, it seems."

"I only have one question. Does Rosamund know about this?"

"She does. She is in complete agreement that we needed these extra chambers."

Chase raised his eyebrows, just enough to

be irritating.

"What?"

"Nothing. Except —"

There was always an *except* in conversations like this.

"If I did not know you better, I would say it looks like you are setting yourself up for liaisons within a month of taking your vows," Chase finished. "But, of course, you don't have liaisons. Until the one with Miss Jameson."

"If you must know, this place is for the enterprise. We both wanted an address other than our home. Also an office other than in our home. A place reserved for those matters, so they don't intrude where they shouldn't."

Those eyebrows went up again, for a longer spell. "Ah."

"That was an extremely annoying 'Ah.' It sounded as if the expert at discreet inquiries had concluded he had his answers."

"All I have concluded is that you have decided that a business partnership and a domestic one don't sit together well in one place."

That was an understatement. Since their marriage, Kevin had several times cursed the agreement he had signed about leaving Rosamund's share in her hands.

"We had a row," he said. "It was small, but it became a poison affecting everything. I had already proposed that I needed a place to pursue my interests, and we agreed to separate those two parts of our lives."

"So whenever the two of you discuss the enterprise, you will do it here?"

"That is the thinking."

"And you believe that if you argue, you can leave the argument here?"

"Of course. Why not?"

"It is unlike any marriage I know, but you are unlike any man I know, so perhaps you have found a perfect solution. Now, I have to go to the City. I'll leave you and Brigsby to settle in."

The notion of being settled in by Brigsby had Kevin striding to the door in Chase's wake. "I'll ride part way with you."

Rosamund wound her hands around the silken tie that bound her wrists to the bedpost above her head. Her vulnerability excited her more than she expected. Kevin had aroused her perfectly, masterfully. Now he sat back on her legs and watched her, making her wait while she trembled with desire.

Lessons like this had progressed in fits and starts. A week might pass before a new one.

A pattern had emerged. He would tell her, in that quiet, clear voice of his, what he was going to do. One time she had recoiled at his words. He had discarded the idea and never presented it again.

This reminded her of their first time together, when he held her hands together above her head. Nothing else was similar, however. She was not lying but sitting, for one thing.

He spread her legs and kissed up the length of one. The higher those kisses went, the shorter her breaths came. His mouth turned toward the dampness down there. His fingers stroked and his tongue flicked. She closed her eyes and rode the intensity of pleasure that he created.

She was almost there, almost breaking apart, when he moved again, leaving her need bereft of completion. He knelt close to her, rising above. He untied her hands.

He had not described this part, but she knew what to do. She caressed him, her hands rising up his torso, then down to his hips and thighs. She took his cock in her hands and pleasured him the way he liked.

His position and hers allowed her to caress him fully. It also allowed something else. She had heard the women talk about it and thought it among the worst of their duties.

Now the notion did not shock her. On impulse, she leaned in and flicked her tongue up his cock's shaft. She sensed a new tension in him and looked up.

"Do you want this?" She flicked her tongue again.

"Yes."

His ragged voice, his tight jaw, the way he watched her — all of it said he wanted this more than that "yes" admitted.

She grazed him with lips and fingertips, teasing him the way he often did her. Torturing him and making his hunger increase. "I wonder if I can make you beg," she said, before circling her tongue around the tip.

"Never."

"No? I have all night to find out."

He braced against the headboard with one arm. "Do your worst."

Kevin woke to find Rosamund looking right at him. She rested on her side, her head propped on her upright hand, while she regarded him.

He must have fallen asleep after collapsing. She had exhausted him. She lacked experience, but her curiosity alone aroused him. And charmed him. Feeling her explore and experiment had left his blood scream-ing.

Now she wore a self-satisfied smile. "I expect decent women are not supposed to do that," she said. "Is that why you never asked it of me?"

It was a hell of a question. "I thought later, perhaps."

"I told you the women talked. I know that men like it."

"Yes. Well . . ."

"You liked it enough to beg."

"I don't think one 'please' is begging."

"It wasn't only one 'please' but a good number, along with some 'yes, like that' and 'deeper' and —"

He grabbed her and tucked her close so she would not feel obligated to repeat every desperate muttering he had made.

He began to drift away again.

"Tell me about Lady Greenough."

Suddenly, he was alert, staring at the underside of the bed's drape that billowed above them. "What about her?"

"I was told that you had a liaison with her last year. I thought you didn't have lovers."

His response shouldn't matter, but an acute sense of caution made him hesitate. "For the most part, no."

"Do you mean she was the exception?"

Damnation. "Yes, although it was so brief that 'liaison' is not the right word."

"I thought you had no experience in discretion, but you must have had some after that."

"Not really." Discretion wasn't needed when a man lived in a woman's private chambers for four days. It had been a calculated orgy of two, a reckless gamble with a cynical goal.

Nothing else came for a good while. Then . . .

"Did you love her?"

He looked down on Rosamund's crown. "No."

She turned on her back with her head in the crook of his arm and shared his examination of the bed drape. "I don't understand something. Why didn't you tell Chase you had been with her when he was investigating your uncle's death? It would have cleared up the questions about you right away if he talked to her."

A series of comprehensions lined up in his head, each one more astonishing than the last.

She had known about the questions regarding his whereabouts on the night of the duke's death.

She had never asked him about those suspicions.

She had ferreted out more information than Chase had.

Yet despite all of that, she had married him.

He could end this conversation by saying it had nothing to do with her and was not her concern. Or he could explain a few things that he had never told anyone, and that did not reflect well on him. Whatever he chose, this marriage, this forever, would probably change. He admitted that what it became mattered to him.

He turned on his side so he could see her. He kissed her cheek. "I want you to know that I never harmed my uncle."

She turned her head so she looked in his eyes. "I believe that. I would not be here if I didn't."

The final discovery. She had weighed all of this before agreeing to marry. She had lined up evidence that could damn a man, and had chosen to believe in him.

He didn't deserve her.

His gaze warmed after she said it, but she could see part of his vision had turned inward. She waited for whatever else he wanted to say. Perhaps he would drift to sleep now, content that he had reassured her.

"I was there the night before," he said. "I went down to Melton Park to tell him I needed the money for Forestier. My uncle had invested, as had I. He saw the potential. However, he refused me more funds. We had a row. I told Chase this when he learned I had returned from France earlier than I claimed."

"Did you think he had left his half to you in his will?"

He hesitated. "Yes. As far as I know, only Chase was aware the will had been changed, and even he did not know what it said."

She didn't point out that this hardly helped. He would know that.

"And you were with this lady all that time, being intimate?"

"Not all the time. Even I need my rest." She did not laugh at his little joke. "I did stay there on that visit home, however. It was a flirtation. A momentary madness when I thought we might suit each other, only to discover we didn't."

Madness. Not love, but enchantment. Enchanted enough to consider marriage. Or maybe not. Perhaps it had only been desire. He knew all about that. Maybe he really wanted this woman's money and had used his sensual powers to encourage such a match. He would find that an agreeable arrangement. Marriage and money in return for pleasure.

It was what he had done with her, wasn't it?

"I was told by Minerva that Chase made a report to someone important," she said. "It included all the people who could have done it, if it was done at all. You were one of them, as was she."

"I don't know the details about that. I do know that before he made that report, he told me to go to the coast to prepare to leave the country if necessary."

"Did you do what he said?"

"I didn't fancy hanging for something I had not done."

Now that she talked about this with him, she only grew more worried. Felicity's gossip was one thing. Knowing there had been a real danger was another.

"The conclusion it was an accident — could that change? Might someone in the future decide differently?"

"I expect so. It has weighed on me, of course. With each month that passed, it got better, however."

She could not imagine what that had been like. Horrible. He had lived with a noose's shadow on a wall of every chamber.

"I trust if it came to it, you would break your silence about where you were that night. You mustn't be a stupid gentleman about it, to protect your lover's name." She returned her gaze to the drapery because if she saw anything like love in him when he thought about that woman, it would be hard to pretend it did not hurt her.

She scolded herself in the silence that stretched between them. She had not married for love. He surely hadn't. As practical marriages went, this was probably better than most. To be jealous over some affair from a year ago was stupid. Childish. It was almost as bad as clinging to the dream of Charles.

Knowing that did not stop the sadness, though. He had said he was never enthralled, so she didn't mind so much that he was not enthralled with her. Only it seemed he had been, at least once. She admitted that she was jealous mostly because her own feelings had changed. Deepened.

Beatrice had once told her that when a new woman joined them, all of them spent the next month reminding her never to fall in love, never to misunderstand what she was to the patrons. Someone should have done that with her and this marriage. "It is a practical match. A marriage of convenience. Don't be so stupid as to fall in love with him unless you want your heart broken."

He had been with that woman for days, but not in a domestic way. She wondered how far they had gotten in the lessons.

"I will explain where I was, if necessary," he said. "I would be a fool to remain silent."

"I want your promise about that."

He turned her face toward him and gently kissed her. "I give you my word as a stupid gentleman."

CHAPTER TWENTY-ONE

Rosamund hired a carriage to take her up river. She left from the shop, where she had said she would be all day. In her reticule she carried a note. It had come two days ago from Mr. Lovelace. It thanked her for her help with the mechanical problem and invited her to visit his works. Kevin had not been mentioned, nor had he received his own invitation.

A good wife would probably inform her husband of her intentions. Rosamund did not. This would probably come to nothing, so why encourage storms to form? She had not forgotten about that row when she went to find a man to make her toy. She was curious, however. She had liked Mr. Lovelace and wanted to see just what he made.

The carriage took her through Southwark, then into the countryside. Some farms still flourished, but others had been given over to small factories. They dotted the river bank.

Mr. Lovelace owned one of the larger works. Men moved through a big yard, entering this building or that, some carrying iron objects and others moving coal in wheeled vehicles. She asked the carriage driver to go in and tell the owner that she was outside.

Mr. Lovelace emerged, smiling a welcome. "I didn't think you would come, but I was hopeful."

"I am curious about your industry."

"Come with me and I'll show you."

They entered a long building. Men sat at tables, using files and hammers on metal. "They are making parts," Mr. Lovelace said. "There ain't a lot of room for error in them. This is not work for a blacksmith. Every wheel, every piston, every cog needs to be as close to perfect as can be made." He pointed to one group. "They make the molds for cast iron. It can't be rushed."

At the end of the building, a group of men fitted parts together. The result was approximating the engine Kevin had shown her, only much bigger.

"I pay for each one I make, to those who hold the essential licenses. Even so, there is enough wanting them that I make a profit."

"What if something goes wrong after they are in use?"

"I send a man to fix it. Except for one part. It is a secret, and if it looks to be that, Mr. Watt sends one of his men." He gave her a meaningful look. "There's been a lot of thieving in this industry, I'm sorry to say. I can't blame Mr. Watt for being careful. But I'm not happy being beholden to him for both the part and the upkeep. What's to stop him from stealing too? My patrons, I mean."

She admired the engine a while longer, then they walked back to the building near her carriage. He invited her to share some refreshments, and they sat on a small, wooden terrace overlooking the river. Barges floated past, as well as one pleasure yacht.

"Mr. Radnor was not happy about my visit, I could tell," he said.

"Not really."

"Yet he sent me that explanation of how to fix my problem. A different machine it was, of course. Not an engine."

"I asked him to help."

"I thought you might've. That's why I asked you to come here. You seemed inter-ested in what I had to say."

"It matters little if I am."

"My thinking is, wives have more influence than they're given credit for. Mine certainly does."

Lemonade had been brought, and he lifted one glass in his gnarled, big hands and drank. He surveyed his little place of respite with contentment. "Let me tell you what Forestier said to me, after he told me that he wouldn't license that gauge to me. He said Mr. Radnor had a better use for it."

"And he does."

"He also said that there are inventors and there are makers, and Mr. Radnor was the first. That is why he gave me his name. He said inventors need makers. I'm a maker. I couldn't figure out how to improve or change the engines I build, but I build them better than anyone. I've sent engines to France and one to Russia." He pointed with his thumb to the building downstream. "Those men know their craft. They work metal like artists. My machines don't break, because the parts are done right."

Precision, in other words. Kevin had talked about that, and how important it was.

Mr. Lovelace speared her with a direct look. "I don't know what he's invented, but I can guess. Not the look or function, but what it does. He has what is called an indicator, I'm thinking. One that maps the pressure, so it can be seen how the steam is working and whether more force can be sucked from it. Forestier invented a gauge for pressure, so it makes sense they would go together."

It sounded right to her, but she looked back blankly. "I am not an inventor or a maker, Mr. Lovelace. I really don't know if you are right or not."

"Of course not. But I think you know that your husband might do better to turn his mind to more inventions than to waste his time trying to run a factory like this. I'm only asking if you might encourage him to hear me out, that's all. I think together we can do great things."

She liked this man. For one thing, he had not stolen Forestier's idea any more than Kevin had. He paid those licenses and he hired artists. Some of his works were not far from London. He was a hardworking man with big ideas who knew what he could do and what he couldn't.

"Mr. Lovelace, if you spoke with Mr. Forestier, perhaps he told you that I am half owner of Mr. Radnor's business."

He appeared startled, then perplexed. Finally, he grinned. "You are the lady in red silk? Miss Jameson? Well, that explains a lot. When I saw you, I thought it unfair that he had two beautiful women in his life. If you will pardon my saying so."

"We married soon after returning from France."

He laughed. "Well, now, I might have said things differently if I knew you owned half of it."

"I think you said everything just fine." She thought fast. Kevin would be angry if she encouraged this man in any way. Furious. And yet . . .

"Mr. Lovelace, you know my partner is not inclined to take this path. However, I am willing to hear what you propose."

Kevin moved the large sheet of paper full of sketches to one side of the table. He took a clean sheet and began copying the only drawing he had made that satisfied him thus far.

It had been a long time since he had embarked on a new project, but this idea would not leave his head. He might as well see where it led. Right now it presented more problems than solutions. He didn't mind that. It wouldn't be interesting otherwise.

A soft cough interrupted his thoughts. He looked behind him to see Brigsby, staring down at the floor. "Would you like me to pick those up, sir?"

Kevin looked down at the dozen or so papers strewn over the carpet. "That isn't necessary."

Brigsby toed at the closest paper. "They might be trampled here. Ruined. I'll stack them on the writing table." He bent and began collecting the papers.

Kevin suffered it and waited for the papers to be stacked neatly on the writing table. "Did you come in here to see if I needed tidying, or was there something else?"

"You mentioned that Mrs. Radnor will be visiting this afternoon. I could make a small cake if you like. It would be nothing elaborate."

"Brigsby, Mrs. Radnor does not visit here. It is hers as well as mine. One does not visit one's own apartment."

"Of course, sir."

"Good." Kevin turned back to his drawing. After a minute, he realized Brigsby was still there. He turned again. "What else?"

"The cake, sir. Will you be wanting it?"

"Fine. Excellent. A cake. Very good. *Now go away.*" He again turned to the drawing while Brigsby passed on his way to the door. "Small," Kevin called after him. "Very small."

Satisfied that he had both ensured Brigsby would be busy, and also averting the chance that the small cake would be ten inches wide and twenty high, Kevin again returned to his work.

It absorbed him enough that Brigsby's reappearance became one more intrusion. "I thought you were making a cake."

"It is done, sir." He eyed the chairs, then moved two an inch or so each. "I'll bring it with coffee soon. Mrs. Radnor is on her way up."

Kevin checked his pocket watch. Hours had flown by.

Brigsby hurried out and returned escorting Rosamund like the visitor she was not. Although she did not come here much. Other than one arranged conversation when they had together examined the drawings and sample of Forestier's gauge, she had not "visited" at all. Her note at one o'clock announcing she would arrive later had thus been of passing curiosity.

Now she looked around the sitting room. She strolled over to the windows and checked the prospect as if she had not seen it before. She sidled near his writing table and angled her head to examine the top drawing. She turned her head and peered in the direction of the big table where he had been working.

"What is this?" she asked, lifting one of

442

the discarded drawings.

"It is just an idea I am toying with."

"It looks like a house. What are these lines here, running up and down?"

"Pipes."

She set it down. "I suppose if I spend time making hats in a workroom behind a shop, you can draw pipes here."

Brigsby arrived again, bearing a tray with coffee and cups and the cake. Kevin would not describe it as small, but it could have been worse.

Rosamund appeared delighted, however. They sat, and Brigsby served, then left.

"This is delicious," Rosamund said. "How nice of him to think to make it."

"The man is underfoot. Irritating. Distracting. Chase was very sly in giving me both space and manservant. They went together, of course. Now I know why."

"He can't be too distracting, considering that stack of paper over there."

"Perhaps not. I'm accustomed to being alone, though. I'm not used to having someone fussing around behind me."

Rosamund gave him an amused smile, then bit into her cake. "We were very naughty last night. I couldn't imagine what that bowl of custard was doing there when I retired. I should have known at once that you had some wicked plan."

Her mention of it brought memories that eliminated lingering thoughts about those pipes. "I had a taste for some custard, is all."

"Most people use spoons."

He crooked his arm around her neck and eased her over for a kiss. "How boring." He eyed the cake. "We could bring this into the bedchamber."

"We agreed none of that here. That is for Chapel Street and this is for the enterprise." She glanced at the papers again. "And whatever else you are doing."

"I didn't think we had anything to discuss about the enterprise. Our next steps are set. We are having another gauge made and will test the two pieces together as soon as it is finished."

"Of course."

He saw hesitation in her eyes and manner. She bit her lower lip. Usually that aroused him, but this time it made him cautious.

"You are looking like a guilty child, and not only because cake crumbs are on your lips."

She wiped her mouth. "I have done something you are not going to like."

"There is only one thing you could do that I wouldn't like, Rosamund."

She took his hand. "That is sweet, but it is not true. In fact, you may prefer that. You see, four days ago, I went to visit Mr. Lovelace at his place of business."

She was right. He didn't like this. "Why?"

"I think you should have listened to what he wanted to say. So I did instead."

"I made it clear that I wasn't interested."

"And I was equally clear that I was. I think his proposal is worth considering."

He stood and paced away. "Did you tell him everything you know?"

"Of course not. How dare you accuse me of that."

He turned on her. "Because a man can't have a proposal unless he knows what in hell he is proposing about." He paused while he leashed his temper. "Even if you spoke of an indicator, he would guess most of the rest."

She stood as well, with eyes narrowed. "Well, I didn't. Nor could I say anything that would give him clues, because I don't understand how the damned thing works. He is not stupid, however. He knows the industry. He could have figured out what you have without one word from anyone."

"Unlikely."

"Very likely. I know that to your mind you are the smartest person alive, but others are also thinking and inventing. He was most explicit about that."

His jaw was so tight, it affected his neck and whole head. He did not see the woman he desired right now. He saw an interfering woman who had ignored his judgment and held conversations behind his back.

Her expression softened. She came over to him. "He wrote it all out. Just read it. You can still reject it if you want. I can't stop you."

"But you would if you could, is that what you are saying? You do not trust me to see this through."

"It isn't about trust, Kevin. It is about being practical. This is past thinking now. It is time for acting, for making this thing and having it available for use. It could take us a year if we proceed on our own. Maybe longer. How much better for someone else to help, so it happens right away." She placed her hand on his arm. "Already your mind is moving on to other things. Wonderful things, I'm sure. Brilliant ones. This invention will have to be shared with someone in order to be made, and I like and trust Mr. Lovelace."

He looked down at her hand. That touch brought him halfway to sanity, but no farther. "What does he want?"

446

"If you read the proposal —"

"What in hell does he want?"

Her hand fell away. She stepped back as if he had hit her. She blinked once, then assumed a firm expression.

"Two companies. The one that we have, then his. We would own part of his, and he would own part of ours."

"No."

"What do you mean, no?" she said, her voice rising. "For the love of grace, Kevin, his is busy and successful and ours is still a dream. It is more than fair."

"I did not spend three years doing this to hand it to someone else."

"No one is asking you to. Right now, all I am asking is that you consider it, and visit his works to see what they do there. I think you will find that they have the precision you say we need."

"Are you an engineer now, as well as being a common hat maker? Stop interfering in things you know nothing about and are incapable of understanding. Damnation, sometimes I think I would have been better off if that half had gone to my fool relatives."

He threw that out to silence her relentless harping. He regretted it as soon as the words left his mouth.

She gazed at him silently for a long time.

Moment by moment, bit by bit, the warmth left her, along with the anger. By the time she turned and strode out, she might have been looking at a stranger.

"Would you like to dine here, sir? It is too late for me to cook, but I could bring something back from a tavern."

The voice pulled Kevin from his thoughts. He noticed the day had waned and deep twilight showed. He must have been distracted for hours.

Unpleasant thoughts could do that as well as contemplations about probabilities or pipes did. He had veered between fury and regret, over and over. Now Brigsby stood in front of him, looking suspiciously sympathetic. The man had probably heard the argument, even if he hopefully had not made out the actual words.

He faced a choice. Stay here or return to Chapel Street.

"Get something in. I'll be here tonight."

He told himself he was not being a coward. His head was still too hot to talk to Rosamund again.

The next morning, he woke feeling at least halfway normal. A tasteless meal and half a bottle of wine had gone far to dulling his mind. Sleep had finally come, although the

448

chaos did not leave him.

Brigsby insisted on helping him dress and had even ventured into the bedchamber to retrieve his shirt and cravat for ironing. A breakfast waited that helped his mood. Finally, he went to the stable in the mews for his horse.

It had been wise to let these chambers from Chase. He could now return to Chapel Street, and that row would be from another time and place. He would still apologize to Rosamund, though. He had lost his temper and spoken rashly. In a few days, they could meet again on Bury Street and he would explain his reasoning more carefully.

He was rearranging his thinking about how to do that when he entered the house. As he mounted the staircase he realized that the house felt different. Bigger. More vacant. It reminded him of a ballroom at the end of the night, when most of the guests had departed.

He entered his apartment to find Morris busy in the dressing room. A firm welcome and a quick nod, then Morris muttered about needing to see to the mail.

Kevin went looking for Rosamund, but she was not in her chambers. He descended the stairs, but she was not in the morning room either. The first alarm of concern sounded when he saw there was no food laid out.

Morris came in with the mail. He set a stack near the place where Kevin normally sat, then held the others with a puzzled expression. "Should I send them off, sir? Forward them?"

His chest emptied out. When he breathed, it filled again, too full. So full that it crushed against his heart.

"She left last night?"

"Yes, sir. In the early evening. Her maid, Jenny, said they were going to visit Mrs. Radnor's sister first, then see to other business. She asked the housekeeper to inform those tutors not to come again unless they were called for."

Kevin wandered back up to her apartment. Some dresses still hung in the wardrobe, and he took reassurance from that. He looked around the bedchamber while he tried to conquer the bleakness that threatened to claim him.

He avoided looking at the bed, so he was leaving before he noticed the papers on it, between the pillows. He reached for them to see if she had left a note. Perhaps word had come about her sister being ill, or some other mishap.

No note. Instead, he saw Lovelace's proposal. Kevin let it drop to the bed while a spike of rage stabbed into his mind. That man was the cause of this. The rows, the harsh words, these empty chambers. Anger held self-recrimination at bay, but it was there like a shadow, waiting.

Another paper fell away from the first and garnered his closer attention. At first it made no sense. Then he realized it was a legal document of sorts, or at least Rosamund's attempt to imitate one. She had written it in her own hand, with only a few errant dribbles of ink and smears from a blotting paper. He pictured her bent over the task, frowning while she tried to form her letters into something an elegant lady might write.

The document itself left him numb. In it, she signed over her share of the enterprise to her husband, Kevin Radnor.

She might return to London, and even to this house, but he knew then that she never intended to return to him.

CHAPTER TWENTY-TWO

Rosamund poured some water into the flower pot outside the shop door. She examined the window display, then went back inside. She paused to watch how the new woman, Mrs. Hutton, served a customer. Mrs. Hutton knew her trade, that had become obvious. Upon her first arrival back, Rosamund had been impressed at how well things were managed.

She mounted the stairs. Here in Richmond, the workroom was on the first story, and she entered it and took her seat under the window so she had good light for the fine sewing she was doing. Beside her, the apprentice Molly was teaching Lily how to hide a seam with some trim.

Lily pricked her finger. She did that a lot, but most new girls did. Her first time she had complained and moaned. Now she only dabbed some salve and wrapped her finger in a clean strip of cloth.

"Wait for it to stop bleeding," Rosamund said, keeping an eye out while she worked. "We don't want blood on that bonnet. Not even one drop."

Lily set the bonnet aside and bided her time. She kicked her feet like a child and wound a finger in one of her long, unbound blond locks. Rosamund smiled at the image she made. Half child, half woman. Some hours one side showed and the next hours, the other.

"This is more fun than school," Lily said. "Maybe I should stay here, or at the shop in London. I could be a milliner like you."

"You will do better than that if I have a say in it."

"I think school would be wonderful," Molly said.

"You wouldn't say that if you met the girls I live with. They are horrid and proud and conceited and —"

"And you have made two friends who are not," Rosamund said. "One week more with me, then you are going back. We will stop in London on the way, and have some dresses made."

New dresses ended the argument, as Rosamund knew they would. Lily was not truly unhappy at the school. She only complained like girls did at her age.

She had arrived without notice to take Lily away. She just needed Lily with her for a while. So much of what she had done was because of her sister. She needed to see Lily, and reassure herself that at least that part of it had been a good idea.

Lily came over to show the trimmed seam. "The stitches are too big at the end here," Rosamund said. "You will have to rip it out and do it again."

"No one will notice those few stitches tucked under there."

"One day your patron will be looking at the bonnet and she will see them. Then she will decide you are a careless milliner. We need to make every detail as close to perfect as it can be."

The words echoed in her head, only now in Mr. Lovelace's voice. That led her memory to the row with Kevin. A familiar, deep sadness spread in her.

During the day, she escaped that sickness of the heart. She kept busy at the shop. She remained close to Lily and enjoyed her company. It was at night, when she was alone, that she hurt the way she had when her father had passed.

She reminded herself now that she had not left London because of that row with Kevin. Not in itself, at least. They had had them before about the enterprise. Always about that.

She had always known he merely tolerated her as a partner too. It was something he could do nothing about, so he accepted it. But he didn't like it. Still, she thought they had found common ground, especially after Paris. But maybe not. Perhaps desire and pleasure had blinded her, and him too.

The argument ran through her memory, word for word, his outburst at the end ringing loud and hard. Something had happened then. To her. It was as if she suddenly stood to the side and watched, and realized exactly what was really occurring in front of her eyes.

Mostly, she saw herself too clearly, from the prospect of her own heart as well as his words. That Kevin considered her an interfering, common hat maker, and mostly an irritation unless they were in bed — Possibly she could have accommodated that. She might have learned to live with it. However, knowing that he not only did not love her the way she loved him, but also that he probably never would — accepting that hurt badly. She had again experienced the humiliation she'd known in the garden with Charles.

She did not want to live like that, so aware

that he scorned one part of her life. Their life. One part of her, really. It would affect everything, even the pleasure. Even now she was seeing some of the time they had shared differently.

Her thoughts distracted her. She pricked her finger, something she rarely did anymore. She set aside the hat and reached for the salve. At the other table, Lily had gone back to her own work.

She wrapped her finger and waited while she looked out the window at the sky. Blue today, after so much rain. The garden at Chapel Street probably had all its roses in bloom.

With time, maybe she would go back. Once she conquered the love. She had no intention of spending another five years living a dream, though. She was too old for that.

The rest was no more or less than she had bargained for, if she was honest. It had been her fault, not his, that she had forgotten that.

He had guessed where she was. A letter had come ten days ago. One sentence:

"Are you well?"

She shook her head and laughed. His wife

456

leaves without warning, and that was his only question?

She had responded just as briefly.

"Yes, quite well."

Then another letter, four days ago. Nothing about her health in that one. He had simply informed her that Chase had announced that Minerva was with child. He thought she would want to know. Two sentences this time.

Steps sounded on the stairs. Mrs. Hutton emerged, first her head and then the rest of her.

"Molly, I'll be needing you below now. I've some things for you to do," she said after she entered the workroom.

Molly set down her work and left, her dark curls bouncing. Mrs. Hutton did not follow. She came over to Rosamund and placed a card on the worktable. "He is below. He wants to see you. What should I say?"

It was Kevin's card. *Not yet,* her heart said.

That would never do. She stood. "Come with me, Lily."

Lily followed her down the stairs. Rosamund paused on the last step and took a deep breath. She turned her head and spoke to her sister. "Lily, Mr. Radnor is in the shop. I want you to meet him."

Lily's eyes widened. She stretched her neck to see around the stairwell wall and almost fell. Rosamund took the final step that brought her into the shop. Kevin stood near the window at the far end, angling his head to examine a hat.

"You didn't tell me he was handsome," Lily whispered.

He *was* handsome. Especially today. Or perhaps several weeks apart made him more handsome than usual.

He looked down the workshop and saw them. Rosamund pushed Lily forward like a shield until they joined him at the window. "Kevin, this is my sister, Lily."

Lily executed a curtsy the way her school had taught her. Kevin bowed, then smiled. Lily beamed a big smile in return.

Rosamund exhaled, proud of herself. She hadn't shown how flustered she felt. She hadn't cried.

Lily was a beautiful child. Rosamund had probably looked much like this at that age, before she grew into a woman. He knew nothing about talking to children, but he asked her how she liked school, and she chattered away, telling him about the other girls and the teachers. While she talked, he stole glances at Rosamund.

It had not been long, but he felt as if he were seeing her anew, standing at the door of Chase's library, stunning him. She smiled softly while her sister talked, but when the girl paused to breathe, she placed a hand on her shoulder.

"Save some for later," she said. "Why don't you find Molly to see what Mrs. Hutton needed her to do?"

"Before she goes, perhaps you want to give her this." Kevin turned and lifted a box he had brought with him. "It arrived a few days ago."

Lily's eyes widened. She looked at Rosamund, who nodded. Carefully Lily lifted the top of the box. "Oh, my." She reached in and brought forth a metal doll. Together she and Rosamund admired it front and back.

"What is this?" Lily asked when she discovered the key.

"Turn it, then set it on the floor," Rosamund said.

Lily did so. The woman smiled. Then she raised the hand that held a hat, and placed it on her head. Lily gaped in wonder and Rosamund beamed with delight.

"Can I show Molly?" Lily asked.

"Of course," Rosamund said.

Lily lifted the mechanical doll. She made another little curtsy and ran off.

"Thank you for bringing that," Rosamund said. "She will be the envy of every girl at her school when she returns with it."

"She is charming."

And then they were there, looking at each other. He had rehearsed all manner of clever things to say, but they deserted him.

The door opened and a woman entered. Another woman came forward from the back to greet her. Both of them glanced in his and Rosamund's direction.

"Is there someplace we can talk?" he asked.

"There is no privacy here, if that is what you mean. We could take a turn if you like."

It would have to do. Outside, they fell into step together.

"You did not answer my last letter," he said.

"I wrote to Minerva. She is the one who is pregnant."

"Of course. Still —"

She laughed. "Kevin, what was there to write? Two sentences, and all about her." She smiled broadly and shook her head. "You are a poor correspondent, aren't you?"

"I like to think of it as being succinct."

"I understand. Truly. No doubt you were

busy thinking about things. Like pipes."

"I have thought very little about pipes while you were gone."

"Has the enterprise been keeping you busy instead? That is good to hear."

He looked down the street. The noise made it hard to talk comfortably, and people kept pushing by. "That is one reason I am here. I need to tell you about it. I have a chamber at the Dark Horse Inn. We wouldn't have to shout over carriages there."

She stopped walking and looked at him. He didn't have to hear her voice the question. He knew what it was. It pained him that she even wondered, but then, they had parted in anger.

"I am not the kind of husband who would demand his rights, Rosamund. I hope you know that much about me." She nodded, and they continued on to the inn.

She had not wondered if he would demand anything. She had wondered if he thought to seduce her. She wasn't sure she could resist if that happened.

His words reassured her. They walked up to the chamber he had taken. It was a nice one that overlooked the street, not the yard. No horse smells, at least.

A half bottle of wine stood on the table.

"Do you want some?" He gestured to it while he moved a chair to join the one already there. "You can sit here, if you want."

She normally would not drink wine in the afternoon, but right now, it sounded like a good idea. She sat and accepted a small glass of the claret. She noticed his brushes and razor near the wash basin, and a frock coat visible through the wardrobe door that had been left ajar. A stack of papers rested on the bed. Pipe drawings, perhaps.

Time stretched as they silently sat together. She could not resist looking at him, even though memories flooded her that made her heart alternately joyful and sad. This was what she had hoped to avoid — a lifetime of moments like this, when her love expanded just on seeing him, only to pain her when she accepted love had been a foolish error.

"That looks to be a fine shop," he finally said after drinking his wine.

"I am very proud of it. Even more than the one in London. It was good to see it again."

He swirled the wine around in his glass, watching it move. "Do you intend to stay here?"

"For a while. I'm enjoying my time with

462

Lily. It has been years since we have been together for more than a few days at a time. We have been growing to know each other again."

"Should I have followed you?" he asked. "Were you expecting me to?"

How like Kevin. A few pleasantries in a vain effort to be polite, then, abruptly, on to what he really cared about.

"I would not have liked that at all."

"A different kind of woman might have expected it, but I didn't think you would."

"You mean it is something a lady might expect? Common hat makers don't make games out of such things."

His gaze reflected she had used his own words to describe herself. "You did not give me the chance to apologize for my behavior that day. You just left."

"I did not leave because of you. I left because of me."

"I apologize anyway."

"We can pretend that you said things you did not mean because you were angry if you want. Only people tend to say exactly what they mean then. The parts they don't normally speak come out. I don't blame you for it. I don't even mind, although pretending would have been easy to do. Only you reminded me of who I am. What I am. Why we married. I needed to live with that a bit, without your distracting me."

He got up and walked around the bed. "I have something here that I need you to sign. It is one reason why I have now intruded." He picked up the stack of papers from the bed, then returned to his chair. "It has to do with the enterprise."

"I gave my half to you. My signature is not needed now."

"Your attempt to give it to me was not valid. You had no witness. There is no proof you signed it at all. Also, as I recently learned from Mr. Sanders, if you ever do want to sell or give it away, you will be expected to say so in front of a judge before it is binding, lest it be thought I browbeat you into it. The law is suspicious of married women divesting themselves of property, because it might be under coercion."

"That's a bother. Did you have Mr. Sanders do it up right? Is that what this is? We'll find witnesses and start it today."

"I didn't think to do that. I need you to sign something else." He handed her a folded document. "We will still need witnesses."

She recognized the scrivener's hand, all flowing and elegant. She unfolded the thick vellum until it hung down to her lap. It took a good while to make it all out. Partly that was because she kept going over sections, to be sure she understood it.

"This looks like a contract with Mr. Lovelace, Kevin."

"That it is. One quarter of the enterprise to him, and one quarter of the company he will form to make it comes to us." He held up another folded document. "The other side of the bargain is here."

She set down the vellum, astonished. "You spoke with him?"

"A very shrewd woman advised me to. It took several days to get to it, but I eventually read his proposal."

"Did it take you that long to stop being angry?"

He took the vellum from her and set it on the table. He leaned forward until he was so close that their noses almost touched. "It took me that long to begin conquering my shock at discovering you had left."

His closeness, and the warmth of his breath, made her tremble. "Did you conclude Mr. Lovelace's proposal was a good plan?"

"I could not deny it was very practical. Sensible. Convenient. So he and I talked, and I viewed his works. I even traveled to Shropshire to see the rest of it. You were right, Rosamund. He will make it well."

She bit her lower lip to force some control on her stupid love. "I did not mean for you to spend days in shock. That was not my intention."

"I know. Yet there it was. I did not want to face that you might be gone for good. I disappointed you in more ways than I know, I think."

"You didn't. You were true to your word. To our agreement. As for the enterprise, I never really expected you to share that easily." Her mouth quivered when she tried to smile. "You once said you were never enthralled by women, except that brief madness with Lady Greenough. I understand why too. You had bigger things to captivate you. Of course you would be possessive about your creations. I feel that way about my shop and my hats."

He listened so carefully, as if every word she spoke mattered. A small frown formed part way through and his attention on her became more intense, if that were possible.

He sat back and turned his attention inward, the way he so often did. She had never been jealous of how he could isolate himself in his own mind. She had always found that mysterious and even exciting.

He gazed over at her again. "Rosamund,

did you leave because you thought the enterprise meant more to me than you did?"

"No, because I accepted that of course it did. It is why we married, after all."

He sat back and closed his eyes.

He stood abruptly and paced away, then stood with his back to her and his hands on his hips. She heard a deep sigh. She had exasperated him again. She couldn't imagine how.

He turned again just as sharply and walked back. He threw aside his chair and dropped to one knee in front of her. He took both her hands in his.

"Rosamund, it is why we said we married, but for me, this has been much more than a practical match. I wanted you from the first time I saw you. With each revelation of who and what you were, I wanted you more. I did not lie when I told you I was never enthralled, but I could never say it now without lying, because I have been enthralled for a long time with you. Captivated. Enchanted. You have stolen my heart, darling, and the better part of my soul. I can't promise I will never be rude, or angry, or all the things everyone accuses me of being. I can only promise that I will love you forever, wherever you are."

He bent and kissed her hands and left his

lips there, pressed against her skin. Her eyes blurred as happiness spilled through her, and her heart released its love. It touched her that he had declared himself like this. He hadn't even asked her to return to him. He just wanted her to know this, no matter what she did or where she went.

She kissed his crown. "Thank you," she whispered. "I could not bear pretending I was not in love. Not speaking of it and accepting pleasure and friendship, but denying this other emotion that overwhelms me. If you love me too, I won't have to."

He looked up. The relief in his expression twisted her heart.

"You will never have to." A moment's hesitation. A flicker of caution. "Will you come home?"

She nodded.

He smiled, then glanced at the bed. That smile turned wicked.

Laughing and crying, she plucked at the tie of his cravat. "You may be too good to demand your marital rights, but I am not." She worked at the knot. "What will you do without the enterprise to occupy you? Pipes?"

"And other things." He shed his frock coat, then eased her feet out of her shoes. "I will leave the resulting practicalities to you.

We are a good match, Rosamund. Perhaps the duke guessed we might be."

His hands slid up beneath her dress and sought her garters. She squirmed when they got high enough to remind her of what awaited.

Her fingers trembled while she went to work on the buttons of his waistcoat. "Did you know that there are men in the City who would purchase a share of any invention you had, sight unseen and ignorant of its purpose?"

"That is ridiculous."

His shirt occupied part of her attention. She made quick work of his upper garments, so his naked chest was available to her gaze and her hands. "You must have impressed some people even while you insulted most of them."

He rolled down her stockings and cast them aside. "I can't imagine how. However, it is good to know that if we ever want to defraud dozens of shareholders, the means are at hand." He stood and lifted her into his embrace.

How like Kevin to be indifferent to the perfectly legal possibilities those investors might present. She would explain it to him eventually.

Their first kiss made her heady and so

grateful for the warmth and love encompassing her.

The power of her arousal awed her. "It has not been very long, but I . . ."

"I know. Me too. No games or lessons this time. I want to hold you in my arms and against my heart."

No words either, except those of devotion spoken again and again while they reclaimed each other within a loving union.

ABOUT THE AUTHOR

Madeline Hunter is a *New York Times* bestselling author with more than six million copies of her books in print. A member of RWA's Honor Roll, she has won the RITA Award twice and been a finalist seven times. Her books have appeared on the bestseller lists of The *New York Times, USA Today,* and *Publishers Weekly,* and have been translated into thirteen languages. She has a PhD in art history, which she has taught at the university level. Madeline loves to hear from her readers, and can be reached through her Website at MadelineHunter .com, on Facebook, Facebook.com/ MadelineHunter/, and at Twitter.com/ MadelineHunter.